I0699598

SPIRIT'S END

THE RIVEN TRILOGY

BOOK THREE

A.R. KNIGHT

OTHER WORLD

I had been alive the last time I kissed her lips. Soft, cool to the touch. Mine were likely the same. Selena's eyes, though, still had life. Her soul was still there. Mine too.

We parted, grabbed our things from around the gray, ashy apartment. I slipped on my long black coat, a reminder of something I no longer was. A guide, meant to take the spirits of Earth's dead stuck in Riven and send them on. Send them to the Cycle to keep them from crowding out this world. This grand, desolate place.

My home.

I hooked my lash into my belt, a ten foot long cord splitting into metal points at the end. On my left side, I stuck in a long knife, a foot and a half of pointed desperation. On my back went the great sword I'd taken from the man who killed me. The sword stood half my height and took both hands to swing. Its black and silver metal blade would have been heavy, but without a real body and its limitations, I had no problems hefting the weapon.

I didn't get tired anymore.

My crossbow hung over the sword, three sets of bolts looping around the shaft. Normal black-tipped quarrels meant to deliver pointed pain to anything they struck. Next were blue ones, ready to spit out wrangling fire that would deliver a spirit to its peaceful end. Last came orange. A shot that could be as dangerous to me as it was to the enemy. My favorite.

"You're sure this is what we should do?" Selena said as she set her cleaver, as long as a knife and as thick as my sword, with biting ridges on the front edge, in its holster attached to the front flap of her coat.

"I don't know," I said. "But if Nara doesn't have an idea, we're stuck. Breaches are erupting everywhere, and the guides don't have the numbers. We need a miracle, and unless you've thought one up in the last couple of hours, that spirit is our best shot."

I didn't bring up the other reason for speed. The voice whispering at the edge of my mind, calling me to drop everything I had and start on that long walk to oblivion. The Cycle murmured, always there. A honeyed hush inviting me to give up my troubles and embrace peace.

And they said the dead had no worries.

"Is it strong today?" Selena noticed my closed eyes. "Bad?"

She asked me every morning. Her passion kept the Cycle in check. If I focused on her, on what Selena was saying, what we had, then the Cycle's siren call would diminish. Selena gave me a reason to stay, one far more compelling than the Cycle's push to leave.

"No worse than any other." I ran my hand over my face, threw her a slapdash smile.

Selena gave me a hard stare for a moment. She knew when I wasn't telling her the whole truth. I didn't have time for that discussion now, though. Bigger things to worry about.

"You ready?" I moved to the door. "Alec and Anna should be coming soon."

"You're the one with a dozen weapons." Selena didn't need blades to be deadly, though the two she carried were enough. One harsh look from those icy eyes and any spirit ought to run away.

LAB WORK

We left the apartment, the top floor of a three-story building that we kept frantically maintained as the rest of the city crumbled around us. Riven's gray light burned through the glassless windows, omnipresent and lifeless. A reminder of what I'd lost when Piotr had me murdered. The color of dawn's sunrise, the sounds of birds singing in the morning, even the roar and rumble of passing traffic. Riven stood a quiet ruin.

Most of the buildings in the city were decaying after centuries without care. Broken by fighting, by the tormented destruction of angry spirits, or left to rot away according to Riven's mysterious laws. Normally the gray sky was a blank slate, but now sparks peppered its dull infinite with colorful bursts. Guides alerting and communicating with each other across avenues and miles of city blocks. Letting others know of a breach, a swarm of angry spirits bent on revenge or chaos or both.

On the ground floor we walked into a bustling lab, a large square space full of burbling machines, twisting metal, and fiery forges. Devices constructed in Riven's harsh world by a madman I'd found years ago.

Nicholas Salzer looked up as we came in and gave a quick wave before turning back to a large piece of fabric he'd spread out on a table. He held a stick with a burnt end in one hand. Paper was hard to find in Riven, so you used whatever snared dark ashes.

"What's burning up your mind now?" I asked and Nicholas paused, turned to me with a spacey look on his face, a man arising from the depths of concentration.

"I've been trying to find a good way to solve this problem," Nicholas said, holding up the ash stick as if it explained everything.

"This problem?" I tried to get a look at what he was writing, but the slew of mathematics etched on the fabric were foreign to me.

"The spirits," Nicholas said. "It seems the bottleneck is simply that the Cycle takes too long. That the spirits are allowed to stay past their expiration."

"You've found the obvious." Selena leaned against the wall, arms folded. "But what are you going to do about it?"

"That's precisely what I'm trying to determine." Nicholas talked at the table, his back to us. "When I have a suitable hypothesis, I'll be happy to let you know."

A probing question came to my mind, but before I could ask it, the scientist broke out rhetorical mutterings. Meant for his equations, no doubt. I glanced at Selena and shrugged. Nicholas was his own man, and he didn't suffer interruptions.

"Wait outside?" Selena said. I nodded.

The lab opened onto a broad road with various buildings on either side forming a low canyon. The occasional spirit wandered up and down, looking lost or, in rare cases, nattering to themselves. Riven didn't have any bias. Spirits from anywhere could show up, well, anywhere. You might be walking down the street and see a soldier from the war on one side and a tribesman from a land you didn't know existed on the other. The afterlife was the ultimate melting pot.

Yet, among the ashen flakes and empty sidewalks, Alec and Anna were nowhere to be seen.

BACK ALLEY BREACH

The skies were clear of sparks. No panicked shouts came down the avenue. Unexplained absences in Riven usually led to dire conclusions, but I clung to a nicer reason.

"Did I lose track of time?" I asked.

Riven had no clocks, no day or starry nights with which to navigate the passage of hours. Only my intuition, that general sense of history inching forward, kept me from losing all idea of when I was.

"It feels right," Selena said. "Which isn't a guarantee."

Before, when I'd been alive, I had felt time. My body, still on Earth, on the other side, would tell me when to wake up. When I should cross back over. Anna had buried that body somewhere. Or burned it. I never asked her what happened to it, and she hadn't told me. I never planned to.

We both shouted at the same time we saw Anna, saw her stumble out from an alley half a block away, clutching at her side. Bleeding claw marks, the jagged lines left from fingernails, rending through her coat. Her flail, chain and spiked ball extended, dragging on the ground. Limping.

"Alec needs help," Anna said as we ran to her. "There's a breach just back there. It opened on top of us."

We didn't hesitate. I yelled back into the lab, told Nicholas to come out and help Anna, and then Selena and I took off running. Our feet pounded on the stones. We ducked between the buildings. Hit a back alley and then saw the breach to our right. In a small clearing formed when the rear halves of some of the structures had collapsed into a large pile of rubble. Now a glowing pool covered those broken boards and stones, only instead of water, the surface reflected up part of Earth.

Spirits climbed through the breach, their hands rising up into Riven like swimmers emerging from the water. People dying from violence, from disease, or even simple old age. Normally scattered throughout Riven, the breaches drew spirits together. Pulled them into single areas where their confusion, their rage and despair over their lost lives fueled each other and drove them into the hysterical rage that made the dead so deadly. They crossed over in ruined clothes, in uniforms, young and old, however the spirits saw themselves as they traveled that final line between life and loss.

A guide stood in the middle of those clutching hands, snarling mouths, and wild eyes. Alec bounced from one spirit to the next, delivering a series of short jabs with the ridged gauntlets that cloaked his fists and forearms. Spikes on those gauntlets burned with blue fire that enveloped every spirit they touched and torched away the anger showing in those dead eyes. Pacified them and sent the spirits on their final walk to the Cycle.

It would've been easy to watch that dance, to stay back and admire Alec as he wrangled one spirit after another. Only we could see the toll. Cuts appeared here and there as one hand or another swung a lucky swipe. A sidestep that dodged one sloppy tackle led Alec into another spirit's bite. Being outnumbered in Riven was a death sentence, no matter how good the guide.

Selena and I waded in on either side. I struck with the lash first, sending its pointed tip out and wrapping around a spirit reaching for Alec's back. The lash looped around the spirit's arm and its point bit into his shoulder. The spirit, a posh gentleman in a suit that looked as though he came directly from a wedding, turned and snarled at me. His eyes burned with the pale fire, a lost mind.

I twisted the hilt of my lash and fire erupted along the cord, blue flames that matched the hue of the spirit's eyes. As the spirit lunged towards me, the fire caught up to his body and wrapped him in its purifying burn. I felt his hand touch my shoulder, but rather than rend, it fell away and I looked up into a vacant stare. The empty eyes of a pacified spirit.

"Your arrival is most fortunate." Alec dodged another spirit, delivering three swift strikes to its middle and sending it stumbling away, wreathed in a wrangling blue glow. "I have a tablet, and it is very nearly ready."

I glanced Selena's way and saw her with her cleaver in one hand and a knife in the other, dashing between spirits and severing their anger with stab after stab. A beautiful storm, a partner that I'd never realized I had next to me. I did not know where Selena found her ability, but watching her carve her way through those grasping arms and spitting mouths filled me with a kind of pride, a love that comes only from seeing the one you care about most exceeding your wildest hopes.

Yes, watching the love of my life carve up a bunch of dead spirits was the highlight of my day.

"Back away," Alec called.

I looked as the guide pulled a tablet off of his belt, a stone block with a sapphire set in the middle. A sapphire that glowed a deep blue, ready to fulfill its mission. To close the breach and drive the remaining spirits away. Alec put it down on the ground and pressed in on the sapphire as two more spirits reached for his back.

Blue tendrils lanced out from the tablet, striking through the spirits and wreathing them in fire. Others shot towards the edge of the breach, seeming to dive into the ground and pull the portal closed. And then Selena tugged at my arm, pulling me away.

"We've got to run," Selena said. "If that thing gets us, we're gone."

My legs kicked into gear and we sprinted away down the alley. I'd forgotten. I was a spirit now. That tablet would destroy me as surely as it had our enemies. So many rules I had to relearn.

"Thanks," I said. "I'm not used to it."

"Pretty sure it was you who told me that Riven doesn't give second chances," Selena said. "That I had to keep watching my back."

"Not as long as you're around," I said. Selena rolled her eyes.

I looked back down the alley and saw nothing left of the portal. Only Alec, picking up the tablet. Content spirits staring at nothing. In another minute or two they would shuffle off and start a days-long journey to a mountain west of the city. Into a cave and down to its depths, where they would find the Cycle, a great blue lake.

Each and every one of those spirits would drop in and erase themselves from existence.

TO THE EAST

So far as scratches went, Anna's weren't dangerous. Tears in the coat, a gash along her leg. Bruises on her wrists where spirit hands had gripped too tightly. Alec shared similar injuries. The common cost of doing business in Riven these days.

"Remember the times when we'd be able to walk in and out pain-free?" Alec stared at his wounds, shaking his head. We stood in the lab, getting ready for our jaunt to the other side of the city. "When all we had to fear was a little bit of bad luck?"

"I'm not sure what Riven you were in," I said. "It's always been dangerous."

"It used to be fun," Alec replied. "Now I cross over because it is my job, not because it is something I wish to do."

"You're talking to someone who's trapped here," I said. "Forever."

"Not if they break a hole," Anna said. "Then you could come back."

"To enjoy the world for the brief hours before the dead overrun it completely," I said. "What a happy thought."

"Which is the reason for this adventure, no?" Alec said. "This woman, this Nara, she has a way?"

"That's what we're going to find out," I said, glancing at Selena. "Speaking of that, we should move. Anna, are you going to be okay?"

"I can handle it." Anna rose to her feet, her shoulders were set. Her head high. "Alec shouldn't be alone out there anyway."

THE WALKING WENT SLOW. Anna still had to limp, and we were more cautious than usual. Kept our eyes scanning alleys, side streets, with one of us always watching our backs. I never relaxed while walking Riven, but now I stood on edge. Every moment my eyes flicked in a different direction, trying to see into all the corners and shadows.

From the apartment we headed east, cutting through the central part of Riven. Streets broadened into wide boulevards and buildings grew to five and six-story heights. Hotels and offices that had never been used. As if a child had dreamed them up and discarded the idea halfway through. Dollhouses with no dolls.

We saw guides. Guides by the dozen. Dashing in teams towards popping sparks. Carrying wounded back towards where they could cross over, to where guides could heal and return again after some hours away. Cries for help mingled with shouts of victory down the corridors between the walls. Several times we broke off to help guides seal away spirits, close a breach or wrangle a cluster of mauling souls. Selena and I, with our coats and guide weaponry, stayed low. Didn't talk, didn't give our names. Did what we could while avoiding recognition.

Only once did another guide push the issue. He'd recognized Alec and, after we'd closed a breach together, the guide congratulated each of us in turn. Hesitated when he saw my battered features. His eyes, bagged and tired, squinted. Looked me up and down.

"I know this face," the guide said. "What is your name?"

"His name doesn't matter." Anna put her hand on my shoulder. "He's with me. And Alec."

The guide gave her a side glance. "Our laws are not kind to those who help fugitives."

"I never knew a guide to turn on someone giving them aid," I said.

The guide took a step back. "I cannot deny your efforts. And I have neither the energy nor the desire to deliver justice to you today. On another morning, however, I will not hold back. You have lives to answer for, Carver Reed."

He turned and walked away, the other guides in his group following in silent judgment. His words hurt, but the pain filtered into the same numb part of me that had grown in the days since I'd been cast out as a guide. I made no pretenses that I was a saint. That I hadn't done terrible things in the name of grander objectives. But losing friends was never easy. Losing my place in life stung every day. Every hour.

As we neared the east edge of the city the buildings thinned out; broad courtyards became the norm. Patterned white stone broken up with the occasional statue or domed building. The largest of these, the Palace, marked the spot where Alec and I had fought our first ghoul months ago. A time when my life was different.

When I *had* a life.

"So when do you think you'll be back?" Anna said.

"That's an impossible question," I replied. "Nara might give us an answer in fifteen minutes, or she could hold us there for fifteen months."

"Riven won't last that long." Alec glanced at his gauntlets, as though they were directly responsible for Riven's survival.

"We'll move as fast as we can," Selena said. "I won't let Carver waste time."

"You won't?" I asked. "But it's my favorite thing to do."

Riven's east gate stood large and proud. An archway built of stone and bordered by twin turreted towers. The four of us stood beneath that arch, looking out to the hundred yards of clear space before the endless fields of waving white grain began. There was something inevitable in the stance, the feeling that we might never see each other again. This parting, this moment where the two pairs separated, with Alec and Anna returning to the war-torn streets while Selena and I ventured into the unknown.

"You are sure you don't want me to bind you?" Anna said. "I can keep you from the Cycle. We can talk over long distances."

"You need your strength," I said. "Can't afford to be anything less than your best. If you die because the binding saps your energy, then I'd be right where I am now. Binding me wouldn't help Selena either."

"We can keep each other sane," Selena said.

"The opposite of most loves of known," Alec added. We laughed, but it was the dry sort. Low and laden with future burdens. Still, I welcomed the chance to smile. In my head, the Cycle continued its whispers.

It never stopped.

THE FOREVER FIELDS

Selena and I put one foot in front of the other. Alec and Anna turned back and disappeared amongst the statues and the columns. Back to the world that I had known. In front of us stood stalk after stalk of great white grain. Some taller than I was, most at least three or four feet in height. All shifting back and forth in Riven's eternal breeze.

I took the lead, pushing and shoving the stalks apart. Like making our way through a thick forest, or swamp. There simply wasn't a motion I could take that didn't involve pushing aside the plants. If they could even be called that.

"How did you manage to walk this far before?" Selena batted a stalk away from her face. "Find your way to anywhere?"

"Nara showed me," I said. "Pointed me in the right direction, led me most of the way. Until I could see the walls."

"I remember the conversations," Selena said. "You talked about how endless this all was. I didn't really believe it but now these plants are the only thing I can see."

The last time I'd been through here Selena and I had been bound to each other. I'd been alive and we could send our thoughts, our emotions over any distance in Riven to each other. It'd been my only comfort as I'd wandered through the endless field alone. Even Nara, when she'd been there, acted less like a companion and more like a distant teacher.

"When we find her," I said, "let me do the talking at first. I don't think she'll be expecting you."

"You think that'll be a problem?"

"I don't know what to think." I parted a pair of stalks with my hands, stepped between them and held them apart for Selena to follow. "She told me that she was old. Hundreds of years. That she'd seen Riven built from the ground up and turned into what it is now. You tell me whether you'd go crazy being in here that long, with no friends, no seasons, nothing other than this."

"Alone? I don't think I would last a month. I don't think anyone would."

"You came close."

Even after I'd found her, even after I had bound Selena, she'd spent most days in Riven waiting and watching. Drawing on the walls of the apartment; cityscapes that she could see from her window. I'd worried whether she was going to fall apart, whether I would come to visit her one day and find Selena destroyed by this world's unchanging pallor.

"I've always been a survivor," Selena said. "I leaned on you. I leaned on Nicholas. I leaned on the memory of my children and what it took to raise them."

Selena didn't mention the husbands she'd murdered. The willpower it must've taken to plot their ends and actually pull them off. To leave one life after another behind as a weeping widow until it finally caught up with her. That scar running along Selena's face an ever-present reminder of the sacrifices she'd made and the pain she'd suffered. And had inflicted.

Perhaps that was what drew me to her. What kept us together in this crazy world. She and I had both lost so much, had endured broken lives and broken dreams. It was fitting that Riven would prove to be our home. The only place two souls like us could make an existence. Such as it was.

"How long will we be wandering?" Selena said later, as the city walls disappeared on the horizon and we continued our march.

"Depends on whether I can find her," I said. "If I get lost, then we might just be here, pushing through the stalks until Riven implodes."

"You're inspiring a lot of confidence."

"Hey, it was your idea to come with," I said. Selena had insisted on it, actually. Declared that if I went off on another quest without her, one of two things would happen: Either I would go insane and fall victim to the Cycle's constant whispers or she would. Made it a pretty easy choice.

We continued pushing further and further into the vast field for what felt like a day or more but without a body's fatigue or a sun's pattern to tell you the time, it was hard to know. Eventually, though, we both saw the wispy smoke rising into the sky. Nara's fire. Burning the grain one stalk at a time seemingly forever.

When I shoved through the last line of stalks and into the clearing, it looked the same as it had before. Nara's hut, a thatched structure, stood alone beyond a fire chewing its way through a large pile of grain. I wasn't sure if it was the same pile that'd been there when I'd first found the clearing, or if Nara actually cut more stalks. Either way it didn't seem like her constant burning was making headway. The grain crowded as close as it had been before.

"Where is she?" Selena asked. "Didn't you say she would be waiting?"

I nodded towards the hut. "Guessing she's in there, or we've come all this way for nothing."

"For nothing?" Nara's voice came out of the hut's door, frosted and scratched. "For nothing? You have a very low opinion of your journeys, Carver. Even if you simply had to turn back now, would you not have gained even the slightest insight into who you are?"

Nara emerged from the hut, wearing the same dark robe I'd seen her in before. Her hood pulled up to cover her eyes, keeping her face in shadow. That strange combination of age that had Nara looking both wise but far from frail. Etched lines over strong arms, thick skin, and bright hair. Movement with purpose.

"Does she always talk like that?" Selena asked.

I could only nod.

THE LORDS OF RIVEN

Perhaps it was the way Nara looked in her robe, her slow purposeful walk as she crossed the clearing to stand in front of Selena and I, but I shivered. Wanted to but resisted backing away. As Nara came closer the light sneaking under her hood revealed more of her face, a look that had just enough wrinkles to convey wisdom if not desiccated age. If this had been Chicago I would've given her a senior's due, respected her as an elder. Here, in a place where spirits determined their own guise, choosing such a look had a purpose.

"You brought someone with you? Who is this?" Nara bent her head towards Selena, kept her eyes on me. "A spirit. An unusual choice for a guide."

"I'm not a guide anymore," I replied. "This is Selena. We're here for your help."

"My help?"

"You said you had a way to keep Riven from falling apart. It's only getting worse; the spirits continue to pour in and breaches are opening everywhere," I said. "If you have a solution, I'd like to know what it is."

Nara stepped over to me, reached out with her hand and touched my face. I flinched away. There was something strange about a person you didn't know touching you. Nara's cold skin, the wisps of her fingernails glancing on my cheek sowed unease. I noticed Selena's hand drift towards her cleaver. But then Nara stepped back, a frown crossing her lips.

"She and I are not the only spirits here," Nara said. "What happened to you, Carver Reed?"

"You see this sword?" I said, my hand rising to the hilt of the great blade on my back. "The man who owned it had me killed on the other side. He paid for it."

"Then you succeeded. I'm impressed. For you to be back, Riven must truly be in dire shape."

"Please," Selena said. "If you can help, we need a way to close the breaches quickly. A way to help the spirits get to the Cycle faster."

Nara gave Selena a frosted stare. "Riven is not a product of nature. It is not a random world of chaos, like where you came from. Where I came from. It is a construct. Built by those who refuse to take the last leap into the Cycle. I am one of those."

Nara held up one wrinkled hand.

"Before you start to ask your questions, before you panic, or assume I am something greater than what I am, take another look at the world in which you find yourselves. A place where natural law is scattered. Where the things you take for certainties come and go with the breeze. Where a house might be nothing more than bits of rubble and yet the next stands perfect. All of this, every inch you walk upon, comes from us."

I heard the words. They sounded like Piotr's. The mad ramblings of someone who thought they were above and beyond everyone else. Even if Nara was telling the truth, even if she was some sort of ancient spirit that had a hand in molding Riven to what it was, she was still here in the middle of the endless stalks of grain, alone in a hut. Hardly the existence I'd imagine for someone with the power to craft a world.

"If you are so strong, if you are truly what you're saying, then why let Riven slide into decay?" I asked.

"Because I cannot," Nara replied. "Because, for everything we have learned over our centuries in Riven, we were once human. And humans are imperfect."

"That's not an answer to my question."

"I asked you to return," Nara said. "Because I want to save you. I want to save your guides and your order. To keep Riven safe. In our folly, in our fear, we bound ourselves. I can no more leave this clearing than you, a spirit, can choose to cross back home."

"Carver," Selena said. "She's manipulating you. I've seen it before. I've done it before."

"Your friend is astute," Nara said. "I do want something from you. I want you to go and find the other two. Bring them here. Together, the three of us can make Riven into what it needs to be. Can prevent this catastrophe and make it so that the guides never need die again."

"That's one hell of a promise," I said.

"It is one I can keep," Nara said. "Is it one you can afford to ignore?"

I glanced at Selena. Her mouth pursed, her eyes squinted at Nara. I'd been the subject of that scrutiny before. Had my soul weighed and measured. But it didn't matter. We had come out here for one purpose; to try and find help for the doomed city and our friends who were, right at this moment, battling for their own survival. Even if Nara wasn't giving us the whole truth, could we walk away?

"You said there are two others," I asked. "Where are they?"

Nara moved over to her burning fire and grabbed the unlit bottom of one of the stalks of grain. Held the torch up high. Her lips moved, a silent whisper that I couldn't make out. The flame at the top of the grain twisted, curling in on itself before launching out to the north and west. Back towards the city and then above it.

"Mali is the first," Nara said. "You will find her playing with her creations. If there was any one of us that truly wanted to be a god, Mali was it."

Once again Nara whispered to the stalk of grain. Once again the flame crawled in upon itself and shot out, south and west this time.

"Dolan is the second," Nara said. "He should be as idle as ever. Caught up in a past he cannot return to."

"And once we get the two of them, you'll be able to work together?" Selena asked. "You'll be able to close the breaches?"

Nara gave a withered nod. I continued to get the sense that Nara hadn't spoken with anyone other than me for years. Possibly decades. The sheer act of holding a conversation was a struggle for her.

"We will do more than close the breaches," Nara said. "We will prevent them from ever happening again."

"That sounds too good to be true," I said.

"When you're dealing with gods, that is often the case. I suggest going to find Mali first. She will be the more difficult one, and you will need all your strength."

Nara turned her back to us and walked into her hut. I watched her disappear and held a thousand questions on my tongue. If there was one thing I'd learned from Bryce and the other guides, it was that information often came according to the wishes of others, not my own.

"She showed us the way," I said. "I guess we better start walking."

"Wait a minute," Selena replied. "We're just going to follow her orders?"

"You have any better ideas?"

"We could get more information." Selena looked towards the hut. "I get the feeling she's not telling us everything."

"She's not telling the whole truth," I said. "But I don't think pushing her is going to get us a better answer."

"Carver, she said the three of them created Riven. If that's true, then why does she need us to do this? You don't buy that nonsense about being bound, do you?"

I didn't know what to do. Or know what to say. All at once the feeling of being trapped, being locked into Riven forever seemed to compress around my mind and fracture into pieces. I was never leaving this place. Never seeing another sky that wasn't gray, never actually breathing real air or drinking another cup of coffee. I'd gone from a world of order and laws, where reason ruled the land, to a world where the dead walked and mysterious figures claimed unimaginable power.

"Selena," I said, wrapping her in a hug so suddenly that her eyes widened with surprise. "I don't know what to believe. I don't know what other choices we have. If we turn our backs on this, then what else is there? What else do we do except fight and fight and fight until the Cycle claims our minds and turns us into nothing?"

"I . . ."

"We died, Selena. Our lives ended. And yet, somehow, we found each other here in this terrible place," I said, without really knowing the words I was speaking. They rolled out one after another as though coming from instinct instead of my mind. "Riven is great and hideous, but it is all we have. I'm willing to do anything we can to save it. Help me."

I felt Selena's arms wrap around me, return the hug. It was both ridiculous and utterly necessary for the two of us to hold ourselves close. I could not hear her heartbeat, because she had none. I didn't feel the rise and fall of her lungs, because she wasn't breathing. I didn't feel the warmth of her body beneath the coat, because we were not warm. But I felt her love, and I embraced that.

A long moment later I released, stepped back and met Selena's eyes. "Are you ready to go find a god?"

"After all we've done already? I get the feeling I'll be underwhelmed," Selena replied.

THE EMPTY CANYON

We marched north for what must've been hours before noticing any change. Anything other than the endless grain. If Nara had been speaking the truth, then the vision her and the others had for Riven was a bland one. Who needed a field this large in a world where nobody had to eat?

Selena, looking around, was the first to notice we'd found our way back. My eyes had been buried too low into the stalks, pushing one after another out of the way.

"I think I can see the walls," Selena said. "The north side of the city."

"Then we're far enough west, according to Nara," I said. "Time to go north."

"Have you ever been up there? North of the city?"

"The farthest I've been was when we escorted that girl, Honora, from New York," I said.

There'd never been much interest in going north of the city. There weren't enough spirits to make it worth your time. The Warrens and the Shambles were more fruitful hunting grounds. The crumbling factories in the Tar Pit more exciting than the dead grass and broken mansions on the north side.

I lived in Riven now, though. Might as well explore my new home.

We made our way to the wall, into that blessed hundred yard clearing between the end of the grain and the stone of the city. No gate in sight, only turreted stone splitting us from the chaos inside and the nothingness outside. I looked for sparks, but none lit Riven's gray sky. Either we were too far away from the fighting, or it had already ended.

"Never thought I'd see these walls and feel relief," I said, touching my hand to the smooth rock. "I'd be happy to never go back in that field again."

"Something tells me that's not likely," Selena said, glancing back at the stalks. "Unless Nara decides to relocate."

Nara's spark suggested we should continue along the wall until we hit the city's north gate. Compared to the trek through the field, the clearing beyond the wall made for easy walking. Every so often I'd remember how long Selena and I had been going, how I hadn't actually slept, well, at all since Piotr murdered me. I should have been exhausted. My body, after walking miles and miles, should have been aching. Instead, I felt the same. Not good, not bad. Just . . . there.

When we came to the north gate, we found it an equal partner to the one on the east side, a single curving arch with room for ten to fifteen to walk underneath abreast. Both Selena and I took a long look into the city. Back that way went home. To the east, the field dwindled and died, as though cut off by an invisible barrier. There were waving stalks of grain, and then, not a foot away, hard dirt. That flattened land extended north as far as we could see. A razed, empty landscape.

"Can't say much about their imagination," I said, staring at the emptiness.

"Nara lives in a hut in the middle of that field," Selena replied. "I don't think they were the most creative group. If I could make a world, Carver, it would be the most amazing place."

"Oh? Tell me," I replied as we set off on our walk north.

"First, there would be an ocean," Selena said. "Because I've never seen one. Towering waves along a beach that goes for miles and miles."

"Not a bad start," I said.

"The beach would transition into a city. Not like Riven, or Chicago," Selena continued. "No, it would be both bigger and smaller. No pollution, friends and neighbors you actually knew. Buildings that flowed together so that you could walk from one end of the city to the other without seeing the same thing twice."

"I guess your sketches weren't all of your creative side," I said. The charcoal and ash drawings covered the walls of her, our, apartment. Riven cityscapes that Selena captured from the balcony.

"Maybe all this blandness brings it out in me," Selena said. "In the middle of the city, though, there would be this grand tree. A trunk miles wide. Whole species would live in its branches, and the most delicious fruit would hang down for anyone passing by."

"I like your Riven more than this one," I said.

Selena kept talking as we walked, adding more and more details to the world of her imagination. I contributed commentary, and we were so immersed in the idea that when we saw Riven split apart in front of us it was disappointing to leave the dream behind.

Canyons. That's the word that came to mind. Great rifts in the ground in front of us, the earth descending and spitting into trenches carved out of the surface. To the east and west we could see more, their ridged edges poking over the otherwise hard-packed earth.

The canyon in front of us stood wide, likely half a mile or more in distance. As though someone had stuck a shovel into the ground right at this point and declared this spot the start of it. I'd seen drawn pictures of, and read accounts about, the Grand Canyon back in America. Its painted sediments forming murals on the wonder's walls. Here, though, Riven once again proved its ability to reduce nature to its most desolate form.

Grays and blacks shaded up and down the canyon walls, though I couldn't account for the colors. Riven's light cast shadows, certainly, but the gradients along the ridged sides ahead of us followed no established pattern. More like someone casting about with a jar of ink, splattering its contents on a giant canvas with no thought to where it would lie.

"And we were just talking about how boring this place is," I said as we stood and stared.

"Riven always surprises," Selena replied.

Surprises. What might be lurking down in that canyon? I didn't see any spirits—this definitely wasn't the way to the Cycle. The canyon bent not far beyond where we stood, and anything could be beyond the corner. I remembered the ghoul in the forest, that age-old monster waiting to devour any poor soul that wandered by. Why wouldn't there be another one here as well?

"I'm guessing Mali is down in there somewhere," I said. "This is where Nara sent us. We'll just be careful."

"Because we haven't been careful before?" Selena replied. "Come on Carver. Whatever comes, we'll be ready for it."

Smart, creative, and cocky? So many reasons why I loved this woman.

LIFE IN DEATH

We went into the canyon, walls going up on either side. As we went deeper I noticed that what I'd thought was shade, or colored rock, was in fact a mossy plant. Something like the dark leaves on trees in the forest. It grew in strings and stretches threading its way between rocky outcroppings and crumbling dirt. In fact it seemed as if this stuff might actually be holding the canyon up, preventing it from collapsing in on itself. After the trees and the grain, I wasn't exactly surprised over a new form of half-life in Riven.

Beneath our feet the ground became more uneven, the dirt filling with rocks and divots. More natural. The ever-present ash flakes faded away, as though being filtered out from the sky. A sky which had lost some of its gray cast. I even picked out a note of blue. The farther north we went, the more Riven changed to resemble the world I'd left behind.

"I don't understand this place," I said. "Riven isn't itself."

"Mali's a creator, isn't that what Nara said?" Selena replied. "What if she's making this?"

"Then why isn't Mali changing everything in Riven? Why only affect these canyons?"

"Carver, you're trying to ask why a spirit that's been stuck here for centuries isn't making sense."

"Point."

As we went further, the plants began to change. The black spidery moss shifted to green. This too looked odd in its own way. The vines and leaves were perfect, spotless in their emerald color. Like the ghoul had been in the forest. Every so often flowers popped from one of the vines; florescent purples and blues. Beneath their feet the hard earth gave way to cushioned grass, all of uniform height. As though manicured by an especially attentive gardener.

Trees began to jut out around us, not the tall dead statues west of the city but brown, bark encoded with leaves. Between their tangled branches, more vines looped and swayed. Ferns, all sharing the same sort of banded leaf sprung up between the trunks. The same designs, appearing again and again. It was on one hand beautiful and on another unsettling.

"Even when Riven does something incredible," I said. "It can't help but be a little bit creepy."

"I'm curious." Selena traced a finger along the bumped bark. "If Mali made all this, then Mali made the city and the forest and the Mountain, but those are not identical. The buildings in the city aren't one and the same repeated over and over again. This, though, it's the opposite of natural."

"I'm thinking we'll need to ask her a few questions," I said.

Of course, we'd have to find her first. The canyon widened around us until I couldn't see the walls anymore. Blocked by the jungle, the thick vines. We were moving forward, pushing through the brush and hoping to find some indication that we were heading the right way.

Yet, I would be lying if I said the yellow light filtering down on us from a blue sky didn't bring me joy. And homesickness. For a few miracle moments I could pretend I was back on Earth.

"How does it feel for you?" I said. "You remember things like this? Sky this blue?"

"Were you ever told stories as a kid?"

"It depended on who I was with. Sometimes, the guide would tell me tales. Or read from a book. More often, I was left to my own devices."

"Seeing the sky, the sunlight, it's like remembering a fairytale. That's how I recall the life I used to have," Selena said. "A story that I was told years before and now all I have are vague memories. Feelings and impressions."

"I suppose it all has to go eventually."

"You'll replace it." Selena threw me a smile. "You'll make new memories. Find new things to love here. Riven might not be everything you want, but it isn't empty. There are things here worth knowing. Worth loving."

"I can think of some."

I was in the middle of returning Selena's smile when I noticed a glint coming from the tree to our right. There's a certain shine to metal, a clear clue that it's not natural. A harsh glare. Living in Chicago I'd seen that reflection every day. Among the leaves and rock of the canyon, there was no hiding it.

With a single move, my right hand reached over my back and pulled off the crossbow. Caught the weapon in my left and aimed it at the light. Selena froze, followed my pointing.

"Tell me who you are and I won't shoot," I shouted into the jungle. I turned the crank, loading a normal bolt. It wouldn't wrangle a spirit, but it could hurt it plenty. Give us time to react if whatever held the metal proved to be less than friendly.

"Shoot him?" said a voice behind me, curious and light. "Why would you do that? Neither of you look like you are members of the Right Hand."

I gave Selena a slight nod, didn't move my crossbow or my aim. Selena drew her cleaver and pointed it over my shoulder at whomever had spoken.

"Same goes for you," Selena said. "Who are you and what you want?"

"Me? I'm Cheo, and we're part of Mali's Left Hand," the man said. "Would you please come with us? It will be such an honor to bring two such as yourselves for the collection."

THE TWO HANDS

The glint moved from the trees. Shuffled down through the branches and leaves. I kept my crossbow aimed at the shape as it shifted lower. Cheo, behind us, whispered words, names I didn't recognize, into the jungle. Around us more people came out from behind tree trunks and dropped from other branches. All of them dressed in orange garb, each and every one of their shirts bearing a left hand printed in smeared, dirty red.

"You can put your weapon away now; there are no Right-Handers here," Cheo said.

"You're going to have to forgive me," I replied. "I don't plan on taking my hand off this trigger until I know what you are."

"Carver, that's not exactly the best way to make friends," Selena said.

"It is okay. I understand. The Right-Handers are devious. Dangerous," Cheo said as I turned to face him, still keeping the crossbow ready. "Keep your weapons. We will take you back to our village. Teach you why we are not to be feared."

"We don't have the time," I said. "We need to get to Mali. You know where she is?"

"Mali?" Cheo said "The great one? Mali is all things. The giver and taker. The creator and the destroyer. We are not worthy of her. Neither are you."

"That's presumptive," I said.

Cheo shook his head. "No, it is only fact. None of us can be worthy while the Right-Handers survive. As they cannot so long as we exist."

I glanced at Selena. "Do you think they know they're spirits?"

Cheo slanted his head. "Spirits?"

"I don't think so," Selena said. "Nara said Mali could shape things. Maybe this is something that she's doing?"

"Cheo," I said. "Do you know about the Cycle? Do you ever feel a compulsion to leave here and walk away?"

Cheo shook his head. "You're both very strange for wanderers. Most do not ask so many questions."

"We're the curious type," I said. Sounded like Mali had her own little slice of Riven and was making something very strange out of it. If Mali could change all of this, though, then maybe she really did have the power to save Riven. To block the breaches or blunt the anger of the dead.

Power. That word, ever since Piotr and Graham, had taken on new meanings. Graham had shown me that spirits could have goals, and could work to achieve them. Piotr had bound both guides and spirits, formed a deadly force that chased his desires without heed for the consequences.

Riven wasn't as simple as it used to be. Wasn't only about wrangling angry spirits and going back to Chicago for a drink in the afternoon.

I missed that life.

The group of people that had surrounded us—I counted eight of them—stared with smiles on their faces. The blank happiness that comes from a life unburdened. Now that they were close I could see that each one carried a variety of weapons. None of the quality the guides had. Sharpened sticks, bows and arrows with metal tips, some crude knives and axes. Whatever war Cheo and his Left Hand planned to fight, it wasn't going to be a fancy one.

"So you're saying that the Right-Handers need to go if we're going to see Mali," I said, and Cheo nodded, this time with a vigor that had me worried he was going to pop his head off.

"Yes, yes that's it exactly," Cheo said. "Come with us. Help us. When we defeat the hideous Right-Handers, then you will get your audience with Mali. Then the world will be righted."

"What do you think?" I asked Selena. For their part, the group seemed endlessly patient. Willing to beam at us with hopeful grins as we took our time.

"It's either we try to fight our way through them," Selena said. "And keep wandering through these canyons, or help them and get a direct path to where we want to go."

"Agreed," I said, then, to Cheo. "You're up, captain. Lead on."

Cheo clapped his hands in what may have been the most pure display of sheer joy that I'd ever seen. Then he strode off into the forest, beckoning us after him. The rest of the Left-Handers filed in behind us as we marched, though I noticed more than half of them disappeared as we moved. Vanished back into the trees.

"Where are they going?" I asked Cheo after the third one dropped away.

"We are not done with the collection yet," Cheo replied. "They are going to find more lost ones for us."

"Lost ones?"

"Like you," Cheo said. "Wanderers that can help. Most, though, are not so well-armed as yourselves. So great and powerful."

"Great? Powerful?" Selena said. "Don't feed his ego, Cheo. Carver doesn't need that."

"Apologies," Cheo replied. "We are a band of lost souls. What we have for weapons comes from what we can find. What we can build. I look at your might and see hope. Things that could win our fight forever."

"That's the idea," I said.

"Are the Right-Handers like you?" Selena said. "Spirits?"

"They may share our face, but not our hearts," Cheo replied. "All they are is evil. Terrible anger."

"How long have you been fighting?" I asked.

"Forever," Cheo replied. "There has always been a Right Hand and a Left Hand. Never has one completely wiped out the other."

I heard heat come into his voice. Cheo's shoulders stiffened, and he glanced at me with a twisted vehemence that I'd only seen in a spirit consumed by uncontrolled rage.

"That changes with the two of you," Cheo continued.

"Mali requires that you wipe them out completely?" Selena said. "She sounds vicious."

Cheo didn't reply. Didn't say anything as we continued moving through the jungle. Perhaps Selena had struck a nerve. Caused the spirit to revisit just what Mali was asking of him and the others. Then I caught myself.

Who cared if the Left- and Right-Handers destroyed each other? They were already dead.

ETERNAL WAR

The plants thickened as Cheo led us through more groves of spindly trees and vines. He recovered, breaking out of his funk and promising that we would find ourselves amazed and awed by what the Left Hand had accomplished. By the paradise that they had put together here in the harsh land of the canyons. And of course, Cheo emphasized, they had done all of this despite the cold attempts by the Right Hand to hurt and kill every last one of them.

Cheo wasn't wrong. Whereas in the rest of Riven, the buildings and the cities had been objects of ruin and decay that lasted for centuries, moldering remains of dreams left to founder, the Left Hand had a home. A village of tree houses and thatched huts. A large square with a central dominating pillar inscribed with runes that I could not read or understand. Fires burned in large grilling pits, though I didn't see any food actively cooking. Spirits wandered, men and women and even children going about building more homes, weaving clothes from plants, or bending and shaping wood into weapons. Here, perhaps, was Riven's only society. A village of the dead that nonetheless felt alive.

"But all of you are spirits?" Selena asked. "How are you doing this?"

Cheo looked at her quizzically. "Spirits again? What are you meaning with this word? We are all members of the Left Hand. We have all been collected and called to our duty. This is our home, our sacred place to protect."

Our sacred place. The words had a weird ring to them. Spoken with a reverence that I'd not heard in a long time. The same sort of reverence that, as a young child, I'd heard in churches. Or in town squares as criers delivered sermons of the day. Whomever these spirits were, I didn't think they believed themselves to be dead.

"Cheo, how many of you are there?" I said. "How big is the Left Hand?"

"Nearly a hundred," Cheo beamed. "One hundred souls ready to pick up spears for Mali and vanquish the Right Hand."

"And the Right Hand? How big are they?"

"Sadly, they are larger still. I fear if we do not bolster our number soon, they will come to crush us."

Cheo said the words and frowned. Then turned to one of the larger huts, one that was more than three times the size of Nara's. He pointed to it. "Please, follow me over there. We can talk more about the plan."

"The plan?" Selena asked.

"Of course! Our grand attack to bring down the Right Hand. It must begin soon. Before they know we are coming."

As we walked through the village the spirits of the Left Hand looked over at us. Some even offered waves. All of them looked conscious and cognizant. None had the vacant stares of spirits caught by the Cycle. None had the pale fire eyes of one lost to Riven's insatiable hunger. No, whatever the spirits were, they'd found a way outside of what made Riven a brutal universe. Selena and I caught each other's eyes and nodded. Mali had created her own little corner in this dead world.

Inside, the hut lacked even the basics. Only a small pit for a fire, this one unlit. Some sparse bundles of plants and grass forming little circles around the inside. As though someone had put the house together and forgotten how to fill it. Cheo sat down on the hard ground and motioned for us to do the same. I looked for beds, for any sign of the usual life comforts. The sort of things that any permanent village would have to have. But I saw none.

"Tell me," I asked Cheo before he could launch into his plan. "Has this village been here as long as the Left Hand?"

Cheo cocked his head at me. "Of course. How could there be a Left Hand without a home for them?"

"That doesn't make sense," Selena said.

"It doesn't have to," Cheo replied. "But it is, nonetheless."

Selena and I waited a moment. To see if Cheo would offer some additional explanation. But it seemed like with that recitation, the statement that sense and logic need not apply, that the matter was settled.

"When we go to attack the Right Hand," Cheo said. "You should know that it will be hard fighting. It always is. They will not hold back, and neither will we."

"We're used to it," I said.

"I expected so."

Cheo laid out an intricate plan of assault on a village that seem to be much the same as the one we were now sitting in. A series of huts in a large clearing. At least, that's what it looked like going by the rocks Cheo laid out on the floor and the marks in the ground he drew with a stick to illustrate exactly how we would be approaching. If there was one thing I took away from the plan, it was that Cheo harbored an undying hatred of the Right Hand. He infused every sentence with insults and anger. Until I couldn't handle it anymore.

"What do they do? The Right Hand?" I asked. "What makes them so terrible?"

"They tried to kill our goddess," Cheo said, his voice falling into an almost stunned reverie. "They tried to take her from us. There is no act more unforgivable than to try to destroy one's creator."

"How did they do that?"

"They attacked her temple," Cheo said, "and we defended her. The Left Hand, we came to her aid and stopped them. Struck them down. But the Right Hand, they are like a disease. They will not leave us for long. They will try again. We must make sure they cannot."

Before another question could come to my lips, three more spirits entered the hut, some of the hunters from earlier. They bore the same bright smiles on their faces and waved their arms. They shouted that they had found more. More that were ready to join the Left Hand.

The collection had been successful.

THE COLLECTION

We went outside the hut to a changed scene. Where before the spirits had been meandering around the village in what seemed like a reasonable imitation of life, as if they had one, now all those same spirits gathered around the pole in the center. Men, women, and children stood staring at that pole, and the five figures assembled around it. A quintet of confused and lost spirits; two were dressed as soldiers, another a child no more than ten, with the sunken look of one who'd fallen to disease. The last two were older women in flowing dress from a region I didn't know.

Cheo guided the two of us to the front of the circle, calmly pushing aside spirits in our path. They made way for us with deference, bowing at our faces and our backs. I couldn't quite comprehend what was happening here. So unlike any other part of Riven. The spirits acted so differently. They didn't seem to be bound, and yet they moved with purpose. They didn't seem to have any recollection of who they used to be, but they were able to find a shared objective.

Riven made it difficult to communicate with many spirits. Language and ideas didn't transcend death. While I might know English, a spirit may not. What I took as a gesture of hello, another spirit might interpret as an attack. All of which made Riven a dangerous place to make assumptions. Here, though, it was as though the spirits were wiped clean. Replaced with a common personality, a common goal, a common mind.

"Every second we're here, I get more worried," Selena said. "These spirits aren't normal."

If Cheo heard her, he didn't react. Instead, he led us to our part of the circle and then moved to the five in the middle. Cheo turned and held up his hands to the crowd. They began to murmur. Not individual speech, no, but the same three words over and over again in a low and constant hum.

We are Mali.

"Nara thinks this person is going to help her?" I whispered to Selena.

"I suppose Mali has an army of spirits? She could use them to help cleanse Riven," Selena said.

"Or rule it," I replied.

The murmur built up in volume and speed, until it became a shout. All the spirits yelling in perfect unison. The five in the middle cast their eyes around, curious but unconcerned. Unafraid. Difficult to be scared when you were already dead. When you didn't know what you were or what, if anything, was at risk.

"Bring the water," Cheo announced as the chant reached its height, loud to the point where I winced with every cadence.

A path parted through the crowd of spirits, a wide berth filled with a moving vat. A cauldron of black stone. Eight spirits carried it, the vessel suspended on wooden sticks held above the ground. I couldn't see over its lip, but it seemed, with the bend to the spirit's shoulders, that whatever was in that pot was not light.

"Set it down before our new friends," Cheo commanded and the carrying spirits put down the pot in front of, first, the young girl.

Now on the ground, I could see over the edge and into the vat. If you would have shown me the liquid back on Earth, on the other side, I would've told you that it was water. Perhaps dirtied, or tainted with some sort of dye. In Riven, the liquid's pale blue cast reminded me of the Cycle and the fire that both drove spirits mad and made them sane.

"Now she shall be the next to join us," Cheo announced. "How do we welcome a new soul to the Left Hand?"

"With the tightest grip," the crowd shouted back.

"And how do we thank them?" Cheo continued.

"With the sweetest wine," the crowd replied.

"I drank my fair share of wine," I whispered to Selena. "It never looked like that."

"Carver," Selena said. "If they offer that to us, I don't think we should drink it."

"I'm not thirsty anyway." I moved my hand to the lash's handle. We still had our weapons. Cheo hadn't bothered to take them away. Perhaps trusting that we were indeed his newest friends. His greatest allies in this strange war.

The young girl walked up to the pot, placed her hands on the edge, and lifted herself up. Stared into the shimmering waters. She hesitated. Cheo walked up behind her, put his hand against her head, and dumped the spirit into the water.

"Drink," Cheo said.

Another first in Riven. I'd never seen a spirit drink anything here, not that there was much in the way of liquid. I wasn't even sure they could until that moment. I certainly hadn't tried it since Piotr severed my cord with the living. The girl, though, took a large gulp. We could see her throat work as she swallowed. After a moment she stood back, turned to Cheo, and embraced him.

"Welcome sister," Cheo said. "Welcome to the Left Hand."

The rest of the five worked in turn. Each one going up to the pot, taking their drink, and coming back a loving member of the Left Hand. New additions to their village. After the final hug to welcome the newest brother, the second of the two soldiers, Cheo held up a hand. One hand, his left.

"With this collection, we are finally ready. Ready to make a last end upon our great foes. Go now and prepare. We will march on the third cry," Cheo announced. One of the spirits that had carried the pot put his hands around his mouth, curled them, and gave a sharp, high shout.

"The first cry," Cheo told us as the crowd dispersed. The same eight spirits that had carried the pot in, hefted it once more on the wooden carrier and lifted it away. "Are you ready?"

"What was that?" I asked, ignoring Cheo's question. Selena and I were as ready as we were going to be. As ready as you could be in a place you suddenly no longer understood.

"The collection?" Cheo said. "They were pledging loyalty. Joining us in our crusade."

"Why didn't you try to do that for Selena and I?"

"Because you do not need it," Cheo said. "You are not lost. You are not searching for a cause."

"How do you know that we'll help you?" Selena said. "Maybe we're on the Right Hand's side?"

I shot her a warning glance, but Cheo laughed. Nodded past us. I turned and looked, followed Cheo's eyes and noticed that on many of the treehouses, standing on roofs and on thatched decks, were spirits with bows and arrows. Rudimentary stuff, but their points had an unmistakable blue tint.

"Dipped in Mali's boon," Cheo said. "Lethal to the Right Hand. Perhaps also to you."

"A threat. Because that's what this was missing," I said.

"Only a warning," Cheo replied. "One that will be unnecessary, I think. With your help, the Right Hand will fall. And then all of this can cease to be."

For the first time I saw Cheo's smile falter. I saw something in those eyes that spoke of a deeper longing, something beneath his drive to ruin the Right Hand.

"What are you looking for, Cheo?" I said.

"For an end," Cheo said. "To be free of this burden. To be free of this hate. To be free."

Another spirit sounded a cry. The second one. Cheo bid us a short farewell to go and get himself ready. To arm himself for what would be the last fight of his life, such as it was.

SOULS ALONE

Selena and I went into the hut to grab a moment alone. Outside, spirits shouted at each other, called for this or that or the other thing. Making ready for a war. Something not even death seemed to exorcise from existence.

"You know, you really do look ridiculous," Selena said. She stood across for me, the meager fire pit between us. Her hair splayed around her face and touched the collar of her coat. Normally she kept it up, out of the way of any potential danger. Yet when we started on the trek to find Nara, I noticed she'd let it flow free.

"I'd venture to say most of us do," I said. She stood there, messing with one of her gloves, trying to make it a perfect fit for her fingers. Her eyes and her smile followed me.

"Most of us don't have a sword, a crossbow, a lash, and a long knife sticking out of them," Selena said. "I have to say though, it's growing on me."

"Now that I'm dead, you start giving me compliments?" I said. In Riven, you didn't age. Selena would never change until she ventured to the Cycle. On the outside, at least. Beneath the skin, she was completely different from the woman I'd found wandering the streets.

"Don't want to miss my chance," Selena said. "And someone ought to. You've been looking awfully sad lately."

"Guess that'll happen when you die," I said. I didn't talk about how Selena had changed too. Riven usually had a dark effect on the soul, could desolate the most positive of people. Yet over these last few months, Selena had gone from dependent on Nicholas and I in order to crack a smile, to being the cause of our own.

"You'll get used to it," Selena said. "Death has its advantages."

"Does it? Like what?"

At first I think I fell for Selena because she was like me. Entirely without anyone else. I was an orphan, she was a spirit. Our secrets were shared with each other, because there was nobody to tell. Now, though, it wasn't about what kept us apart from the others but what brought us together. Literally, Selena kept me safe from the Cycle's song, and I did the same for her.

"It strips away your needs," Selena said, placing her hands above the small fire. "I don't need the warmth from these flames. Don't need to find food to eat, air to breathe. I'm never sick, nor tired. Centuries could pass without aging a day."

"But without any of those things, what do we have?"

Selena stepped over the fire pit, slipped her hand beneath my chin, leaned in for a kiss. Our cold lips touched, and though I may not have had a drop of blood in my body, I may not have had a heartbeat, I had a soul. And in that moment, my soul found a partner.

"You make a compelling argument," I whispered into her smile. A smile that faltered as she stepped away from me. Back over the fire pit.

"In a way, I think what we have is more pure now than it ever was before." Selena threw a look out the door, at the spirits getting ready outside. "Our survival is dependent on each other, and there are no other needs getting in the way."

"I won't think of it like that," I said. Now it was my turn to chase her around the fire pit. Gently fold her in my arms. "This isn't about survival. It's about you and I. Together."

"Careful, Carver, you're getting too sweet," Selena laughed. "Don't tell me my gruff guide is going soft?"

I didn't know whether the kiss made me soft or not. I didn't care.

"You realize we're about to fight a war for a bunch of spirits?" I said when we parted. "That we left the city looking for an end to the fighting, and only found more?"

"You and I have been fighting our entire lives." Selena started checking her weapons, arranging herself . "Why did you think it would stop once our lives were done?"

The great sword went over my back, the crossbow on top of it. No bolt loaded, as I wasn't sure what I'd need to shoot first. The lash coiled and slotted into the belt holster on my right. My long knife, sharp and ready, on the left.

"For a while there," I said. "I held some strange hope that you and I would find a way. That we could curl up in this imperfect corner of the world and make a life. Or I'd find a way to bring you back."

Selena tied back her hair, and we stood across from each other. Two guides, heavily armed and ready to dive into another fight. Seeing Selena stand that strong pulsed a thrill through me. Seeing the one you love confident and capable, that rush didn't go away with death.

"You already did," Selena said. "You gave me a purpose. You taught me what I needed to know to survive. Now I'm returning the favor."

The third cry sounded. The call to yet another battle. I wouldn't be fighting it alone.

DEAD MARCH

We flowed through the jungle with the Left Hand. Cheo's band whispered between and above the trees, sliding through branches and around trunks with little more than the chatter of leaves to announce their passing. Cheo himself, along with us and some other spirits that I gathered hadn't quite mastered the art of forest travel, trod along on the ground, trampled ferns and fallen leaves beneath our feet.

"Have you ever noticed, Cheo, that it all looks the same?" I asked our leader as we moved along.

"The same?" Cheo replied.

"The plants, the trees. They're all copies. The same types, and they grow the same way."

"When I first came here, every branch stood unique. Flowers of every color bloomed. Creatures even whistled in the night or scattered at our approach." Cheo's voice fell into reverie. "Over time, such things have gone."

"Over time?" Selena asked. "How long have you been here?"

Cheo looked at us, the corners of his mouth having trouble deciding whether to turn up or down. "Mali is a wonderful goddess, and I stay at her pleasure."

A goddess? Her pleasure? Mali's private world kept getting more and more strange, and Nara wanted this person to help her?

"Do you serve someone?" Cheo asked me when I posed the questions. "Have you ever lived and died to help another?"

"Only with my own choice," I replied.

"Then perhaps you do not understand. Mali is not simply a master, or a person we obey. She is with all of us. Inside us. When we triumph, she celebrates with us. When we fail, she mourns our loss."

"Does she control you?" What Cheo was talking about sounded more and more like a group of bound spirits serving out Mali's whims.

"She expresses her wishes, and we do what we can to make them real." Cheo never stopped moving forward, always kept his eyes on the next piece of jungle to move out of the way. "You ask these questions as though you disapprove, yet you came here, yes?"

"We need Mali's help, but I'm not a fan of binding unless it's necessary."

"I have seen what happens to those who lose Mali's gift. This binding that you mention. They wander, lost, and disappear never to return."

Cheo didn't sound too disappointed by the prospect, though. In fact, I'd have argued the Left Hand leader looked losing Mali's gift as a blessing.

Cheo seemed to realize his own tone betrayed him, and he gave a heavy sigh. "If I am weary of the bow and the arrow, the spear and the sword, it is because Mali's service is not easy."

"You could lose, right?" I said. "Throw yourself into the Right Hand's attack?"

"Mali compels me to fight as best I can. Such an act would go against her wishes. Therefore, I await the day a Right-Hander bests me in combat. May it come soon."

I didn't know what to say to that. A spirit with a lingering death wish they could not fulfill. Riven never ceased its surprises.

The hike felt long, but without exhaustion or a day's passage to tell the time, it was impossible to know. Only when Cheo held up a hand did we discover that we were close.

"Beyond the next glade," Cheo said. "We will find their village. They will not be expecting us, so if we move quickly, then victory should be ours."

"How do you know they're not expecting us?" I asked.

"Because they have completed their collection. We have not," Cheo said. "They no longer scour the jungle for new ones to add to their numbers, which means they are preparing to attack us. Which means we have one moment to capture the surprise."

Cheo unslung a crude bow from over his back, held an arrow in his left hand. His eyes adopted a focused glint that I'd seen in my fellow guides ahead of a battle; that iron focus, a steeled reserve against whatever ruthlessness was to follow.

"Guess it's time," I said to Selena, but she'd already drawn out her cleaver and knife. I followed Cheo's lead and brought out the crossbow. Slotted in the blue bolts and cranked one into ready position. Did I want to use any of the six bolts I had in a random fight with jungle spirits? Not particularly, but I didn't want to die either.

And if victory meant an audience with Mali, then there was no point in holding back.

Now we crept. Kept ourselves low as we shifted through the brush. Cheo and I on either side and Selena between us, just behind. The positions gave us clear firing lines while leaving Selena free to step up and engage anyone rushing us. Standard tactics for engaging spirits. As for whether they'd work against the Right Hand, who knew?

The clearing looked identical to the Left Hand's village. The same number of huts in roughly the same places. A central pole standing tall, though the runes were different. As were the spirits crowding around it. The many spirits circling the pole. Far more than the Left Hand.

"Cheo, we're too outnumbered," I said. "They must have double ours, maybe more."

"Surprise, my friend," Cheo said, "is the great equalizer."

Cheo stood, nocked an arrow. The Right-Handers continued to

chant—I picked out Mali's name amid unfamiliar words—and glanced around the perimeter to see the other Left-Handers settling into positions. Picking their shots. I supposed I'd better find mine.

Looking down the crossbow, I squinted my right eye and took aim. Like the Left Hand, the Right Hand had spirits of all backgrounds, ages, races. Mali's devotees didn't discriminate.

I found a frightening man, one bearing a series of jagged scars around his face, body, and arms, and leveled my shot. He'd likely died in an accident, sudden and vicious. Crossed to Riven without realizing, without having a chance to change his soul to suit himself.

Now, I'd wipe what was left of him just as quickly. My finger tightened on the trigger, and I squinted. Dead on.

Cheo fired.

STRIKE

The arrow flew silent. My only clue came from the slight *twang* as the bowstring snapped. Cheo's aim was true, and the arrow re-appeared wedged in between the shoulder blades of a spirit on the outside of the circle. A man that yelled in wounded surprise, a yell that cut off abruptly as pale blue fire erupted from the arrow's point.

I hesitated. Blue fire? These spirits had arrows capable of wrangling? How?

Battle cries jerked me back to the present. Left-Handers calling from the trees as they peppered the Right-Handers with arrows. The Right-Handers scattering and calling for arms. Both sides wished Mali's vengeance upon the other. Both sides damned their foes in the name of the same goddess.

"Are you going to use that thing?" Selena said as Cheo loosed another arrow.

"Waiting for the right moment," I said, covering. Took aim with the crossbow. My scarred man had vanished into the swirling crowd, so I picked a target at random. A frenzied guy whose lanky arms waved, directing traffic. Pointing out Left-Handers in the trees and jungle. I pulled the trigger.

My blue bolt lanced out, pierced the spirit's chest, and wreathed him in the same blue fire as the Left-Hander's arrows. He stopped his arm waving and, a moment later, wandered off towards the jungle. A long, long walk to the Cycle from here, but the spirit would get there.

The first counters started from the Right-Handers. Arrows of their own shooting out from hut windows, or from spirits crouching behind stacks of wood, piles of brush. Our ambush had taken a good fifth of them, I estimated, based on the number of idling and wandering spirits staying in the middle of the clearing. That still left us outnumbered.

"We can't afford to let them get settled," I called to Cheo.

"Agreed!" Cheo replied, and then he cupped his hands and gave a ululating cry. "Charge with me, friends!"

"And now it gets interesting," Selena said as we took our first steps out from the brush.

"Stay close," I replied. "If those arrows hit us, we can't save each other. Can't use a binding to recover."

"You mean we might die again?" Selena laughed as we ran towards the village. "Carver, all that would give me is peace!"

I raised the crossbow as we charged, cranked the next blue bolt into position. Directly ahead of us stood a pair of huts, Right-Handers starting to pour out of the main doors. Hard to aim with every footfall pushing the crossbow up and down. Thankfully, a point-blank shot wasn't hard to find.

A hulking spirit shoved his way out of the hut on the right, and I blasted the man's monstrous chest with my shot, sending him falling back into the hut with blue fire burning along his body. A tattooed woman took his place, raising a pair of knives and starting towards me.

I threw the crossbow hard, striking her in the face. Keeping her in the hut's doorway, the only thing limiting the number of spirits coming at me. As she recoiled, I grabbed the great sword with both of my hands, planted my right foot into the dirt, and, leaning forward, drew the weapon in a long front slash. The sword sliced through the hut's walls, cut through the spirit's pitiful knives, and diced her in fire.

The doorway collapsed, the roof sagging as my cut undermined the hut's integrity. Instead of one, now three more spirits stood in front of me in the wide opening. Two with crude axes and a third holding a bow, arrow knocked and ready to fire. I braced for the shot.

A knife flew by my right shoulder, embedding itself in the bow-wielding spirit, causing the man to stumble back. Selena followed it, sidestepping an ax-man's swing to chase down her knife, grab the weapon with her left hand and twist the hilt. Blue fire raced down the blade, sending the bowman to blissful peace.

The first ax-man came at me, crying out in a language I didn't know and bringing his short-hafted weapon in an overhand strike towards my head. A suicide play—the spirit left himself wide open, ready to give up a hit in order to deliver a crushing blow. Instead, I pushed off with my right foot, went to the left of the wild swing and sliced with my sword as the spirit went past. My swipe caught the spirit in the back and sent the ax-man sprawling, burning blue lighting him up.

In front of me, Selena matched her ax-man blow for blow, clangs ringing out as the cleaver caught the ax-man's strikes again and again. The ax-man feinted a right-handed cut, which Selena moved to counter, and struck out with his left hand. Punching at Selena's face.

My love was too fast. She saw the punch coming, ducked it, and threw her right shoulder into the ax-man's chest. As he stumbled back, Selena reversed her right arm, sweeping the cleaver out in front and catching the ax-man with his arms wide. A burning blue cut opened in the spirit's stomach, and he looked at Selena, mouth agape, as all the rage and ruin drained from his eyes.

"Cheo!" Selena yelled as the ax-man fell away. I followed her eyes and saw our Left Hand leader pressed by a quartet of Right Hand spirits. At first I thought Cheo's end was going to be quick in coming, but our guide to this misbegotten land had no intention of going out quietly. He spun and kicked, blocked and countered, content to keep the swiping axes and knives at bay rather than expose himself for a killing strike.

"Guess we'd better help him," I said, running back out into the clearing. Beyond Cheo's dire dance, the rest of the Right Hand village had blown into one of Riven's surreal pitched battles. Vacant spirits, standing stunned or starting to walk off to the Cycle mingled with the furious fighting between both sides. The Left-Handers, either out of arrows or unable to find good targets in the melee, had left their ambush spots and dove into a Right Hand force gathering into its own.

Strategy's part in this play had ended. Chaos had taken hold.

Something smashed into me as I ran towards Cheo, picked me up and threw me ten feet across the ground. I hit the grass and rolled, keeping the great sword's blade flat against the ground. Looked up to see a foot sliding towards me. Felt it strike my head and snap it back.

Spirits in Riven couldn't suffer serious injury for long. Without organs, bones, or blood, there simply wasn't much to actually damage. Pain, though, that stayed. Not because of a natural process, or so Nicholas had told me, but because our minds still believed we had breakable bodies. Still believed we could be damaged and destroyed.

So when the kick connected, a banging blossom of thwacking agony wracked my mind and the jungle overhead spun like an over-wound clock. Instinct was the only thing that saved me. I rolled with the strike, lifted the great sword in the way of the attack, and caught my assailant's club on it.

My enemy's weapon was a nightmare instrument: a warped wooden shaft with shards of metal sticking out of its end at odd angles. Like the crooked claws of a hideous monster. Each and every one of those glinting pieces shimmered with pale fire waiting to be unleashed. I couldn't let it touch me.

I shoved up against the club, and against the corded arms that held it. Arms covered with scars. My first target, come back to find his would-be killer. The shove brought me a bit of breathing room as he stepped back to stay upright. I curled forward, planted the sword against the ground to get to my feet. Took my first good look at my foe.

The first thing I noticed was his club, coming right back towards me in a crashing blow I had no time to dodge.

THE PRIZE

So I didn't try. I dropped the great sword and ducked into his swing, hoping to get close enough so that I dodged those metal pieces. I felt the club strike my shoulder and the left part of my neck. The thwack nearly drove me to my knees, but I didn't feel any sting. No slicing cut. No blue fire. My shoulder, had I still been human, would have been dislocated. My shoulder, because I was dead, merely flashed between aching pain and numbness.

With my right hand I drew my knife and tried to stab the spirit in the stomach, but his left hand grabbed my wrist, holding my knife out wide. He reached back with the club for another strike and I slipped around him, pulling his left arm across his chest as I went underneath his right. Or at least, that's what I tried to do. As I moved behind him, the spirit dug in his left foot and pulled me back, whipping me down to the ground. Raised the club above his head and brought it smashing towards my face. I stabbed up with the knife, catching the club on the point of my blade. The knife drove into the wood, splitting the club and shattering it into pieces, the shards sprinkling down around me. The spirit stared at the stump in his hand, a few inches of splintered wood. Until I stood up.

"Quality matters, my friend," I said, brandishing my polished, forged knife.

The spirit growled at me, his face a menacing mishmash of crumpled bone and skin. His exit from life had been a truly miserable one. He threw the club stump at me and followed it up with a reckless charge, head down and arms outstretched. I ducked under his hands, caught his waist and, bracing my feet, lifted him up and over my shoulder and sent him flying behind me.

As he hit the ground I turned and drew my lash. The spirit planted his hands and shoved himself back up, just in time for my lash to wrap around his neck. The metal end pierced the scarred man's skin and I twisted the hilt, sending the blue fire along the length of the cord and wrapping the spirit in its pale glow, ending his pain.

I withdrew my lash and turned around, hoping Cheo still lived. Saw that Selena had come to his rescue. The two of them were finishing off the Right Hand spirits. Cutting and slicing and tearing with wild abandon. Behind them the pitched melee died down. Cheo's surprise play had worked. Without a chance to get themselves formed up, the Right-Handers had been trapped inside huts, or scattered across the clearing where teams of Left-Handers divided and skewered their foes. Despite the numbers, the Right-Handers had no leadership, had no organization, and were picked apart.

Selena and I joined in the cleanup efforts, taking care of the scattered resistance and making sure no other threats remained. Eventually, when the jungle returned to its normal quiet, the two score Left-Handers that had survived the battle joined us in the middle of the clearing. Clusters of vacant-eyed spirits stared at us, while others wandered out under the Cycle's siren call.

"Then it is done," Cheo said to the group. "The Left Hand is victorious. Our enemies vanquished. Now, our peace can finally reign."

I glanced at Selena. "What peace do you think he's talking about?"

Selena shrugged. "You don't think they can live in their village?"

"Did you see it when we were there? Did you see this one? The only things they were doing were getting ready for war. Recruiting more spirits. They don't have a peace time function."

"Maybe now they get to find one," Selena said.

Cheo continued extolling their victory. He claimed the battle in the name of Mali. Claimed her grace caused the Left Hand's triumph. The rest of the Left-Handers echoed each of the statements with wild shouting. The sort of delirious victory I'd seen on occasion with guides when we closed a breach. When we took down a ghoul. Even so, the ecstasy on these spirit faces as Cheo pronounced them the favored ones had me shivering. I'd seen loyalty like that before. I'd seen the spirits in Barth's tower, the guides that followed Piotr. That sort of fervent obedience only ended in terror.

After Cheo's speech ended, the crowd dispersed. The Left-Handers wandered the clearing and found what weapons they wanted to take. Collected arrows and spears and axes. Then they disappeared back into the jungle to walk back to their home village. Cheo kept us behind, until only the three of us stood in the clearing. He held out his hand and shook each of ours.

"It's been a long time since I fought alongside a pair of your caliber," Cheo said. "Thank you."

"Glad we could help," I said. "This is what you wanted?"

"The Left Hand won. The Right Hand lost. I achieved Mali's goal," Cheo said, but the pronouncements sounded oddly hollow. "Now, I imagine you would like to see the goddess herself?"

"That is why we're here," I said.

"Then I will take you to her, as promised."

RUNES

We struck out from the village a few minutes later, not heading back east towards the Left Hand's town but instead striking north. Deeper into the canyons whose walls seemed to grow ever higher and the jungle ever more dense. Even though the trees and ferns were the same, there were more of them. They pressed tighter around us until the thought of leaving the path and leaping to the branches as the Left-Handers had done, looked an impossibility. Instead we moved in single file, the thick trunks closing in on either side. All signs of the blue sky above faded away as leafy canopies closed off light. Rays filtered down through tiny gaps, spotlights illuminating our steps. As though we were shifting between night and day.

"Quite the atmosphere," I said.

"Mali made beautiful things, once," Cheo replied.

"Once?" Selena brushed a low-hanging vine from her face.

"She hasn't left her temple for a long time," Cheo answered. "I suspect she has lost interest in us, in her people."

"How long have you been here?" I said.

"You know that is an impossible question." Cheo led us across a bridge, made from tree branches strung together with vines, over a shallow crevasse whose smooth bottom suggested it once ran with water. "But I feel as though it has been many, many years."

"I ask because you understand English. You understand our words. Yet, I don't think you came from America. Or England."

"I speak many tongues," Cheo said. "I have to collect many spirits, teach them and train them. As I find new ones, I endeavor to learn. When time is no object, mastering a new skill is not so daunting."

"And Mali? Will she understand us?"

"Mali will hear what she wants to hear. That is why you must choose your words with care."

Not really an answer, but as with most things Mali, it seemed like the only way we would know was when we met her face-to-face. Around us, the jungle shifted from its copycat form. Where similar trees had grouped together, now arced large trunks with spiraling bark. Mushrooms bloomed up to our waists. Flowers, static without any breeze, stood straight up and searched for any sunlight poking through.

"Mali's garden," Cheo observed. "What energy she expends is focused here, closest to her."

"Beautiful." Selena went over to one of the flowers, a purple and black menagerie with long, spindly petals. She ran her hand along the ends, then frowned. "It's hard. Not soft, like a flower should be."

I took a turn, ran a finger along the edge. The petal felt like stone. Rough and scratching. When I pressed on it, the flower didn't move. Cheo, standing behind us, said nothing.

"Can I say I'm uneasy?" Selena said as we continued our walk.

"You can. I'd even agree with you," I replied. "Whatever Nara expected Mali to be, I don't think this was it."

"Keep that sword of yours handy."

"Always."

I wasn't lying either. My hands had taken to resting themselves on the hilt of the lash, the long knife. Comfort in the thought that no matter what sprung out at me, I'd have a decent chance of sticking it first.

Such was our world.

Our single file walk ended with a rock wall. Only, unlike the black mossy vines that covered the rest of the canyons, this section, maybe two hundred feet wide, was carved out in gold. Or at least, rock that looked like it. Every square inch molded into one symbol or another. Characters I didn't recognize, swoops in lines and diagonals looping around each other. Some carried on for yards, climbing up to the very top where the leafy canopy brushed up against it. All of it sparkling as various spots of light slipped their way through and bounced off. An opening, twenty feet wide, yawned at us. Bordered on the edges by set stone. No light came from that cave, only a deep night. Alongside the entry stood a pair of pillars, on which the same four characters repeated from top to bottom.

"I'm guessing that's her name?" I asked.

"My goddess is not a humble one." Cheo gestured at the face of the temple, the patterns laid into the rock. "Before, we brought spirits here for the collection. This served as their first introduction to the greatness they were going to see. Until Mali tired of the ceremony."

"There are so many symbols on these walls." Selena stared at the columns, and I watched her eyes move along the etchings. "They're hard to understand."

"You can read these symbols?" I asked.

"It's in an old tongue," Cheo said. "I no longer hear any spirits speakings its language. Earth must have forgotten it."

"I can't read it, Carver." Selena walked up to the left pillar, traced her hand along the carved runes. "But I've seen the symbols before. In museums."

"Do you know what it says?" I asked Cheo.

Our guide ran his eyes along temple's exterior. I chose to call it the temple because that's what it seemed to be. Mali's place of power. A goddess's palace of strength.

"My translation is imperfect," Cheo said. "But I believe it says that this domain belongs to the maker. This world belongs to the one who built it. All those who do not recognize its brilliance, you are not wanted. Those who wish to pay their respects, enter and be recognized."

"I'm sensing arrogance is a thing with Mali," I said.

"That may be all she has left," Cheo replied. "If you have come to offer something Mali wants, you will fare better."

"I have no idea if Mali wants what we're offering."

"Who wouldn't want an invitation to walk through a bunch of dead grain to meet with a creepy old spirit?" Selena said.

"We're not giving her a choice," I replied. "She's coming with us."

Cheo looked at the both of us, confused. I shook my head, and nodded towards the doorway.

"Shall we?"

"Before we go in," Cheo said. "I would caution you; be careful and courteous, or be prepared to face the fury of a goddess."

"Cheo, anyone ever tell you how good you are at giving ominous warnings?" I said. "Selena and I have seen the worst Riven has to offer. I think we can handle it."

"For your sake, I hope so."

We followed Cheo through the entry, into Mali's temple.

Into the dark.

TEN THOUSAND TIMES

As a child, I'd been scared of the dark for years. I think it had something to do with moving all the time. Never having a parent or someone that I could crawl into bed with, someone to chase away those phantom monsters. Instead I'd had one gruff guide after another, people whose nights were spent in another world. Who, when I cried out because of some nightmare, did not wake up. Did not come to comfort me or drive away my fears.

It took me more years than I cared to admit to come to own my terrors. To fight the shadows. The night became a battleground, a place where I waged endless wars with the black corners of my room. When I started crossing into Riven, the spirits added shape to the monsters I'd been warring with for years.

So as we stepped into Mali's temple, as the details slipped away until only the silhouette of the door behind us was visible, I refused to be afraid. Refused to fear what I could not see. I placed my hand on Selena's shoulder, and felt Selena put her hand on mine. We walked side-by-side.

"Have to say," I said, my voice sounding strange in the dark. Disembodied; coming from everywhere and nowhere. "I love the ambiance."

"There used to be lights," Cheo said. "Burning torches that never went out. Mali tired of the paintings."

"The paintings?" Selena asked.

"Hold on." I reached down to my belt, pulled out the long knife, and twisted its hilt. Blue fire wrapped the weapon, and lit up the hallway in its pale glow. Around us the walls burst forth with colorful images. Finely detailed strokes outlining landscapes and telling stories. Three figures repeated among all of them. Two women and a man. One woman with silver hair, one with black. The man had none.

One painting on the left wall showed the trio standing on a disk surrounded by lava. Or some other glowing, hideous liquid. The next one showed the three of them marveling at the land around them, the dark-haired woman's arms raised to the sky. On solid ground, a mountain soaring in the distance.

"Who made these?" I said. "Mali?"

"I don't know," Cheo said. "They have always been here. Since before even I. If Mali made these, then they were the only ones she ever painted."

The fire on my knife went out. It was not a torch, it would only burn for seconds at a time. I reset the hilt and was about to twist it again when Cheo, in the dark, put his hand on my wrist.

"Please," he said. "You come as a guest. It is best to obey the host's wishes. If Mali wants these paintings hidden, it is best that they remain so."

"And if I want to see them?" I asked.

"Do it after I am gone," Cheo said, and I could hear his grin. "That way Mali will know who to blame."

I thought about it. True, I didn't want to annoy Mali either, but I wanted another look at those paintings. What they seemed to show. Three spirits, and one with Nara's silver hair. Mali, perhaps, the other woman, the one appearing to make the world. Who the man was, I had no idea. Nara had mentioned a name, Dolan?

"Are you thinking what I'm thinking?" I asked Selena.

"Carver, I learned a long time ago never to assume you and I are thinking the same thing," Selena replied.

"Fair point. When we get out of here, let's talk."

"We've got a long walk back to the city. Plenty of time."

Cheo ushered us along. Further down the dark path. I could feel the walls closing around me. The stone floor shuffled with the scuffing of our boots. No other sounds played out. No flowing water, no rustling of a breeze. No crackle of far-off flame. Riven was never a loud place, unless you were in a pitched fight with howling spirits or standing next to a building as it finally succumbed to a slow collapse. But the passage achieved a new silence altogether. As though I'd truly died, as if all of my senses had disappeared.

I bumped into Cheo's back. Our guide had stopped.

"We are nearly there," Cheo said. "When I enter her chamber, I will cease to be myself."

"What do you mean?"

"I am Mali's subject," Cheo replied. "Under her rule, and her will. Do not interrupt. After it is done, you will have your chance. I wish you every bit of luck."

"You won't stay?"

"I will do as Mali wills," Cheo said. "I do not think it likely that, after all of these years, she will have changed. It has been a pleasure to know the both of you. May the Goddess grant you good fortune."

"Not sure we want her blessing," Selena muttered. Cheo didn't reply. He started walking again and we followed.

I almost didn't notice the light. Didn't realize that the walls fell away as we walked into a larger chamber. A room with twin pools on either side. One glowing a faint blue and the other a lime green. A stone pathway ran between them. It led to a dais, on which, in a chair, sat the goddess we were seeking. Next to her, resolute and staring at us with non-existent eyes on its metal face, stood a ghoul. Its golden skin shimmered in the pools' light. The ghoul wore a tunic coated in jewels, a rainbow of gemstones. Two arms, two legs, each a pillar of precious metal. As though Mali had molded the ghoul from both spirits and the earth.

Mali herself sported a silver dress, one that flowed around her and the throne on which she sat like liquid mercury. She wore no crown, sported no jewels. As if she didn't want to compete in opulence with her own ghoul.

Cheo kept walking as we stared. Left us standing there gawking at Mali's chamber. He took five steps forward and dropped to one knee, placed his hands on the ground and lowered his eyes to the floor.

"As it ever is, I have returned," Cheo announced. His voice dropped any friendly affectation. Every syllable spoken as though giving an official notice. As though pronouncing, sentencing someone to their death.

"As it ever is," Mali replied from her throne. She spoke with a light voice, earnest. A person trying to seem more excited than they really were. Disguising the weight of her centuries.

"Shall I perform the rite?" Cheo asked.

"Ten thousand times," Mali spoke softly. "Ten thousand times, Cheo, you have led the Left Hand to victory. And ten thousand times, you have conquered my realm for the Right Hand. It seems you are my greatest creation."

Ten thousand times? Both the Left Hand and the Right? I wanted to ask questions, but the idea of interrupting felt so far removed from any aspect of politeness, that I felt rooted to the spot. Unable to tear my eyes away from these two. From a goddess and her servant.

"I have fought many battles for you," Cheo said. "I will fight however many more you choose for me."

"I wonder, my Cheo, why you keep on winning?" Mali said. "Every time I pass the mantel to a new spirit, you wind up the victor. Are you truly the best that time has ever seen?"

"It is because you give me the strength I need."

"Yes," Mali replied, leaning forward in her chair and giving Cheo a glittering smile. "As long as I live, so will you. No matter how dangerous your duty becomes, so long as I am here, you will return victorious."

"As it ever is," Cheo said.

Mali nodded and Cheo stood, went over to the lime green pool and dipped in his hand. Took a sip of the water. Shivered.

"I stand for the Right Hand," Cheo announced to the chamber.

"With your blessing, I shall destroy the Left Hand. I will end their vicious attempts to hurt you. To damage your kingdom."

"Go then, and seek their most deserved doom," Mali replied.

Cheo turned to her, bowed, and then marched past us. I thought about stopping him, but it didn't look like our friend lived anymore in those eyes. The Cheo that had brought us here was gone.

THE CREATION

Have you ever had an elder stare at you? A look from someone who seems to know who you are and who you would become?

When Mali turned her gaze to us from Cheo's departing back, I felt those eyes. Her Riven-gray colored pupils on me. They ran to and from every inch of my soul. And when Mali slid over to Selena I'd be lying if I didn't say I relaxed.

But exchanging stares wasn't going to get us anywhere.

"Mali," I said. "Nara sent us. We need you to come work with her to save Riven."

Mali sat back on her throne. Her fingers bounced constantly up and down, as though playing a piano that no one could see. I watched her eyes flick towards me. Instead of matching mine, Mali's look landed somewhere over my shoulder. In a space and time far away from the temple in which we stood.

"Nara sent you," Mali said. "Are you certain?"

"The woman in the field of grain," Selena replied. "Riven is falling apart, and she said you could help save it."

Mali laughed. A sort of strange, despairing chuckle that comes when someone hears about yet another folly committed by a notorious friend. Another error in an endless series of mistakes. Where redemption is so far gone that the only reaction is a sad chuckle.

Then Mali, goddess of her own making, stuck out her arms, palms up, and began to hum. The water in each of the pools started to rise up, droplets breaking free of the rest, hanging in the air like diamonds. Then the drops shifted to the center, over the walkway and between Mali and us.

They formed a square, a moving sheet of water hanging in the air. The droplets began to shift, re-arrange themselves. Some combining to darken their color and others splitting, becoming lighter. Until before my eyes sat an image like that of the painting in the hallway. A deep green disk on which stood a trio of blue figures. Two women and a man. Around them a sea of light blue, nearly transparent water.

The water moved, blue droplets gathering and weaving through the green. Smaller figures. Blue lines stepping off and scattering away.

"I think that's the Cycle," Selena said, and I agreed.

The parade of spirits continued as the three figures watched. Then one of the women appeared to reach out with her hand, to touch one of the blue lines. The droplets stopped their walk across the green disk. Waited until the blue figure pointed above. Then droplets marched their form up and off of the disk. Once more, they scattered into the transparent sea.

Now the second woman moved, tracing her hand along the outside of the green disk. More drops from the green pool raced up to join the water curtain, adding their color to the expanding disk. Widening it until nearly all the transparent water had been pushed off the edge. As the disk grew, the first woman continued reaching out and touching the smaller blue spirits, keeping them in a large huddle. Building an army.

The transparent water, the Cycle, had almost been removed from the curtain entirely when the male figure reached out. Pointed to the first woman's growing group of spirits. At the wandering blue lines that no longer had a place to go. The second woman shifted, her arms corralling the Cycle into a small circle and sending it to the left side of the watery curtain. Surrounding it in a triangle of deep green.

The Mountain, and the Cycle within it.

I noticed now, wandering through the curtain of water, more deep blue figures appeared. Not so large as the main three, but more defined than the spirits. The man reached out to those figures, and each one he touched seemed to alight their hands and arms in light blue drops. The pale wrangling fire. The first woman, the one with the expanding army of thin blue figures, grew agitated. Some of the thin blue figures surrounded one of the man's burning allies. And quenched it. This prompted the man to send his other servants after the woman's army. They clashed around the disk, with many of the woman's thin blue figures racing off towards the mountain as they fought.

Meanwhile, the green disk changed. Instead of a flat and uniform surface, everywhere the second woman brushed her hand, new features arose. The green lightened and darkened, clustered and shifted to form a familiar outline. A map I knew all too well.

"This is Riven's history," I said. "How it came to be."

"But who are they?" Selena said, pointing past me at the three figures. "I get that the one making all the green things, that must be Mali."

"The other two? I don't know."

"You think the other woman is Nara?"

"The one binding all the spirits?" I said. "Possibly."

That would explain how Nara knew so much about bindings. If she had been the first one to learn, with centuries to perfect and perform the process. Only in this rendition, it almost looked like Nara was the evil one. Her army of spirits fighting constantly against the man's smaller, pale-fire-wielding force.

In the water play, it looked as though the man and first woman had fought themselves to a stalemate, an equal line of figures continually replacing and destroying each other. The second woman, Mali, moved apart from them and watched. The view changed. Zoomed in on the city, the droplets shifting and expanding to show alleys and blocks. Thin blue figures moving and appearing to work with each other. Spirits running a town. Moving carts of goods, illustrated in green droplets. Operating stores. Gathering together.

Then, from the left and north sides, came the deep blue figures and their pale-fire arms. Streaming down through the streets and burning away the spirits. Sometimes they appeared to smash through buildings, scattering green droplets. The swirling battles went on for a while, until the view shifted out again. The smaller figures vanished entirely, reforming into the man and first woman, standing on a green plain. They grappled, their fingers locking with each other. Behind them, the green shifted and broke, droplets scattering and forming themselves back together.

Mali entered from the right, her dark blue form appearing to plead with the pair. Being ignored. And, finally, raising her arms to the sky. Deep green lines came down the water curtain, splitting the man and woman. Splitting Mali apart from them. Mali's figure hung her head, and then the water curtain dissipated. Scattered back to the pools.

"Now you understand," Mali said. "I cannot free them. I cannot free Nara, because she will try again."

"Try again to what?" I asked. "Bind spirits? It didn't look so bad, there, in the town."

"She kept them," Mali said. "All the spirits. They did her bidding. Worshipped her. You believe Riven is in danger now, then freeing her would only bring the hordes under her control. What you saw there was a city bent to the desires of its leader."

"Then why did you make it in the first place?" Selena asked.

"Because Nara asked me. We were the first ones. The first who kept ourselves from taking that last step into the Cycle. No doubt you have found its call easier to resist when you work together? So it was with us. When Nara wanted a city, I built it. When Nara wanted the Cycle gone, I tried to destroy it."

"You put it in the Mountain," I said.

"I would have sealed it off completely, were it not for Dolan," Mali said. "If he hadn't held me back. Argued that there might yet be some use for it."

"So if you think Nara is going to ruin Riven," I said. "Can you help us? Can you drive the spirits into the Cycle?"

Mali shook her head. A frown came over her face. "Meddling has only brought me pain, little spirits. I should have vanished into the Cycle when I first came here. Instead, here I am. Trapped in a prison of my own making."

"I don't understand," I said.

"I learned to create this world. I do not know how to destroy it. There is no way to free the Cycle. And I will not let Nara go. Whatever befalls Riven, she will not have a hand in it."

I glanced at Selena. If Mali wasn't going to help us, then there wasn't much use in staying here. We were wasting time.

"Let's go back," I said. "Nara might have another idea."

"Didn't you hear her?" Selena said. "She's saying Nara's evil."

"Mali also said she didn't want to help Riven," I said. "That makes them the same to me. At least Nara gives us a chance. Maybe she's changed after all these years."

At my nod, Selena and I turned back to the passage. The dark path to the surface.

"You are not the first," Mali announced to our backs. "Nara has sent others. All begging for her release. All of them turned as you did. Determined to help Nara find a way free."

"What happened to them?" Selena asked.

"I did not let them go," Mali said, her voice dropping to a whisper. Once again, Mali's hand shot forward. The stones bordering the passageway out shivered, then crumbled in on themselves. Blocking our escape.

"We don't want to fight," I said, turning back around.

"You are free to die," Mali replied, then nodded at the golden ghoul beside her. Its head turned, and though its eyes were golden ovals, I met its gaze.

And when the ghoul marched towards us, Selena and I met its advance.

AUTOMATON

Selena ran towards the ghoul, cleaver raised in her right hand, her long knife held at her waist, point forward and ready to stick Mali's creation. The ghoul more than tripled our height; Selena didn't come up to its waist. As the two approached, the ghoul swung out with its right hand and connected with Selena's side, knocking her across the ground and into one of the pools. The ghoul didn't bother to look at what happened to her. Came right on towards me.

Most of the other ghouls I'd seen had been horrendous creatures. Misshapen masses of arms and legs and limbs that bore no other description. The spirits that they'd consumed shifted beneath their skin, faces popping to the surface and giving you a reminder of who had been consumed to create the abomination. Mali's ghoul looked different. Golden, pristine, a model of a person, if one without any clear gender features. Smooth skin and sporting a long gold tunic that stretched from collar to knees. I'd seen similar things before, in museums of ancient artifacts. Exhibitions on tours through Chicago. But it was one thing to stare at an artifact beneath a glass case and quite another to have an object of antiquity reaching for my throat.

I cracked the lash, wrapping around the ghoul's outstretched hand. Waited for the telltale sign that the metal tip had pierced the ghoul's skin. Then I'd start the fire and send it to its next life. Only the lash's point bounced off the ghoul's skin and hung, limp, as the ghoul continued its advance.

"It's skin isn't . . . skin," I shouted to Selena as she pulled herself out of the pool. The bluish liquid clung to her, bits of it dripping off onto the ground. Thicker than water.

"Maybe if you actually hit it harder," Selena shot back.

I didn't have time to hit anything. The ghoul swung at me with its right hand again, just as it had attacked Selena. I dropped to the floor, flattening myself and feeling the ghoul's fist fly overhead. Through the ghoul's legs, I saw Selena coming up behind, cleaver ready. If I could get its attention for another moment, Selena could hammer home.

I glanced up and saw the ghoul's left fist rising high. Ready to deliver a strike to my back that would bash me into nothingness. Then Selena's cleaver bit into the ghoul's calf. She swung her large knife with two hands, hacking at the monster's skin. This time, unlike my lash, I saw flecks fly off. Selena's blade breaking through. I expected a roar, but the ghoul stayed silent. A look at its face confirmed that it didn't have a mouth, only a metal line. Still, her attack made the ghoul pause, turn and regard the flea biting at its leg. Which let me get back to my feet.

Selena's cleaver had another trick. She twisted the hilt, the blade sticking into the ghoul, and wreathed the cleaver in blue fire. I waited for the cleansing flames to wash over the creature, to burn it to a cinder and leave nothing standing. Except the flames failed. They didn't burn. They didn't catch on and torch up and down the creature. They stayed on the cleaver, as though the ghoul were made of water. As though a steady breeze blew the flames back. Selena stared at her weapon as though it had betrayed her.

"Watch out!" I said.

The ghoul, rather than smash me with its fist, swung its left arm back, catching Selena with its barrel-sized hand. Again she flew through the air, this time landing at the foot of Mali's throne. Crumpled to the ground.

"Hey," I said to the ghoul. "My turn."

I did not want the creature mashing Selena to spirit-mush. The ghoul didn't seem to care which of us it crushed, so long as it was crushing. Its right fist came at me in a lumbering hook. I sidestepped the attack, backed out of the ghoul's reach. I let go of my lash and drew my great sword. Lifted the weapon out as the ghoul pulled its arm for another swing and brought Piotr's large blade down on the ghoul's hand. It cut through, lopping off three of the creature's fingers. They hit the ground; heavy, solid gold blocks.

"Have to be more careful," I said. "You only have ten of those. Well, seven now."

The ghoul didn't seem to care about my jabs, physical or verbal. Its left hand made a grab for my head. I pivoted, swung the great sword at it, and at the last minute the ghoul jerked its hand back. My strike missed by inches. That was okay. All about buying time.

"Mali, call it off," I shouted. "We don't want to fight you. I don't want to break your toy."

Mali, for her part, ignored me. Ignored the fight. Her eyes were closed, her hands still playing that rhythm in the air. Either living in a memory or doing something I didn't understand.

If she wasn't going to stop the ghoul, then I'd have to destroy it.

The ghoul swept its broken right hand towards my legs, bringing it in low. I crouched, and then jumped over the swing, bringing the great sword down on the ghoul's wrist. My blade bit in, and, as I fell back to the ground, I twisted the hilt to send blue fire down into the creature. Again it failed. I stared at the cleaving cut, incredulous. The fire should burn away the rage, clear the binding that held a ghoul together in Riven. If it didn't work, then we had no hope.

The ghoul's left hand caught me unaware, bashed me into the side of the room. I bounced off and landed on my knees. My head rang with the impact, and I realized the great sword still hung from the creature's right wrist, stuck in the ghoul. The monster turned towards me, and I drew the long knife from my belt. A pathetic choice to go against the giant creature.

So I ran.

I went around the ghoul and towards the blue pool on the far side.

The ghoul turned, but its bulk made it a slow mover. A good thing, as I had to figure out a strategy. My knife wouldn't help much. I had my crossbow. The normal bolts would be useless. A blue bolt, that would only send the same fire that had so far failed to hurt the creature. The orange. That was an option, if I wanted to bring down this entire temple on top of us. The space was too small; Nicholas's invention would burn its way through the rock and us in its quest to devour anything within reach. So I backpedaled. Tried to get my distance. For its part, the ghoul didn't seem to be in any hurry. Why bother running when the rat has nowhere to go?

My retreat around the pool brought Mali, and her throne, into view. A thought—if I couldn't defeat the ghoul, then maybe I could take out its creator.

I took four steps towards her before Mali realized what I was doing. With her eyes still closed, Mali held out her hand. The floor around her began to shake, stone blocks rattling loose from their frames. Revealing dirt and grime underneath. They shot together, forming a wall in front of me, between Mali and the point of my knife.

"Please," Mali said. "Stop this. Give in and let the end come. Embrace your fate as Cheo embraced his."

Cheo. That was an idea. If I could get the ghoul to the right place . . .

INTO THE DRINK

But I'd run out of time. The ghoul had closed, its hands wrapping around each other in a heavy overhead smash. I tried to dodge, squeeze around to the left along the chamber's back wall. The ghoul, keeping its hands raised, kicked out with its right foot instead of smashing down. The swipe wasn't dead-on, wasn't very strong, so I only flew up and bounced off of the wall, landing near the corner with my head and back aching. The knife out of my hands, which were trying to push me up. I knew the ghoul's follow-up would be coming, and as I scooted forward, the ghoul's left fist flattened the spot where I'd fallen.

I didn't make it past the right hand. Despite only having a thumb and pinkie finger, the ghoul wrapped its palm around me as I ran. Lifted me off the ground. Only, without the fingers, I could still move my right arm. The ghoul's thumb pressed against my head, like squeezing a fruit. I tried to think of what I could grab, but all my weapons were gone. My crossbow pinned to my back. In a second, I'd snap apart.

"Let him go," Selena growled, her voice trembling with pain, strong.

The ghoul turned towards her, letting me see her running jump onto the creature's tunic. Selena climbed, using her knife and cleaver to slice new handholds. With its left hand, the ghoul tried to pluck Selena off itself, but its movements were too slow. Too clumsy. Selena was a wiry spirit, slippery and quick when she wanted to be. She dodged the scrabbling hand and pulled herself up onto the ghoul's shoulders. Took her cleaver in both arms as she wrapped her legs around its neck, and slammed her blade into the ghoul's head, biting off flakes of metal.

The ghoul jumped. Pressed its legs down and elevated, ducked its head. Slammed Selena into the ceiling and crushed her into the stone blocks.

The impact knocked the ghoul's hand open, let me loose from the fingers. I splashed down into the blue pool, its icy water soaking my clothes. The chill seemed to scare away the pain, bring reality back into focus.

"Selena!" I called, sputtering away the water. She didn't answer, her broken body motionless on the walkway. The ghoul, after staring at Selena's form for a second, turned to me. I stood in the pool. Right where I wanted to be.

The ghoul's hands came for me again, smashing down. I dodged back, towards the far end of the pool and the entrance that Mali had sealed. The ghoul's hands splashed into the liquid in front of me, finally shaking the great sword out of its wrist. The blue, gooey water ran into the cuts and holes, the scratches we'd made on its hands. Filling them.

The ghoul shuddered. Paused.

When Cheo drank the green stuff on the other side, it seemed to erase his mind. A trap, or some sort of binding. Maybe, maybe the blue would do the same to the ghoul.

The monster seemed to fall asleep for a moment. It stood back, straightened. I stayed in the pool and watched. Did nothing to interrupt its reverie. If this didn't work, if the ghoul decided again to pound us into dirt, then I didn't think there was anything we could do to stop it.

Instead, the ghoul jerked. Turned towards the chamber's exit and, with a strong swing of its left hand, punched through Mali's broken wall. The golden ghoul walked away, vanishing into the darkness.

"Unexpected," Mali said. "I've never seen that happen before. Not in all my years."

"So glad we could make it interesting," I said, running over to Selena's form.

If she'd been a human, I had no doubt the ghoul would have killed her. Every bone in her body would have been shattered into dust. As a spirit, however, Selena had no bones. Had nothing other than her soul. So when I held her, I saw her eyes flicker. Her mouth move. Selena would come back.

"Indeed," Mali said, her eyes moving to the pool. "Nara's gift, it seems, has proved to be a trap all this time. Always ruining the beautiful things Dolan and I built for this world."

"I'm starting to think you're the evil one, not her," I said. "You keep spirits for centuries, replaying the same conflict over and over. You said that you murdered everyone Nara sent before."

Mali considered. "Let me ask you, spirit, what you think I should have done? Should I have welcomed Nara's pawns with open arms? Accepted her overtures, released her?"

"The way I see it, you all had the power to keep Riven safe. So why didn't you?"

Mali sat forward, looked hard into my eyes. "I wonder if she has her claws in you even now. This far distant, you should be free, and yet . . ."

"Help us."

"There is no helping you. I will not give this cursed world into Nara's grasp." Mali pressed her hands on the arms of her throne, digging her nails into its grooves. "Come now, servant. Let's see if Nara has chosen well this time."

As I held Selena in my arms, my weapons scattered around the room, Mali, the spirit that built the Riven I knew, that crafted its buildings, its forests, its ashen sky, rose from her throne with my end in her eyes.

AGAINST CREATION

Mali slid out of her throne, stretched, holding her arms together above her head. I set Selena back down on the ground, picked up her knife in my right hand, unsure of what to do. What strategies worked against a spirit thousands of years old? What haven't they seen? I decided to flip the knife to my left, lunge forward and stab.

Mali made me pause.

Two stone blocks in front of her feet rattled, broke out of the floor. One flew into each of her hands and melted into a ring, the stone seeming to liquefy and reform in her grip. The rings were as big around as a melon, only with serrated edges. Mali held them lightly, though I couldn't see how she didn't cut herself on the gleaming rings. Perhaps she did. Perhaps she didn't care.

"It's been such a long time," Mali said. "I might be rusty."

"That would be such a shame," I replied. "Really wanted another hard fight after that last one."

"Oh, I wouldn't worry about that."

Mali raised her right arm behind her, getting ready to throw the ring. Which meant I had to strike first. I stepped over Selena, and took a long lunge forward. Bursting out with the knife towards Mali. A third stone flew up out of the ground in front of her, striking the middle of the knife and sending it flying. The blade splashed into the green pool, leaving me barehanded and staring into Mali's devilish grin.

"Come now," Mali said. "Such an obvious attack? You'll have to do better."

"Most people can't pull blocks from the ground," I countered. "Not fair."

"You were expecting fair? How have you made it this far?"

Mali whipped her right arm, then her left, the sharp disks flying towards me. I had no time to dodge—only a few feet separated us. The first one burrowed its way into my left shoulder, and the second into my right leg. They whirled like saw blades; grinding, spinning, and tearing. My left arm went numb, and I fell to one knee as my leg stopped being able to hold my weight. As fights go, I'd had better starts.

"That's all you've got?" I said, trying to buy time. Spirits healed fast in Riven, and if I could keep her talking, I might get some function back. "All those centuries and you make a couple of rings? Why not another ghoul?"

"Dolan gave me the ghoul," Mali said, sending a quick frown up the passage. "I covered it with gold after a while. There's only so long you can stand to see swirling spirits and grotesque flesh."

"That didn't answer my question."

"I don't answer to you," Mali replied.

She sucked another pair of blocks up from the floor, once again pulling them into the circular rings. I still wore the crossbow on my back, but without two arms, drawing the weapon and loading it wasn't possible. Not to mention it would be obvious, and I didn't think Mali would stand there and let me crank a bolt into position.

"The same rings again. Very creative," I said. "It's like you're stuck on them."

Mali worked a smile at me. "When you've already made everything, you find yourself returning to your favorites."

Behind me, Selena groaned. She'd been barely moving since the ghoul crushed her into the ceiling. If she could wake up, then we'd have a better shot. Goddess or no, Selena and I were a tough team to handle.

Mali wasn't going to let that happen. She walked around me, and I watched her. I couldn't do anything, could barely focus over the burning pain from the stone disks, which were still embedded in my skin from Mali's attack. The goddess stood over Selena and looked down at her, shook her head. "I forget how hard it is to actually destroy a spirit. Without Dolan's weapons, you'll keep coming back."

She wasn't wrong. I took Mali's moment of distraction and used my right arm to pull the stone ring from my left shoulder, ripped out the one from my right leg. Tossed them to the ground. Immediately, I felt my spirit tying itself together. Like drinking water after a long thirst—a cool, nourishing glow. It would take hours to get full movement back, but every little bit helped.

"You know what?" Mali said. "Nara and Dolan called me the creator. You call me a goddess. It's an incomplete name. I cannot make whatever I want. Inanimate things, yes. Facsimiles. Those trees in Riven's great forest. The grain covering Nara's fields. All of it is so close to life, none of it is living. The flowers in the canyons, the endless copies of ferns and vines. None of it is alive. All of it stays as I wish it, and will as long as I want it to. But if I want souls to play with, I have to find them. Same as you."

"I don't play with souls. I send them to the Cycle."

"Yes, and how noble of you," Mali said. Selena twitched and Mali gave her a vicious kick, stilling her. Then Mali walked over to the green pool and dipped her rings inside of it. "You feed souls, creatures of mind and memory, love and loss, into the one thing that can destroy them completely. Have you ever wondered why?"

"If I didn't, Riven would be overrun," I said. "This world, and Earth, would only be home to the dead."

"Would that really be so bad?"

Mali pulled the rings out, dripping with green. I knew what she was going to do. I'd seen it with Cheo. With the ghoul. Cut us, get that liquid inside of our souls, and bind us to her. Or to her Left Hand. Or

Right Hand. I couldn't remember which color meant which. I didn't want either.

"You tell me," I said. "You've been living with the dead all this time. You don't seem too happy about it."

I twisted around, faced Selena. The motion tapped the crossbow against my back. An idea, maybe, but I needed a distraction.

"All due to a lack of variety," Mali said. "A little more space. Freedom from this place. Then, I think, I would be as happy as a spirit could possibly be."

"You'll be as alone then as you are now."

"Maybe, but it's worth a try, don't you think?" Mali walked up to me, raised the ring in her left hand. "Now I will give you one last choice. Yourself, or her? Which of you will be the first to enter my service?"

"She will," I said.

And Mali laughed.

AGELESS

"So gallant," Mali said. "Even the men in my own time were better than that."

Mali turned her back to me, and gave me my chance. With my right hand, I reached behind my back. Grabbed the blue bolts loaded into the side of the crossbow and slipped one out. Twisted it in my fingers as I brought my arm back forward. Threw it. Like a dart, hard and fast. The bolt stuck between Mali's shoulders, bursting into blue flame. I could see Mali shudder, and I'm sure her eyes would've been wide had I seen her face. But Riven's creator did not scream. Didn't shout, or howl, or curse my name. As the fire covered her, she dropped the rings to the ground and knelt.

"There's the freedom you were looking for," I said, pulling a second blue bolt out. Just in case.

A moment later, Mali's spirit rose, vacant and ignorant to the world she'd made. The goddess's ghost walked out of the room, vanishing into the dark passage.

After Mali left I stayed in the chamber, sitting on the stone floor for what felt like hours. Letting my soul knit itself back together and playing over in my mind what had happened. Nara had sent us a request to find Mali, to convince her to come back. Instead we found her, enraged her, and destroyed her. A spirit that Nara said was key to saving Riven, and we'd sent her to the Cycle.

Add to that everything Mali had told us. Her show with the water. Her statements about Nara, that the old spirit was playing us. That Nara wanted to undermine Riven and all that it stood for. That all Nara believed in was binding spirits by the dozen; creating a world of her own making.

"Carver?" Selena's voice sounded weak. Tired. "Are we still here?"

"Against all odds, we are," I said. "How are you feeling?"

"Oh fine." Selena groaned. "You know, broken everywhere. Every possible part of my soul is aching. The pain is canceling itself out, I think. As though my mind can't reconcile all of it."

"It'll get better," I said. "We're safe now. Mali's gone."

I replayed the fight for her. When I came to the part where I suggested Mali take Selena first, Selena laughed. Still lying there on the stones, her head flat against the rock, but I saw the smile, and it made me feel happy. Needed those moments. A little bit of love and levity in the twin pool's dim light.

"Of course you'd send me first," Selena said. "Always about you."

"I had to," I protested. "If she hadn't turned her back, then I wouldn't have—"

"Sure, sure," Selena said. "Of course that's the reason. Couldn't you have done that any other time, like when she was dipping her rings in the pool? Had to wait until she was going to take me out?"

"The pool would've been a far shot. I had to be sure."

I could tell Selena wasn't being serious. Could see the play in her eyes. We spent a while there, sitting, then standing, and then limping out of the chamber, picking up our weapons on the way. With every step our spirits put themselves back together. By the time we made it out of the temple, we could make a fairly good pace, leaning on each other for support.

"I feel like an old man," I said. "Like my body doesn't work anymore."

"You don't have a body, remember?" Selena replied.

"If this is what they feel like, maybe I'm glad I never saw mine broken."

Outside, we turned to look back at the temple entrance. All those runes, those stories about the goddess that lived inside. No longer. The temple would stand empty, potentially forever. Riven didn't have natural forces, and unless something came by and actively destroyed this place, Mali's home would stand for more centuries than she did.

"So what are we going to tell Nara?" Selena said as we turned back to the jungle.

"That we tried," I said. "Maybe she'll have other ideas."

"Do you think we should trust her? Because if we don't, and we're wrong, Riven's going to fall apart. But if we do, and we're wrong, then Nara's version might be worse."

"We play it both ways," I said. "If what she says seems to be right, that we do it. If it's wrong, now we know that we can wrangle her just like any other spirit. Mali showed us that much."

Selena nodded. We passed by the same rock-hard flower from before. Again, Selena reached out to touch it. No change. No sign that the flower knew its creator had disappeared. Like the buildings in Riven's city, the only thing that would tear the plant apart would be our weapons, our struggle.

"Strange that this flower will likely last longer than all of us," Selena mused, looking at the plant.

"So will the stones, and the rivers and the clouds," I said. "The difference is that they aren't doing anything with their time. They aren't risking themselves to save this place."

"Doesn't sound so bad."

"You'd get bored."

Selena laughed, then grimaced and steadied herself on my shoulder. Still putting ourselves back together.

We continued walking, past the ferns and trees that took on a stranger cast now that we knew none of them truly lived. That they were all figments of a bored spirit trying to find something to do with her imagination. Onward into the canyon, until the whispering wind gave way to harsher noises. Shouts and cries. The sound of metal on metal.

"Is Cheo already fighting another war?" I asked.

"I don't think we can wage another one."

"We may not have a choice."

Because the sounds were coming straight for us now. A rolling mix of snapping branches, crashing brush, and clashing iron. And we didn't have the strength to run.

NEW GHOUL, NEW GOALS

In front of us a tree simply disappeared, vaporized and blew apart as the golden form of Mali's ghoul smashed through it. Cheo and a group of other spirits came hot behind the monster, all throwing knives, spears, or firing arrows at the ghoul's back.

"Do not let up," Cheo shouted over the noise. "The Left Hand's monster must not be allowed to live! It is a perversion, a slight against our goddess!"

The ghoul ran straight for us, but as it noticed our limping forms, it slowed to a stop. Stared down at us with its solid, unseeing eyes. Behind it, arrows and thrown spears clinked off the ghoul's back, bouncing away. Cheo and the others, four spirits, caught up and stared at us as well, halting their attack as they realized the ghoul had done the same.

"Didn't realize we were that stunning," I said. "Do we really look that bad?"

"Who are you?" Cheo pointed one of his crude knives towards us. "Are you part of the Left Hand?"

"He doesn't remember," Selena said to me. Cheo's other spirits fanned out around us, setting a trap. In our condition, even with our weapons back in hand, neither Selena nor I would be able to fight them off. If Cheo truly had no idea who we were, if he believed we were the enemy, there was no way we could win.

"Remember you?" Cheo said. "I don't understand."

"You know who Mali is?" I said.

"Of course," Cheo replied. "She is my goddess."

"Don't take this the wrong way, but she's dead."

Rather than flying into a rage, or sitting down in despair, Cheo reacted with a nod. A slow, sad motion. The other spirits mimicked the move. "Her voice changed. A whisper, now, telling us to go far away from here. I assumed it was a Left Hand trick."

"The Cycle," I said. "You'll get used to it."

"I do not understand?"

Cheo asked, and Selena and I told the spirits about the Cycle, how Mali fell. By the time we were done, the spirits had put up their weapons. I couldn't tell if the ghoul listened as well, but it stood tall and shining over us the entire time.

"It seems we have nowhere left to go," Cheo said. "Except to this Cycle."

"You've been a spirit for a long time," Selena said. "You don't have to be one anymore."

"And this one?" Cheo pointed at the ghoul. "Does it belong in your Cycle as well?"

The ghoul, standing above us in silence, reached out and pointed at me with one hand. The one that only had two fingers left.

"Think it's mad you cut off its fingers?" Selena asked me.

"I hope not," I replied. The ghoul pulled its hand back. Stared at me with its blank gold face. On an impulse, I pointed to a tree next to me and spoke to the ghoul. "Grab that."

The ghoul stomped around me, reached down with its intact hand, and pulled the tree from the ground. Held it aloft like a club.

"It's obeying you?" Selena said.

"Looks like I got myself a ghoul." I waved for the monster to toss the tree away and the golden ghoul launched it through the brush. "You better be real nice to me now."

"Aren't I always?"

The ghoul, along with the other spirits, belonged in the Cycle. But as I started to tell them to march that way, I paused. The spirits had wrangling weapons, and the ghoul could certainly pound some breaches into pulp.

Bryce and the guides could use a force like this.

"Selena," I said. "I think we've got a new plan."

"I get nervous when you say that."

"This one's good, promise," I said. "How many spirits do you have, Cheo?"

"Between both hands? The number would be around one hundred. There have not been many new collections lately. Spirits are becoming rare."

"The breaches are drawing them south," I said. "Cheo, I need you to gather up both hands. Even the spirits you hate. We're going to the city."

"The Left Hand will not march for me," Cheo replied.

"No." I glanced at the ghoul. "But they will for this."

LOSING GROUND

Convincing Cheo to round up the other spirits in the jungle and hike back to the city with us didn't take much doing. I guess living without a purpose means there's nothing to hold on to. They weren't giving up anything to come with us, and so they took to the new adventure without complaint. The ghoul followed us every-where. Tromping along behind me. I wasn't sure what drove its actions either, except, perhaps, a loyalty to whomever had destroyed its master.

Mali had said the ghoul was a gift from Dolan, the third one of their trio. I'd never heard of anyone making a ghoul before, perhaps this one was different. In any case, I wasn't going to say no to a giant monster for a bodyguard.

After a long trek, we made it back in sight of the city's walls. Then to the north gate. Selena and I walked on our own now, almost back to full strength. Truly, being dead did wonders for one's health.

The north side of Riven held a scattered series of large houses. Parks and dried lakes. Empty, ruined from fighting. We didn't even encounter a guide until we entered the city center. Then a pack poured into the street in front of us. Their weapons at the ready.

Several guides hung out of windows from buildings bordering the street, aiming at us with guns and bows of their own making. Our band, nearly a hundred strong, boasting our own military menagerie, and a giant golden ghoul, probably had them nervous.

Understandable.

"Never expected to see you again," said the guide leading the pack. He pulled up his mask and I knew him. My most likely murderer. Polk stood a thin and wiry man. A weaselly face. I hadn't known the guides still counted him a member. Didn't know what he was doing here.

My hand drifted to my lash. Selena grabbed it. Stopped me.

"Now is not the time," Selena said. "There's too much at stake."

"You know why we did it," Polk said to me. "Piotr's orders. He told us he had a solution that would save everybody. We didn't want to die anymore than he did."

"That's not an excuse," I said.

"Why I'm here," Polk replied. "Trying to pay it back. Closing breaches. Buying you time."

"You want to buy us time?" I said. "Then let us through. This group is reinforcements. To help you. They know what they're doing, and they can wrangle spirits."

"And that thing?" Polk said, nodding at the ghoul.

"He's mine. I'll send him after anyone that annoys me. Like you."

Polk laughed, but it was a weak chuckle. Laced with nervousness. Good.

The guides didn't fight us. They let us into their territory. From there it wasn't a far walk to the square with the fountain, near the clock tower's charred ruins, where Bryce had set up headquarters. We were lucky. We'd come in at a time when both Bryce and Alec had crossed over. They were there, looking over a large board on which a crude map of Riven had been drawn. Markers placed, moved on and off to indicate breaches. Still other pieces, bits of debris cut into squares and circles, indicated groups of guides and where they had been sent.

It didn't take Bryce long after I told him our tale to send the ghoul, Cheo and his army to a new target. The west gate into the city.

"It's the best choke point we've got," Bryce said to Cheo. "You'll have constant action. There's too many breaches in the forest and we can't get out there. But if you hold them with the walls, funnel them to the gate, that will give us time to clear the city. Right now we're just hanging on."

Cheo accepted the new duty with the same solemn expression he'd given Mali. Pledged his devotion to the new cause, and then marched his force off.

Bryce came to Selena and I. Waved Alec over.

"It's not looking good," I said to my former mentor. "We killed the person Nara said was going to help us."

"There's no backup plan?" Bryce said.

"We don't know," Selena said. "We haven't been back to her."

"That's where we're going now," I added.

"Can you spare an hour or two?" Bryce asked. "Anna is missing. She and that sneak of hers, Laurence, were helping us out. I don't have any guides left that I can send after them. Especially not any that want to risk themselves for a sneak."

"I'd go alone, but the breaches make it too dangerous to travel solo," Alec said.

"Where'd she go?" I asked.

"She said she was going back to where they cross over. They wanted a tall building to help scope the city. If we can secure a vantage point, we'll be able to send guides to breaches quickly. Keep us living a little longer," Bryce said. "You know where a building like that might be?"

"The Warrens. We can check it out. How's everything else?"

Bryce sighed. "If there was any hope that we could survive this by strength of arms, I'd have you stay. I'd have you fight with us and close as many breaches as you could. We've lost the forest. We're facing more ghouls every day. On the other side, with Piotr gone, the peace talks are wavering. Nobody wants to give up their stake. While they argue, their armies keep fighting."

Bryce spared a glance to the spark-filled sky.

"Carver, if you don't succeed, we won't hold out much longer. Neither will Riven."

AFTER ANNA

Running through Riven felt familiar, and in a good way. The same back alleys, crumbling buildings, and ash strewn streets felt like home. No more canyons, no more identical jungle flora. Just hard stone and wood. Selena, Alec, and I made our way south from the clock tower and towards the Warrens.

"How's the other side?" I asked Alec as we walked along.

"Chaotic as ever," Alec said. "Chicago, it is a mess. All in a flurry trying to make things for this endless war. On top of that, everyone is sick. This disease continues its rampage. Everyone uses their masks now. Even inside."

"Sounds like fun," I said.

"I used to live like that." Selena's eyes stared into a distant past. "Wiley, my husband, he worked as a meat cutter. We never had clean air in that part of the city. Everyone wore their masks. Sometimes the purifiers would break and you'd wear them indoors too. Because anything could make you sick, we wore gloves all the time."

"Yuck," I said.

"Indeed, of the worlds we have, yours appears the most miserable," Alec said.

"You'd think that," Selena said. "Except we were so careful that few of us actually became ill. We were happy, healthy in our own way."

"I would take a chance with disease in order to breathe out of my own mouth every once in a while," Alec said. "When it's hot out? Nobody wants a mask wrapped around their face."

"The price you pay, I suppose," Selena said.

"Is Ezra's still around?" I asked.

"Carver, you've been gone a week. The world hasn't changed," Alec said.

Fair enough. I hadn't been dead for that long. Only it was hard to tell. Already it seemed like my memories of the time before, of Earth and walking the real streets, were fading. Like childhood or a boring day the next morning. Bits and pieces falling away and being replaced by the perennial gray. I didn't know how to hold onto them. How to hold onto who I was.

We reached the Ghoul's Gateway, the arch that led into the Warrens. Spirits were more common here, the tall, packed buildings providing plenty of space for them to cross in after their demise. Usually you'd find a few angry spirits running around, ready for wrangling. Now, there were guides patrolling in groups and nearly every spirit had already been pacified. Their eyes blank. None of the frightened curiosity you'd see in a spirit before the fire claimed them. No, all of these had been wrangled. If Riven had a scorched earth policy, the guides were employing it.

"Do you think it will ever go back?" I asked Alec. "Where you won't have to walk every block with your hand on your weapon?"

"Can't answer that question," Alec said. "We can choose. If we succeed, then Riven may know some peace. If we fail, then we may know ours."

After four more blocks we came across a large building, nearly a block long in and of itself. Seven stories high and serving as Anna's crossing point. Her room, the place she and Laurence crossed over from their hideaway in Chicago, sat in its basement. We stood in front, looking into its entrance, and saw nothing.

"Should we go inside?" I asked.

"Where could they be?" Alec peered up the building's wide facade.

"Two choices," I said. "Up or down. They cross into the basement, so I say we check there first."

The three of us moved into the lobby, a spacious place that deserved to be decorated with potted plants and marble columns. A bronze desk with a receptionist, a doorman to tip his hat and greet you. Instead stains splattered the inside, faded reds and browns, the occasional black mark of fire. Holes punched in the floor and tears in the walls gave distant fights their due. Large rooms off the lobby on either side played homage to the life the apartment building was meant to have. Restaurants, perhaps. Or meeting spaces. Social clubs, as if Riven had ever had any. Towards the back of the lobby a wide stair opened up, going both down and towards the top.

We fell into the typical silence that guides adopted when investigating a new area. A space where danger might be around any corner. The slightest sound, the quietest laughter could serve to drive a spirit angry. Not a chance we were willing to take. I led, the great sword in my hands. The stairway gave me enough room to swing, though I was less sure about the hallways beneath and above. Then again, these walls wouldn't mind a few extra cuts.

The basement resembled a catacomb. I'd crossed over here with Anna more than a few times, but never alone. Always with her to lead me out. So I had to pull the floor plan from memory. Whether it was because we were standing right there, or because the thought concerned Riven, the layout came back clear.

Who needed memories of childhood when you could recall basement arrangements at will?

"It's a grid," I whispered to Selena and Alec. "We're at the back middle. To the right, there are three main rooms. All square, I think maybe meant to hold supplies. On the left, it's one large space. Ductwork. A lot of ruined stuff. Probably where power would've gone, if this had been Chicago. I say we start there."

I didn't say that the large room would make it easier to see each other. To cover corners and make sure we weren't getting ambushed. Alec, Selena and I needed a warm-up. Needed to get back into the groove of clearing out rooms where angry spirits could hide behind anything. Could reach out from any shadow to grab your throat and tear it apart.

The door to the large room, a double affair, had been ripped away. On the other side, it was easy to see what had done it. A trio of slathering spirits stood at the far end of the long room, scrabbling at its back door. Pounding and tearing. What they were trying to get at, why they didn't just come back out our door, I didn't know. No reason, except that spirits tended to think in straight lines.

We crept into the room, stepping over pipes, rubble, and broken bits of wood. The spirits didn't notice. So focused on that far end. On whatever was on the other side of that door. We made it within five feet of them before one turned, a middle-aged man whose eyes burned bright with that blue angry fire. He opened his mouth to scream and his fellows turned, and then I ended all of them with a single swing. A wide slice with the great sword, its blade wreathed in blue fire.

Each of the three cuts from my slash ignited, burning the spirits and collapsing them to the ground. In a minute they would rise up again, no longer dangerous.

"Quite the weapon that," Alec said. "For a second there I thought you would miss. Give that one an opening."

"Glad you have faith in me," I said.

"You're recently dead," Alec replied. "Figured you need some time to adapt. Might be a little slow."

"Haven't lost a step, believe me."

Selena stepped past us and lifted the door's handle, an action the spirits hadn't thought to take. The back of the basement sat on the other side, a dark empty hallway. We went out into it, and turned to the right. Towards the rooms on the other side of the basement. I recognized this place; Anna and I crossed over into the last room on this side. The door into it was shut, and when I tried the handle it didn't move. Locked. So I did what no spirit would ever bother with.

I knocked.

SPLITTING STAIR

"W ho's out there?" I heard the voice on the other side. Recognized it.

"Laurence, it's Carver. And some friends. We're trying to find you, and Anna," I answered.

The door clicked a moment later, and swung open to reveal Laurence, Anna's fellow sneak and Chicago resident. He looked, to put it charitably, not good. His eyes were wide, and I noticed his mouth had picked up an unnerving twitch like he couldn't decide whether to frown or open up into a chilling scream. Laurence, who hadn't made any secret of his disdain for the guides, hugged me tight. So tight that I had to shift my arms up, keep the great sword out of the way as the man burrowed his head into my shoulder.

"I never thought we'd see another soul," Laurence muttered as he stepped back from me. "I never thought I'd be able to get out of this basement. That Riven would be closed to me forever."

"Seems kind of dire, doesn't it?" I said. "It's not like there aren't a bunch of guides running around."

"How many would come in here?" Laurence asked. "You can't see the breach, not from the street. We realized that after the first day. It's in the middle of the building, along with all the spirits. They weren't making much noise when we came back here. Went up to the rooftop, and they caught our scent."

"Anna's on the roof?" Selena said. "Why?"

"We thought we could find a spot," Laurence said. "This building is one of the tallest in all of the city. From the roof you can see across every neighborhood. You can spot breaches miles away. If we held it, and established a line of communication to Bryce and the rest of the guides, we could direct them to any breaches quickly."

"So why are you down here, when she's up there?" I asked.

"We took the risk," Laurence said. "Anna diverted their attention, and I made a run for it. We agreed that because she had a weapon, because she knows how to fight, that Anna should stay up top while I went down. I barely managed to trick the three spirits in the next room."

"We found them," I said. "They're taken care of."

"Pardon, I believe we should make a move up to the roof," Alec said. "Any delay seems improper."

"Yes, yes," Laurence said. "I had planned to travel to Ezra's. To tell you what happened. But now here you are."

"Always arriving just in time, that's us," I said.

We turned and ran up from the basement. Our feet pounded on the stairs, Laurence taking the back. Up to the lobby, and then to the second floor. Up to the third.

You could hear it, the growls and knocks of crazed hands beating on the walls. The hissing and half-whispered rage. The breach was here.

"Is there another stair?" I asked Lawrence.

I'd been up this apartment building once before, when Anna and I tried to talk to the spirits we bound over at the Mountain. We'd taken the central stair all the way up. She never mentioned if there was a back way, but it seemed strange these steps were so empty.

"Thin and treacherous," Laurence said. "A fire escape. I never understood why one would need one of those in Riven?"

"There's a long story about where this all came from," I said. "I'll tell you later. If the spirits aren't running up this one, then they've got to be going the other way."

"That's a good thing, right?" Selena suggested. "Fewer obstacles before we get to Anna?"

"Theoretically."

"Hold on," Alec said. " I have a tablet. We can close the breach."

"Alec and Selena." I pulled out my long knife, handed it to Laurence. "You too. Find the breach, close it. I'll go after Anna."

"You are sure?" Alec said. "We could split evenly?"

"The breach is more important." I held up the sword. "And have you seen this thing? I'll be fine."

Selena rolled her eyes. I gave her a wide grin. Spirits liked to play hero too.

The trio broke off, headed down the hallway one step at a time. I hefted the great sword in front of me, both hands wrapped around the hilt, and dashed up the stairs. Once again, I was aware of how a spirit's endless stamina made running up floors holding a heavy weapon as easy as a light jog back in Chicago. I just hoped Anna would still be there for me to save.

SAVE THE SNEAK

I hit the fourth floor and things became messy. A pair of spirits stood on the landing, snarling at each other. Fighting over who would get to go first. Two soldiers. Still sporting their ragged uniforms. I'd noticed as the war had gone on that the quality of gear worn by the spirits became thinner, shabbier. Used to be that they would cross over in clean colors, medals and ranks sewn into the sides. Now they wore barely more than rags. Whatever the countries could churn out fast enough to clothe their troops.

And yet, those simple uniforms sealed to the soldier's identity so tight that when they died, those rags came over with them.

"I wish more people would fight over me like you're fighting over those stairs," I said, coming up to the landing.

The nearer soldier glared my way, those eyes burning blue fire. Turned and leapt towards me, hands outstretched. The stair's height gave him plenty of reach, but proved little defense against my great sword. I swept it from right to left catching the spirit mid-jump and throwing him down the stairs as blue fire curled up and over him. Wherever the soldier landed, he would be walking to one place. The Cycle.

The second spirit tackled me back down the stairs, catching me before I could get the sword in position. We bounced off the wall, rolled over each other down the steps. Halfway back to the third floor. I kept rolling until I sat on top, level on a step. The spirit bit at me and I jammed the hilt of the great sword into his face. Knocked him back.

I would've loved to have had my long knife. To grab it with my left hand, take a quick jab to finish the fight. The great sword didn't do much in close quarters. So I did what I could. Raised the hilt again and jabbed the thing in the face a second time. Bought myself a moment of stunned confusion. Used it to bring up my knee and plant my foot on the spirit's stomach. Stood myself up and climbed back a couple of steps. The spirit rolled up after me, grabbing at my ankles. Fine. I rotated the sword in my hands and jabbed it straight downward. Right into the middle of the spirit. Sent him away with a burst of blue.

I went up the stairs, past the fourth floor to the fifth. I could hear the noises at the far end of the floor. Towards where Laurence said there might be a back stair. I had a choice. I could go that way, engage spirits here and fight my way up. Or take these stairs, the easiest route to get to the roof.

I favored the path of least resistance.

Up to the sixth floor and then the seventh. Or rather, to the door opening onto the rooftop. I listened before twisting the handle, but heard nothing on the other side. No clashing metal, no growls, no fighting. If Anna still lived, she'd cleared herself plenty of room.

I used my shoulder, pushed the door open with the sword held ready to stab forward into anything on the other side. Only I didn't see anyone. Not a soul on the entire rooftop. Empty stones and the wide expanse of the city beyond the edge.

"Anna?" I shouted. "Where are you?"

"Carver!" I heard Anna's voice, off the side of the building. Down below the roof.

I ran over, stomping across the flat stones. Stared over the edge and saw that Laurence had been right. A second stair clung to the building, black iron climbing up the side in a crisscrossing pattern. On top of that escape, holding a long line of gnashing and thrashing spirits at bay, stood Anna. She wielded the flail Nicholas had made for her in both hands, crushing it down on a spirit as it attempted to climb its way to her. Anna swung slowly, and I noticed she bled from plenty of cuts. Particularly a long gash above her left eye.

"Mind switching spots?" Anna said without looking up at me. Her voice was layered with exhaustion. "I've been here for a long time now."

"Give me some room," I said. Anna backed up, allowing a pair of spirits to gain a few more steps without her flail sweeping out in front of her. That was a mistake. I dropped off the rooftop, slamming the great sword in front of me as I fell. I caught the platform at the top of the stairs, and brought the sword down on both of the spirits. As I cleaved into the pair, I realized why Anna had chosen to fight here, rather than on the broader base of the rooftop.

The spirits that I'd wrangled stood there for a moment on the stairs, blocking the path forward for the angry ones behind. Confused and lost. Buying us time.

"Not a bad plan," I said. "Though, why didn't you use your sparker? That's what they're for."

"We did." Anna slumped back against the railing. "I used every spark I had. Only the sky is too crowded. So many lights now that it's impossible to know which ones truly need help. Or maybe nobody even noticed."

Coming back into Riven from Mali's canyons, I'd noticed the same thing. The sky a changing rainbow of colors as endless sparks splashed against the fog. Our main method of communicating became less effective the more we used it. If there were sparks everywhere, we couldn't tell which required the first, or any, response.

"So you were trapped up here?" I asked.

"No, I stayed because I felt like it," Anna retorted. "Doesn't it seem like fun?"

"Sorry, bad question."

The two spirits shuffled back through the line of angry ones and I took Anna's spot. Waved my blade at the grasping hands of the next wave, kept them at bay. And if they came too close, carved them in two.

"Did you find Laurence?" Anna asked.

"He was enjoying the basement." I jabbed at a spirit and sent him reeling back down the stairs, burning away. "You have to teach that guy how to fight."

"I will, with all that extra time we have," Anna said, then she perked up. "But if we can take this building, then I think it will help. Bryce doesn't know where to send his forces. We're responding, not being proactive. The more breaches we catch early, the less ghouls we have to deal with."

"We'll take it," I said. "Selena and Alec, they're busy dealing with the breach. Once it's cleared, we should be able to mop up the rest of these guys no problem."

"Thank you, Carver."

"My fault you're in this mess. Think I owe you at least one escape."

We stood there, holding ground at the top of the roof for a while longer. Until shrieks started down below. Alec and Selena had closed the breach and were working their way up to us. When the spirits turned their back to me, I made quick work of them. We met up in the middle, on the fifth floor. Alec and Selena with grim looks on their faces.

"Where's Laurence?" I asked.

"He crossed over, after we saw the two of you up top. Apparently the two of you have spent a little while on this side?" Alec said.

"My body's probably dead," Anna said. "I'm only half joking."

"Then go. I'll tell Bryce about the building. Do not worry."

"We have to get moving too," I said. "Nara is waiting."

"She is not the only one. Everyone's waiting, Carver, go. Find a way to save us. Selena, do not let him mess it up."

"You're asking the impossible," Selena said as we pushed our way through stunned spirits.

"Carver," Alec said, and I saw him holding my long knife by the blade. "Forgetting something?"

He tossed the weapon to me and I caught it, felt the edge cut into my palm. Felt the slash start to knit itself back together immediately as I slipped the knife into its holster. My spirit covering for my mistakes.

We left the Warrens and headed east. The first time we left the city, Alec and Anna had given us a personal escort. Now we had none. Now the guides running around barely noticed us. We didn't have blue fire in our eyes, we didn't have a breach behind our backs, there was no time to investigate a pair of spirits. No reason if we weren't trying to kill them.

Riven was dying from a thousand gashes. The guides had to focus on the largest ones.

ASKS AND EVASIONS

The grain fields weren't as endearing as Riven's dark streets. Something about those endless stalks, knowing that they been made by a sick goddess with no love left for the person Mali had trapped made the waving plants even worse than before. I saw Selena shudder, felt like doing the same as we pushed our way through. Each and every one of these mirrored stalks the product of one person's delusion.

We made it to Nara's clearing quickly. Neither one of us cared to spend an extra minute in these fields. Her fire still burned, the grain stack the same height as when we left. The charred ruin sending thin smoke up to the sky and leaving the air with the smell of dry kindling. Nara herself wasn't out as we came in. Only appeared after we'd been standing there for a full minute or more. As though waiting for the proper moment to make her grand entrance.

Not that her frail form, robed and tired, could pull that off.

"I count only two of you," Nara said.

"Mali didn't like your offer." I sighed. "Didn't like us much either."

I launched into the story. The fight with the ghoul, Mali's water show, and kept an eye on Nara's face throughout. Her expression never changed. Not even when I shared Mali's comments, those harsh statements about whether Nara should be trusted. About whether her motives were true. That Nara would only bring Riven into further chaos. In fact, the only reaction I saw came when I told her how I'd stabbed Mali with the crossbow bolt. The blue fire burning away Mali's power, her consciousness. At those words, Nara closed her eyes for a second and I swore, I swore I saw a tear make its way down the creases in her cheeks.

When Nara's eyes opened again they were as fierce as ever.

"I should have expected that Mali would have lost her sight," Nara said. "Mali was ever the most attuned with the present. With what she felt in the moment. It made her such a great and terrible creator. Her whims built the city, built the forest, built this massive field. She gave no thought to where it was going, gave no thought to what she was doing."

"I wanted to ask you," Selena said. "If you knew why Riven's city is so close to modern? If Mali had been here for centuries, then why would she build a place that must be completely different from her time?"

Nara smiled, glanced over at the fire. "It wasn't always like that. The city has lived and died a thousand times. I haven't seen it in so long that I barely remember how it looks. As new spirits came to us, Mali would have them tell her of the world, and she would remake Riven to suit their tales. You say that she kept new spirits of her own. I assume, whenever she felt like it, Mali rebuilt the city."

"Wouldn't we notice?" I said. "If, say, a hundred years ago, the city changed itself?"

"Perhaps you did. Are there records? Written journals?"

"Some," I said. "But most are concerned with guides. Names and titles. Positions and laws. Riven itself always seemed to be the same. An endless task."

"Then perhaps that is your answer," Nara replied. "If the focus is ever on the spirits, then a world that changes slightly once in a lifetime may not be so remarkable."

Nara had a point. If I'd wandered into the Warrens tomorrow and found it made over with newer buildings, I might be confused for a moment, but at the first sight of a tortured spirit, I'd be back to the usual. Riven tended to kill the curious.

"Mali mentioned prisons," I said, switching back. "With the water, she seemed to show the three of you being divided. Is that why you didn't come with us?"

"When we parted," Nara said, "we had our differences. We realized that we posed a great danger to Riven with our struggles. So we sealed each other away. I had hoped Mali could part the barriers."

"I don't see any barriers."

"The field," Nara said. "That is my prison. Dolan has his desert, and Mali her canyons."

"I don't understand," Selena said. "How? How can you seal someone to a single place?"

"Surely by now you accept that Riven has secrets to which you are not privy? Perhaps, in time, you will understand."

I'd listened to guides give me vague statements all my life. Growing up with one sentence after another telling me to accept what I'd been told and not ask questions. To deal with the fact that some things weren't meant for me to know until some undefined 'time'. I'd bested the leader of the guides in combat, rescued and damned my own parents, and been murdered. What else could I possibly do to be ready to understand something?

"Nara." I unsheathed the great sword. Pointed it towards the woman. I felt Selena's eyes burning into me, but ignored her. "Explain. Or I'll assume what Mali said is true. I will end you here and take my chances with the spirits."

"A bold statement," Nara replied evenly. "And no doubt, Carver Reed, you are willing to take your chances. But what about her? What about your friends back in the city? Are you willing to risk all of them on your rash judgment?"

I narrowed my eyes and she held up a gnarled hand. "Still, perhaps you are right. You want to know why we are sealed? Go, find Dolan. He will tell you. If Mali can't help, then he is our last option. While the three of us would have been better, Dolan and I can still do what needs to be done."

"And why can't you tell us? Why can't you give us the answers?"

"Would you believe me if I did?" Nara replied, and I had to admit she had a point there. Already I'd started taking her every sentence with a heaping helping of doubt.

"You said he lived in a desert?" Selena shoved us past the tension. I lifted the sword away, put it back in its sheath.

"South of the city," Nara said. "In a sea of sand much like this field. If you keep walking, you will find him. Bring him here, and together we can help you."

Nara turned to go into her hut, and Selena looked back the way we came.

"Wait," I said to the spirit's back. "I have one more question."

Nara looked back at me, her face a set line. No surprise, no irritation, no anything. "Ask."

"Mali. What she showed to us, it looked like you bound spirits. Many, many of them. How did you do it, if you weren't alive?"

Nara smiled, but I didn't like the hunger that came over her crinkled eyes. A person reminded of her brilliance and eager to show it. "A living soul binds another through by giving part of their life. Like setting fire to kindling. A dead spirit binds the other way. By stealing what remains of the one they seek to control."

Her words clicked. Barth's tower, on the far edge of the city. The mad former guide had more than a dozen spirits doing his bidding, but most had lost their personality. Had been stock still and silent, save for the one Barth had directed to greet us.

"How many?" I asked. "How many spirits could you bind like this?"

"Why do you need to know? Are you getting ideas?"

"I'm trying to find yours."

"I have told you, time and again, that my true wish is to save my home," Nara spoke, annoyance drifting along the edges of her voice.

"You haven't said how."

"You are in no position to ask. Now, go. Your friends are dying while you dawdle."

I had no argument against that point. As Nara went back into her hut, Selena and I once again set forth through the field of grain. Marching back to the city, and then south, to another part of Riven I'd never seen.

Hopefully the desert, and Dolan, would prove less hostile than the jungle and its queen.

LOVE IN THE AFTERLIFE

To get to the desert, we once again had to choose: go back through the city or around it. We made it to the east gate without facing that decision, and, looking in at the broken Palace and the parade of sparks beyond, I glanced at Selena and shrugged.

"We go in there, we're liable to get bogged down," I said. "You heard Alec, there's no time to waste."

"You hear me arguing?"

"I, uh, no I don't. Guess I wanted to state my opinion."

Selena nodded, matched my eyes through the archway. "Come on, Carver. Let's go around the outside. Bryce and the others can keep it together long enough."

So we followed the wall south. Spent most of the journey bantering back and forth as to whether Nara would turn out to be the worst decision we'd ever made. After seeing Mali's show, I felt less and less like the old spirit in the hut would turn out to be a good call. That in trying to save ourselves, we'd wind up bringing Riven into an even darker ruin.

"Hard to get worse than world-ending," Selena replied when I'd spoken the thought.

"Do you trust her?"

To our right, the city wall continued. We walked on hard dirt, staying clear of the grain off to our left. Above, the same gray sky loomed over a breeze that blew ashen flakes around the air. I never really understood where those flakes came from, but they made Riven feel as though it was constantly snowing. Light flurries. Without any of the seasonal charm of the natural, chilly kind.

"I see someone who wants something, and thinks we're the best way to get it," Selena said. "My first husband, the alcoholic?"

"The one who fell from the apartment window?"

"Matthias, yes. We had a similar understanding," Selena said. "I didn't want to stay in the country. He wanted a wife and lived in the city, where I thought all that really mattered took place."

"That's naive," I said.

"What do you expect from a fifteen year-old girl?" Selena replied. "For a brief time, too, it was everything I imagined. Matthias used me, his new, pretty wife to get into the sorts of clubs and parties he'd not been invited to earlier. It was a deal, and we both made our profits."

"You're such a romantic."

"Please," Selena said. "You're no better. It's why we're perfect for each other. We're so bad at sharing sentiments that it took both of us dying to really fall in love."

I laughed. Couldn't argue with that. Before, when I'd bound Selena, there'd always been our unequal standing hanging over us. I could jaunt back to the other side while Selena had to stay in Riven. If I'd died, the binding would be broken, potentially sending her to the Cycle. Now, we needed each other. Needed each other's stories, their hand to keep the Cycle's whispers at bay.

Riven didn't have dinner dates. Didn't have theaters or a circus. But it did have time. We didn't sleep anymore, didn't get tired. Our moments came when we worked to wrangle a spirit, when we navigated the crowded jungle in Mali's canyons, when we filled the endless gray with stories we'd tell to each other. What we had wasn't a fairy tale, but I loved it all the same.

"So how does Matthias make you trust Nara?" I asked.

"Because she will not change until she has what she wants," Selena said. "And when people get what they want, they let their guards down. If Nara starts to do something we don't like, we take care of her."

"Don't know that there are many apartment windows to push her out of in that field."

"We don't need one. Not here," Selena said. I could tell without looking that her hand rested on the cleaver's handle. In that, Selena was right. If Nara decided to play a different game, tried to change the rules, we could end her just like we did Mali.

THROUGH THE DESERT

When we reached the south gate, on the other side of the Shambles and the busiest spot in Riven, I stopped and stared at the train of spirits. Thousands of them milled through the gate, heading out of the city and towards the Cycle. On a downbeat path that journeyed into the dark forest and up to the Mountain beyond. Technically, the west gate would have been closer, but the path went this way and the spirits followed it.

Maybe that's how Mali had designed it.

To the south, Riven's scraggly dead grass continued off towards the horizon. I wondered if it would be like the canyons, where we would be walking towards nothing at one moment and, in the next, see a new world open up in front of us.

"Why is it so crowded?" Selena said, marveling at the gate. "It wasn't this bad when we rescued Bryce."

"The breaches," I replied. "Normally spirits are spread out all over Riven, but now they're concentrating. When a battle on Earth forms a breach, it pulls in other spirits crossing over. Then you've got a big group. The guides wipe them out, and they walk here together. Join the rest."

"It's eerie."

All of those faces; men, women, children from across the world shuffling their feet one after the other. Looking straight ahead. Quiet and numb.

"It's peaceful," I said and Selena cocked her head at me.

"Suppose you could see it that way," she replied.

"I choose to. Easier to deal with if you look at it that way. A peaceful march to an endless sleep."

We ventured south, padding along the ground until I noticed that it began to give away. My footfalls landed on less firm soil. The dirt shifted, and my footprints left deeper indents. What grass there was died.

"It's white," Selena said, looking ahead. In front of us, Riven's dirt fell into a silky sand, laid out in small drifts as though someone had spread a fine blanket of snow. Ash flakes fell and vanished into the landscape, buried by Riven's slight breeze.

"At least it's not gray," I replied.

Trudging through the sand would have been a slog had we been alive. Able to get exhausted. I figured that's why nobody had explored these regions before. The canyons and the desert were so far beyond the walls of Riven's city that any living guide would have had to turn back. Perhaps with a succession of different spots to cross over you could gradually make your way farther and farther, but that begged a different question.

Why?

For nearly two thousand years, guides had operated in Riven without chasing the origins of its structures. Had stuck to their prime goal: wrangle the spirits, keep the dead moving to the Cycle. Our numbers never gave us the luxury of sending guides out on expeditions.

Our. Still talked like I was one of them. Not only was I a spirit, no longer alive, but I'd killed Piotr, the last leader of the guides. He might have been chasing disaster, but I don't think I still qualified for membership in that esteemed group. I glanced at Selena walking beside me, her eyes bright in the light reflecting from the sand.

I had what I needed.

The column appeared in a slow unveiling. A shaded obelisk on the edge of our vision that resolved itself and its fellows behind it as we came closer. As tall as the ones bordering Mali's temple, and similarly carved in runes. Behind the column, splitting it on either side, were more. A long row leading back to what appeared to be a wide cluster of buildings.

Laurence had a map, back in Chicago, that hinted at a town like this. A ruined place. If there was anyone that would take the leaps to get so far afield, it'd be him. Now I wished I'd studied that map more closely. Much as I enjoyed walking into the trap in Mali's temple, I'd prefer to avoid the same situation here.

"Do you see it?" Selena said to me. "On the statue?"

I took a harder look as we walked up. And recognized it. The disk, the three figures plastered on the hard stone. The same image as Mali's show with the water. Nothing else adorned the statue, just a pile of sandy bricks stacked on top of each other.

The next column continued the tale. The figures moving now, some of the thin blue outlines that I'd taken for spirits appearing on the disk. The same illustrations, the same story. It played out across the statues, each one showing the next scene as we went deeper and farther down the row.

"I guess that means Mali told the truth," Selena said. "Unless she made these too, and it's all a lie."

"Seems like a lot of trouble, but I can't put it past her." I ran a finger along one of the paintings. To see if it would flake off, but the columns were sturdy. "From what Mali said, it sounded like she made all of these places."

We made it to the warring scenes. Where the dark figures with the blue fire attacked the spirits. Drove them into the Cycle. Without Mali pushing the story along, we took some time to examine the figures. The paintings that brought them to life.

"Do you think these are the guides?" I asked Selena. "Wrangling the spirits and sending them back to the Cycle?"

"Can't think of anything else they'd be," Selena said. "Which would make that third figure the reason we exist."

"We?"

"Feel like I've earned it, Carver." Selena folded her arms. "Keeping you alive has to be worth something."

"The pleasure of my company isn't payment enough?"

"If only." Selena gave me a slight grin. "I know I shouldn't care. That it's pointless, given that we're spirits, but I never *belonged* to anything. Not once."

"Until now," I said, earning the full smile this time. "Of course, that means you can't walk away. Can't retreat to the far corner of Riven when things get dangerous."

"Because that's so like me."

"Just saying that the guides don't take freeloaders."

"They took you, so I think I'm fine," Selena replied.

"Good point."

The next column held a picture of the three figures, standing apart and split by thick green bars. Mali had hinted that this had been when the three of them had locked each other away. But she never explained the prisons. Nara said she couldn't leave the field, but why? How?

"Do you think she couldn't leave the canyons?" I mused.

"I think Mali was as trapped as Nara," Selena said. "And Dolan, he's trapped here."

"I hope he knows how to free himself. If we're going all this way as a waste of time . . ."

I went to the next column, the last. Like the first, it stood in the center of the path. The other columns fanned out on either side, regaling us through painted pictures the story of the three spirits and how they had made Riven into what it was today. This one, on three of its four sides, showed one spirit. Mali, Dolan, and Nara. Each one painted with a green circle around the figure. The circle seemed to extend the line from one to the next. Mali, her hand outstretched, appeared to push the circle around Dolan. Who did the same to Nara, who brought the arc to completion around Mali.

Nara's reach cut across the blank side of the column, the entirety of that side a single green line lancing through the stones. As though something could've been there that was left off at the last. I felt a hand land on my shoulder, heavy. At first I thought it was Selena, and then I looked.

The wide, lost eyes of a spirit new to Riven stared back at me.

TO HELP A SPIRIT

Young, a boy not much older than twelve or thirteen. No marks of disease, no mortal wounds. The boy had the presence of mind to turn his spirit into who he wanted to be, rather than what he was.

"Carver, I have him," Selena said from behind the kid, her voice tight. Her cleaver no doubt ready to strike.

"Wait," I said. "Spirits shouldn't be showing up here. He should be pulled to a breach, or one of the other places in the city."

"The city?" the boy said. "Do you know where I am?"

I started to answer, but the boys eyes drifted away and, in the middle of my sentence, he began walking back behind the column. Further into the desert. Not unusual. Spirits had a lot on their minds, and their minds weren't exactly whole to begin with.

"Should we wrangle him?" Selena asked, coming up beside me.

"No," I said. "I didn't see any fire. Let's follow."

We paced the spirit deeper into the desert. Past the columns and into what seemed like a small village. Single-story houses, their pale adobe-style bricks rising up from the white sand in square shapes. They felt old, but also pristine. A set constructed by a historian, or someone making a model in a museum. The spirit moved past the houses, didn't bother checking or looking in any of them.

"Who are you?" I asked the spirit, called ahead to it. Sometimes, pushing a spirit to remember who it was could give it a measure of sanity. Bring it back from the brink. The boy glanced back at me.

"My parents called me Turner," the boy said. "You don't suppose they're here, do you?"

Again, when I started to answer, the boy turned away and walked. Further into the town.

"He's not going towards the Cycle," Selena said.

"Which means he's taking us to where he came from," I replied. "We'll wrangle him there."

After a few more twists and turns through the desert streets, we came to a large courtyard. Stones paved across the center, and the wide square stood surrounded on all sides by more of the brick buildings. Several of these pushing two stories and one, across from us, standing a full four. The large building looked designed with a fine hand, its doorway bordered by twin columns culminating in an arch. Mali's temple, in desert form.

"There's a breach," Selena said, pointing. In the center of the courtyard the wide shimmering pool of a breach stared back at us. More spirits hovered around the edges. Looking around, curious. It must've formed only moments ago. The spirits not yet angry, not yet vicious and intent on tearing us apart.

"Turner," I said. "Is this where you wanted to take us?"

"I thought you could help my friends," Turner said. "We're all lost, you see."

My hand drifted to my great sword. There was only one direction for these spirits.

CASUALTIES OF WAR

I unsheathed the great sword from behind my back, leveled it out towards the boy. Selena drew her cleaver and long knife beside me. The two of us hadn't taken a breach solo, but this one wasn't burning. Not yet anyway.

"Carver," Selena said. "We don't have a tablet."

"Then we clean it up as best we can."

Without a sapphire tablet I wasn't sure how we'd close the breach, but leaving spirits around would, eventually, create an angry swarm. The breach would grow. Swallow the desert town and start pouring spirits north. Delaying that as much as possible still mattered.

Turner didn't move as I went up to him, as I twisted the hilt, as the blue fire burned up and over him. The other spirits turned to watch, gawking as I made my way around, sharing slashes with Selena. Wiping what was left of the spirits out of Riven so that their mindless souls could start on their last walk to the Cycle. Within a minute we'd cleared most of the courtyard. Or at least, that's what I thought.

I almost jumped at the first howl, so at odds with the silence of the place. The rustle of the wind on the sand, the occasional whisper of the breeze looping through a nearby house. Otherwise, the only noises came from the swishing of our blades. Until the newcomers made their presence known.

They crawled from the breach without us noticing, one hand at a time. Hauling themselves out, looking like soldiers. Or natives from a land I didn't know. Breaches didn't discriminate.

A pair of spirits stood up from the pool, looking around. Their eyes flickered with the pale blue fire that meant all shred of sanity had left their souls.

"And just when I was getting bored," I said to them, waving the sword their way. The spirits hissed and charged towards me, their arms outstretched and clawing for my face.

I stepped forward with my left leg, leading into a wide swing that bisected both of the spirits and sent them burning away to the ground. Behind them, though, four more sets of arms appeared through the breach, pulling the spirits through.

"Finish up the rest," I said to Selena. "I'll handle the newcomers."

I ran over to the spirit arms as they appeared, and swiped down. First one, then another, and another with consecutive slashes. Burning them away as they crossed through into Riven.

Something snatched up my ankle, and I fell flat on my back. The breach spread up beneath me, a window into a ruined mountain town. That accounted for the variance. A war-torn village in a country I didn't know, soldiers and townspeople crossing through as shelling continued.

Not that I had time to appreciate it. The same spirit that had knocked my ankle aside clamored out of the breach on top of me. Clawing my coat as he climbed up towards my face. With my left hand, I grabbed my long knife off my belt, and jabbed it into the spirit's chest, twisted the hilt and burned him away. Only those seconds had already cost me too much time.

I pulled up to my feet, and two more spirits hit me from behind. I managed to move with the push, using my jacket's loose skin to tear away from them. Left them holding shreds of leather. The two spirits continued coming for me, joined by another three to my right. Behind me, I could hear Selena hacking away at the others outside the courtyard.

"Guess I deserve this for being cocky," I said. Not that the spirits listened, or cared. Their burning blue eyes were interested in only one thing: me.

I sidestepped left, and the two groups of spirits ran into each other as they turned to follow. Slipped the long knife back in my belt and gripped the great sword, went for a wide slash. One that should've chopped clean through all of the spirits. That would have, except the first spirit dove at me in a frantic tackle. Caught my arm before my swing could build momentum. Knocked away the great sword with his scrabbling hands. The rest followed in.

I raised my arms, tried to knock away the fists and claws, the teeth. "Selena!" I shouted. If nobody came in a second, I'd be torn to pieces. No idea if my spirit could recover from something like that, and I didn't want to find out.

Selena didn't answer, but I heard plenty of growling rage from her side of the courtyard. We were outnumbered, and we were losing. As a spirit bit at my face, I jutted my head forward, bashing into it and knocking the spirit back even if it made the world blur. I reached for the long knife, and when I jabbed it forward, I felt it bite, saw the flames take hold. Then the next spirit swatted the knife away. The lash wasn't any good here, too close.

A pair of hands grabbed my shoulders from behind and threw me to the ground. Another spirit, leering down at me with a smile full of rotten teeth. Wild eyes and frayed eyebrows. A wrinkled, splotchy skin that suggested more than one encounter with the disease. The spirit leaned in towards me, his mouth opening to reveal craggy teeth sinking towards my face.

THE FOUNDER

Pale fire erupted from his chest, as though the spirit had been stabbed through. Then something lifted the spirit up into the air and launched him away. Threw it to the other side of the breach. The other spirits reaching for me paused. A fatal mistake. A man, wearing a tan cloth shirt and pants, stepped over me and swung his arms, stabbing in through the air. Instead of weapons, every time his leather-wrapped hands came close to a spirit, wrangling fire would shoot out from his knuckles, spreading forward and catching the souls in its cleansing burn.

As the man swept the spirits away from me, I heard his laughter; bright, free-flowing joy.

The man, for I didn't know what else to call him, cleared out the breach with smooth strokes. Punches and kicks, mainly, but in the manner of one exercising. Testing his muscles, his reach. Several times the man glanced back at me, apparently making sure another spirit hadn't caught me unawares. He didn't wear a helmet, and his dark head was hairless, his eyes bright and burning around the edges with the same fire as the angry spirits. His teeth were as white as the desert sand, bared in a fierce smile. Before I could say anything, he bent down and picked my great sword off of the ground. Strode to the center of the breach, jammed the blade into it, the point cutting down into the stone. Twisted the hilt.

Blue flame poured out of the sword, spreading and covering the breach like an oil lake lit in flame. Everywhere the fire touched, the image of Earth, the ruined town disappeared. Crinkled away and revealed the white stones beneath. I searched for Selena and saw her at the edge, banishing a remaining pair of spirits with synchronized swipes and slashes from her cleaver and knife. In a minute it was over.

"Been a long time since I've seen this sword," the man said as I stood up, his voice tinged with ash and fire. "Like meeting an old friend. One you never thought you'd see again."

"Dolan?" I said, because who else could it be?

"Seems you know I am," the man replied. "Now I'd ask the same of you? Who comes to play out here, in these desolate ruins?"

"People who come to find you," I said.

Now Dolan's grin faltered. Sank into a line. He glanced at the sword, still held in his hands. "Not much use coming for me," Dolan said. "I had my time, and this isn't it."

"Not sure that's your decision to make," Selena said. "Riven needs you, Dolan. Whether you like it or not."

The spirit laughed, a loud grumbling thing that bounced off the walls of the houses around us. "A bold announcement. And you may not be wrong, as I haven't seen a breach in this ruin for a thousand years or more. Unfortunate then, that I cannot leave it."

"Are you sure? Nara sent us," I said. "She wouldn't have, if you couldn't come with."

When I said the name, Dolan's eyes flared, and his teeth bared into a snarl. Before I could move, before I even knew what was happening, Dolan darted forward with my sword and stabbed me with it. Blue fire ran up and around me, and burned my world away.

When I died, when Piotr had me killed back on Earth, it'd felt like falling down an infinite well. Bits of me disappearing as my soul untethered itself from my body. This, this was more vicious. Whereas before my physical body fell away, now my mind dissolved. My memories, my sense of who I was, where I was, what I was vanished. I would say that everything went black, but that's not true. It didn't go anywhere, didn't become anything.

Just ended.

I came back on the edge of the courtyard. Dolan stood in front of me, his hand on my forehead. His eyes still burned, not in the pupil's center as with the angry spirits, but more as though the edges glimmered with that pale flickering flame.

"I'm sorry," Dolan said. He stared at my eyes, apparently searching to see if I was really there.

"Yeah, you can back off now," I said, pushing him away. "What did you do to me?"

"I brought you back," Dolan said. "Something I haven't done in centuries."

I'd done it before. With a binding, you could restore a spirit to some semblance of their former self. Rescue their mind. I'd brought Selena back after the ghoul on the way to the Mountain demolished her. I hadn't known what it felt like to be torn away and put back together. I didn't want it to happen again.

"Well that's lovely," I said. "Mind explaining why you decided to torch me in the first place?"

"You said Nara sent you," Dolan said. "That alone is reason enough."

"They don't like each other," Selena added.

"Got that, thanks," I replied. "Mali told us the Nara wasn't exactly your best friend. You have to look past it. If you don't, then everything falls apart."

Dolan glanced at the courtyard, where the breach had been. "I believe you. Except, there is a difference. You do not release a river to extinguish a candle."

"Excuse me?" I said.

"Whatever she said to you, Nara will doom Riven more surely than anything you could ever imagine. You are a spirit, and you would be in her chains. She would rule over all of you without a second thought, and you will have no say in the matter."

"Do you have a better idea?" I said. "Because if our options are to die horribly as Riven tears itself apart, or be ruled by a power-hungry spirit, then we might as well torch ourselves here and now."

Dolan stared back at me, then let his eyes cast around the ruins. "You mentioned Mali. I assume Nara sent you to her first?"

"She's gone," Selena said. Before I could speak up, Selena launched into the story.

Dolan took the speech in stride and, by the end of it, nodded as Selena wrapped up with our return to Nara. "Then you have happened on a stroke of luck," Dolan said. "You won't need Nara anymore, because I can do it better."

"Do what better?" I said.

"You are staring at the founder of the guides," Dolan said. "If anyone can lead you to victory against a horde of angry spirits, can cleanse Riven of the foul stench of the dead, it is I. And with Mali gone, at last I am free."

Oh, good.

A LEGEND

Dolan decided our instruction in Riven's history at Mali's hand hadn't been good enough. As we began the long walk back towards Riven's city out of the desert ruins, the ancient spirit told us his version of the tale.

"If you want to know how Riven came to be, it starts with the three of us," Dolan said as we went through the sand. His eyes wandered the distance, floating back through memories. "We came into Riven within moments of each other. Each of us, all of us, victims of an attack on our village by a neighboring one. All of us were young, barely fifteen years old. That didn't matter. The attackers came in fast, slaughtered everyone and presumably took everything that was ours. The next thing I knew, we were standing here, on a flat piece of rock fifty or sixty yards across."

"How do you know what a yard is?" I asked him, and Dolan blinked at me, annoyed that I'd broken his recitation.

"If you want to jump ahead," Dolan said. "I'm happy to do so."

I shook my head, as it was obvious that Dolan was not, would not, in fact be happy to do so. After a moment, the spirit turned back to his story.

"If you've seen what Riven looks like now, it shares nothing with the Riven that I knew when I came here. There were no trees. No mountains. No walls. No city. The dead were our only companions. They came to the one spot they could. An endless river of spirits and souls dropping onto our little patch and stepping off into the great blue ocean of the Cycle. I watched them. I don't know for how long.

"If you think time holds little relevance in Riven today, it held less then. Nothing measured how long we stood there. No buildings to tell a history of wars, no scraps of paper to write down the passing of days. Eventually, the three of us noticed each other. Found in our inaction, in our hesitation to walk off the edge, a common bond. Nara and Mali's eyes, like mine, tracked the endless walk of our countrymen without joining their journey. Mali spoke first.

'Are you alive?' Mali asked us.

"We did not know, then, what had happened. Whether we had died or whether some mystical event had forced us into this strange new place. Our gods had no stories of a world like this one. Our elders had no tales to prepare us for such a void as Riven. So in our confusion and our loneliness we bonded over the endless years.

"Our friendship kept the Cycle at bay. Its whispers quiet, hovering at the edges of our consciousness. As children will do, we started to play. To test the boundaries of the world we were in. The dead spirits didn't mind as we pushed them around."

"You three were the only ones that stayed?" Selena said. "No other spirits came over questioning where they were?"

Dolan hesitated, his foot settling into the sand at the top of a rolling dune. The look he gave Selena held the same sadness I'd seen on a thousand spirit faces. Regret that could not be righted.

"That patch became our castle. Our sanctuary. Anyone that didn't start the walk to the Cycle became a problem. Someone that might attack us. Attempt to rule us." Dolan twisted into a defiant mask. "We are not saints. We were a trio who found ourselves in a strange and unfamiliar place. Without guidance, without knowledge. But Riven was ours, and we kept it."

"That's evil," Selena said.

"Selena," I cautioned.

"She's right," Dolan said. "My, our, only defense is that we knew nothing better. Only that spirits who fell into the infinite blue never returned. That our patch was small. And that, in our experience, newcomers only meant loss."

I could see more questions dance around Selena's lips, but she kept them closed. Dolan waited a moment, then began his march. Continued his story.

"Over time we began to see the cracks in Riven's facade. The pieces of this world that didn't quite connect. It started when one spirit fought back. When I managed to overpower it, and break its neck. Only to have the same spirit heal itself and stand back up an hour later. That was our clue that the normal rules did not apply.

"Nara was the first. She realized she could find a way to attach to the spirits. To hold their hand and gain their trust and eventually, control them. Those were momentous hours. Mali and I watching Nara go up to each spirit in turn, take its hand, and speak softly to it. You must understand, such an act as the binding came to us as out of one of our legends. Magic, you might have called it, though in time we understood binding to be more akin to love than to sorcery.

"As Nara proved to us that our conception of reality didn't hold sway in Riven, Mali played with a different sense. Projected her dreams and desires out into the gray. I never understood quite how, and Mali never explained it to us. A jealous keeper of secrets, that one."

"Seems to fit with her character," I said. "She didn't want to talk much with us."

"Always more interested in her own mind," Dolan said. "It's why I wound up trusting her more than Nara. Mali wanted her own world, but she didn't feel the need to destroy this one to get it."

TRIPLE BOUND

So she didn't tell you how to create things yourselves?" I said. "And you didn't ask?"

"We asked," Dolan said. "Both Nara and I. Except, as you've seen, talent still chooses its targets in Riven. Mali harbored hers, and neither Nara nor I could ever master more than the simplest creations. For me, that meant these."

Dolan nodded at the columns we were walking past, the ones coated with paintings.

"Spots of color," Dolan sighed. "That's all I could ever make. Nara even less. Her attention turned inward, to the workings of the soul. With Mali's growing ability, we became kings and queens, living in grand castles in the middle of the city. Nara bound spirits and questioned them, brought us information from the world outside. I acted as the enforcer, working with Nara's spirits to push any reluctant souls into the Cycle.

"I began, before long, to have Mali make weapons to arm Nara's souls. To arm myself. A few of the spirits had become aggressive, resisting our escorts to the end. With the long shaft of a spear I found my own talent. A curious dip in the Cycle, the spear's point vanishing beneath the surface, sent the pale fire up its length and into my body.

"I should have been destroyed then," Dolan brushed at the edges of his eyes, where the faint blue hue still shone. "Except Nara's spirits, my bound allies, pulled me back from the brink. Brought my passive body to Nara, where she ignited me. Brought me back."

"Then you owe her your life," I said.

"To a degree," Dolan admitted. "A debt I have long since paid, I assure you. After Nara returned me to myself, I could feel the fire raging in my soul. If the Cycle whispers to you, it screams at me. And like a shriek, I found I could let it out. Pour its energy into things, like that spear. Like your sword.

"It didn't take long for the city to crowd with lost spirits. Nara became more obsessed with binding them, demanding that I take care only of the ones that appeared sentient, to know where they were. Nara turned to Mali to create streets and stores, buildings large and small. Replicas of places the spirits would tell us about. Riven's city grew larger, and I found more spirits wandering its alleys. Lost and growing angry."

"So you took action," I said.

"No," Dolan replied. "Though I wonder what would have happened had I started sooner. Before Nara became enraptured with the lives she was spinning in our dead city. As your world grew, more souls crossed into Riven. Nara couldn't bind them fast enough. The spirits would turn on her, on ones she had already charmed. The bright streets became dangerous, and Nara looked to me.

"Mali and I created the weapons together. She molded the edges, I imbued them with fire. At first we gave them to Nara's spirits, and they patrolled the streets with deadly efficiency. Tireless warriors. With only one master."

"You didn't like that," Selena said.

"We were a trio." Dolan nodded. "Now, we were Nara's prisoners. Mali realized it first. When Nara requested a change to part of the city and Mali denied it. Said she preferred that neighborhood as it was. Only when Mali refused, a pair of Nara's spirits holding my weapons appeared at her door. This time, it wasn't a question.

"From then on, Mali and I began to recruit and harbor those sane spirits we found. Built them up and trained them in secret, in a mountain on the edge of the forest. Well away from Nara's fantasy world."

"We've been there," I said. "To the Mountain."

Dolan looked north and west, towards where the Mountain would be. "Mali made it to cover the Cycle, to hide what we were doing. She claimed to Nara that it would allow us to control the spirits coming in, and it did. We took and trained those we could. In time, we had an army of our own.

"I don't know how long the war lasted. Only that Nara ran out of weapons before we ran out of souls. At the end of it, standing in Nara's grand room, we made our worst mistake."

"You trapped yourselves," Selena said. "That's why you split up."

"We tried to bind her," Dolan said. "Rather than simply send her to the Cycle, which is what we should have done."

"It didn't work?" I asked.

"Nara tried to do the same thing. Bind us as we bound her. The conflicts wrecked our minds. Nearly drove us all to insanity. Mali herself leveled half the city, built it up and brought it down. As though a thousand voices yelled in our minds at once. Nara, you don't understand, she can command your every idea. Your every feeling, if she chooses. So Mali and I clung to the only thing we could control, which was our connection to her.

"We sent Nara east, into the fields. Made her walk every step, and then forced her to remain in that clearing. At the same time, we could hear her whispering to us. To Mali and I. Soon after, I found Mali at my throat, coming for me with Nara's curses spilling from her lips. After that, we left the city. I came here, where the desert sand and distance kept Nara's voice quiet. Mali and I would have thrown ourselves into the Cycle years ago, except doing so would have freed our enemy."

"If what you're saying is true, then bringing you back is a risk," I said. "Can't Nara overpower you?"

"Maybe," Dolan said. "Though all things change with time. Perhaps I can resist her urging now, or control her with my own binding.

Better still if we do not test the theory. If we can quiet Riven without involving Nara."

After what Dolan had said, I was all in favor of that.

STRATEGY SESSION

Bringing Dolan, an ancient spirit, into the middle of the guide headquarters went over about as well as I expected. Guides are taught to treat anything new with more than a bit of suspicion. Spirits looking like Dolan, wearing clothes no guide would sport, gave an excuse to take extra precautions. Guides watched us from buildings as we walked, sneaks trailed us from the moment we entered the city.

Bryce had an operation running, and it ran well.

Even so, I saw the cracks. Other guides crossed our paths, dashing by in front of us and ducking down alleys. Calling for help to close a breach, or wrangle a group of spirits. Still, the chaos seemed better controlled than when Selena and I had first left the city for Nara days and days ago. I even let myself feel a rush of hope. That maybe, somehow, we'd manage to control the city. Break out and stem the tide of angry spirits.

Bad idea.

By the time we made it to the clock tower courtyard and Bryce's haphazard command center, the leader of the guides expected us. Alec walked the three of us into a cluster of senior guides, standing around a large table cobbled together from doors torn off of their hinges. On it, marked by chunks of broken stone, sat landmarks I knew.

The Mountain. The city walls. The gates on the south and west sides.

"For a makeshift war, I'm not impressed," Dolan announced after introductions were made. "You are letting the spirits come right up to your doorstep. You should be driving them back. Take the breaches one by one until there are none left."

"I don't know what the numbers were like in your day, sir," Bryce said. "We have neither the manpower or weapons to make such a move."

"With me, you do," Dolan said. "I will lead your finest to the west gate, into the forest, and clear it. From there we will forge a straight path to the Cycle and keep it patrolled. Make it easy for spirits to find their way to their everlasting home."

"You talk as if the breaches are not constantly moving," Bryce said. "They pop in and out. We close one and another appears in a completely different part of the city. There are no paths to patrol, there are no single regions to hold. They are everywhere, and we're not."

Dolan stared back at Bryce, thinking hard. Or at least that's what I thought he was doing. Perhaps, after so many centuries, the idea of holding a strategic conversation was new to him. So I figured I'd better step in.

"Bryce, I think Dolan has a point. If nothing else, cleaning out the older breaches in the woods can buy us time to get rid of some of the ghouls and maybe bring us to another solution."

"Leaving the protection of the walls will allow such a force to be surrounded," Bryce said. "Here, if a breach appears, we have reinforcements. Help is all around you. Out there, in those trees, you will be swarmed by spirits looking for souls to devour. Ghouls by the dozen. The west gate is constantly pressed as it is."

Bryce spared me a nod. "That spirit, Cheo, and his tireless force is the only reason we are not there now fighting for the city's life."

"Your guides are too terrified to risk their lives for Riven?" Dolan said. "Too scared to wade into danger?"

"They have no fear of danger. No love for suicide, either. We have families, Dolan. People on the other side that depend on our return. Throwing that away in an uncertain attempt is not an order I can make."

"Then you are a coward," Dolan replied. The rest the room looked at the spirit, and the stares weren't friendly. Including my own. "I created the guides as a force for Riven. To face its dangers without fear. A sword against the plague of the dead. Now you say that you are nervous about the cost you might pay? You should be honored to pay it!"

All of us sat silent for a minute. I wasn't sure what to say. How to calm the tension. Then Bryce did what he'd done for me countless times: found a way.

"I cannot understand where you came from," Bryce said to Dolan. "I do not know your life. What circumstances brought you here to us. Carver says you are a force for our side and I choose to accept his judgment. But here, in this place, you are not the leader. Whatever you might be, you are not a guide, and here guides make the choices, and we do so without threats." Bryce turned to me. "Carver, you left to find a woman. Where is she?"

Selena and I explained what happened. How we found Dolan, and how Nara still lived in her hut in the field. Dolan said nothing. No outburst of anger, no harsh asides casting aspersions on Nara's motivations and her character. No, he stood there and stared at Bryce. His eyes calm.

If I knew anything, I'd guess Dolan was finally evaluating Bryce. Taking a measure of my mentor's person against Dolan's centuries of experience and finding where Bryce landed among all the spirits Dolan had ever known.

"So you're proposing that Dolan is as good or better than your original option?" Bryce asked me when we concluded, and I nodded. "That we should listen to him?"

"I don't know if his plan will work," I said. "But I do know that doing nothing will get us killed. Going back to Nara may well be worse, if what Dolan says is true. With those facts in hand, in my view, we should at least try."

Bryce turned back to Dolan. Gave the spirit a nod. "We will allow you to take a force of spirits. My guides may follow. Provide support at a distance. If things go well, and I hope they do, then we will commit more of us to the attempt."

"If that is what you can give, then that is what I would ask," Dolan replied, nodding his head. "Now, if we can get started. It has been many, many years since I have had the pleasure of a good fight."

"So who goes?" I asked the group around the table. "Who wants to brave the ghosts of the forests, the ghouls and the breaches? Because Dolan and I can't do it alone."

Dolan caught the inclusion. Adding myself to his cause. The old spirit gave me an appreciative nod. Selena, behind me, chimed in her name.

"I'll go," came Anna's voice, from the back of the room. I hadn't even seen her there. "Laurence can take my shifts watching from the Warrens."

"I can't let Carver get himself killed, so I will go," Alec said. A number of other guides echoed his cheery observation and before long we had a group of thirty ready and willing to risk their lives in our impossible mission.

THE RESET

We started out west from the clock tower courtyard. Went through crowded avenues and by the apartment that I'd long since left to Nicholas. Which reminded me that I hadn't seen the scientist for a while.

Selena and I split apart from the pack and dropped in. I briefly wondered if Nicholas had blown himself to pieces, given that, from the outside, his lab appeared quiet.

What we found inside, what we saw, wasn't what I'd expected. The machines that once covered his lab; crude furnaces and forges, gadgets crumbled together from whatever junk Nicholas could lay his hands on, were gone. The only thing that still remained in the room sat in the center. A spherical device that Nicholas hunched over, back to us, looking like a man madly devouring a meal.

"You've changed things around?" I said to Nicholas and he jumped at my voice.

"Carver," Nicholas said, turning his goggled eyes towards me. I noticed more than a few singes along the man's face, and his ever-dirty coat had reached a stage of filthiness that rendered its definition as clothing suspect. "I was not expecting you. With more notice, I could have prepared a better presentation."

"Presentation of what?"

"Ah, this." Nicholas stepped aside and waved at the object. Without the scientist in the way, I had a better view. The ashen-metal ball resembled what I'd seen of artillery shells used in the war. Nicholas had been reaching through a flipped-up access door. I tried to peer inside, but, without sticking my head in, I couldn't make out anything. "You remember my orange rays? From the crossbow?"

I nodded. The rays jumped from one object to the next, devouring and destroying anything close by. And by destroying, I meant ruining utterly. Disintegrating into nothing. Obliterating souls seemed dangerous, so I tried not to use the weapon all that often.

"This device will send out so many more," Nicholas said. "At twice the range. It will keep burning until there is nothing else to grab."

"Where do you think we would use it?" Selena said. "Spirits don't sit still and wait for you to detonate a bomb."

Nicholas looked beyond us, out the window on the first floor and into the street. "The city is crowded enough. The rays should be able to leap across the streets. If we used the device in your clock tower square, the entire city should go up."

"That doesn't sound like victory," I said.

"I am not aiming for victory. I am aiming for survival. The device will annihilate most of the spirits. If the guides cross out ahead of the explosion, they will remain. Riven will be reset, and we get another chance."

I let the words sink in. A reset button. If we triggered the device as the war wound down, as disease stopped the insane flow of spirits, then a reset might be all Riven needed. A chance to escape. We just had to keep Riven going long enough to set it up.

"I like it," I said.

"You like it?" Selena said. "You like that he's made something that can destroy all we have?"

"Please, Selena. We don't really have anything. Mali thought this up ages ago. It's not ours. It's not real. The only thing that is, is you and I. What we have. That doesn't need the city."

"Nicholas," Selena said. "Who's going to trigger the bomb?"

"I will," Nicholas said. "I'm the only one who can. Who knows how. And I won't teach you."

"What? Why?" I asked.

"Because, Carver," Nicholas said, "you have Selena. Graham and Katherine are no longer here. That leaves me alone. With as much time as I've spent with these cold machines, I'm getting tired. Getting lonely. This device is my way out. A swan song, I believe they call it."

"We'll get you enough time to use it."

Nicholas nodded. It felt strange; talking about the end of someone. Normally, a spirit's end came through the Cycle. A slow walk to peaceful nothing. A journey triggered, perhaps, by my wrangling lash. Yet here was a soul planning self-sacrifice. To remove himself and take our troubles with him.

"You're a good man," I said to Nicholas. "A great scientist."

"Do not tell me what I already know," Nicholas said, the man's smile flavoring his words. "Now go buy me some time. The device is not ready yet."

AT THE GATE

The west gate leading out of the city stood tall and grand, the opposite of the factory remnants of the Tar Pit that came before it. I could make out Cheo's golden ghoul from blocks away, standing in the middle of the gate as though single-handedly barring the passage into the city. Only when we closed did I realize that's exactly what the ghoul was doing. It braced its legs against the ground, a pair of large stones from one of the factories dragged behind it, to help the ghoul keep its balance. Its hands were outstretched, palms spread out against the gate. A gate shut for the first time in my memory.

On the other side we could hear the clamoring of angry spirits. The hammering as their fists struck the solid wood barrier. I couldn't tell how many spirits were out there, not from the ground. So Dolan, Selena and I made our way up to the top of the left turret.

Cheo stood up there, staring down at the horde attempting to gain entry. A true mass. More spirits than I'd ever seen in one place. They stretched out in a wide semicircle all the way from the clearing at the gate to the edge of the forest. A hundred yards or more. All of them were shrieking, wailing, waving their hands in anger at some distress that I could never know. The spirits were all types: men, women, children, grandmothers and grandfathers. Races from across the globe. Cultures equally varied. A man in a soldier's uniform might stand alongside a woman in a tribal headdress, both of their eyes burning with pale angry fire.

"This is not a battle we can win," Cheo said. "The Right Hand does not have the forces for this. The ghoul will not hold forever."

"Seems to be doing a good job so far," I said.

Cheo shook his head. "They are starting to climb on one another. Eventually, they will climb these very walls. Once that happens, the real battle will begin. It will end shortly thereafter."

"Everyone's all doom and gloom today," I said. "First Nicholas, now you. Dolan, cheer me up?"

The old spirit looked out over the mob. The wave of burning blue eyes. "I've seen a force like this before," Dolan said. "Nara did similar things. Brought an endless stream of enemies to our doorstep. Thrust them against us like a battering ram. Do you know how we beat them?"

"Do we look that old?" Selena said.

"We used what they did not have," Dolan tapped his head. "The spirits do not think. They are not bound, they cannot adjust their tactics. We lay a trap, we open the door, and we bring this fight to an end. So think, my friends. What snare can we set?"

"I have an idea," I said, thanking Nicholas for reminding me of the very weapons I already had.

First, we took my crossbow and unloaded the orange bolts. All three of them. Then, we laid them out on the ground, one spaced out from the other across the gate. Safely behind the door as the ghoul held it. Once the bolts had been laid out we drew back, assembled our guides and the Right Hand's spirits around the opening. Far enough back to be out of the range of those blistering orange rays.

"Fair warning; the rays might destroy the gate," I said.

"We won't need it anymore," Dolan said. "After this, we strike out. Carry the fight to the breaches in the woods. Slow them down and end them. If your man on the other side can fulfill his part of our bargain, then that should be enough to tip the scales."

Bryce had crossed back when we left. Crossed back in yet another attempt to warn the world against its cataclysmic course. For his part, Bryce said that the war was dying down anyway. A lack of soldiers. A lack of national will. But the faster the conflicts could be resolved, the sooner we could gain control on our side. The sooner Nicholas would be able to flip a switch.

"Let's go," Dolan ordered and the ghoul complied. The beast rocked back on his heels, his hands leaving the door. Immediately the pounding grew, and without the ghoul's hands supporting the gate, the sheer pounding force from dozens of tireless spirits began to break it apart.

A crease appeared in the gate's middle, then a crack. The hinges groaning alongside the archway. You would've thought that such a massive thing would give way slowly, but no. When the gate lost its hold it was open in an instant. The large doors twisting and breaking along their sides. An endless flood of horrors pouring through towards us.

"Weapons ready," Dolan said. He shifted the great sword, my great sword, into a forward stance with his hands. Point facing towards the spirits. I drew my lash and long knife. Selena held her cleaver at the ready. Then a spirit stepped on the first bolt.

The orange ray exploded, blossoming and dancing and cutting and burning its way into the charging ranks. Nicholas' weapon worked best if the targets were close, and these spirits were as close as you could get. Smothered into one another as the stampede surged forward. The burning orange rays shot through all of them. Jumped and split from soldier to sailor. From bartender to baron. The spirits vanished as the blossoming glow consumed them.

By the time all three bolts had been triggered, by the time the growling roars had ceased, the only thing in front of us was a charred ruin that had once been a gate. The stone walls had burned away, the archway collapsed, but there were no spirits.

I didn't know how many thousands upon thousands had been

obliterated by those bolts, but I did know the idea had come from Dolan. The ancient spirit had proved why he deserved to lead. Why I was happy to follow.

"Do not rest," Dolan announced. "For this is only the start. Ready yourselves, for now we charge."

ADVANCE

Dolan could run. The ancient spirit wasn't willing to wait an extra moment, and after we saw him sprint ahead five long strides, dancing around the rubble and the scorched remnants left behind by Nicholas's burning rays, we joined him in the rush.

The guides fanned out behind Selena and I, along with Cheo's squad of spirits. A motley crew. Our number, compared against the angry souls we'd just decimated, was nothing more than a pittance.

Dolan wanted to get to the breaches before more spirits came through. I knew we wouldn't make it. We weren't that lucky.

We were halfway across the clearing when the next wave began emerging from the woods. The forest's gray trees and their dark leaves hid the spirits until they broke out. Appearing as if from nowhere and running headlong across the open plain towards us. Their blue eyes burned with hatred. Hatred that they didn't know or understand, yet acted upon regardless.

Dolan lifted the great sword high. "Never stop running!" Dolan shouted to us as he led. "Take them as they come and move on to the next. Find the breaches, seal the gates, and reclaim your world."

And then the spirits were upon us.

I tried to stick close to Dolan, to Selena. But in the melee, that was an impossibility.

The first spirit coming towards me looked like a soldier that had caught the wrong end of a mortar. His torn arms outstretched, reaching towards my throat as he ran, and without stopping I cracked the lash in front of me. The point burrowed into the soldier's chest and I lit him up in blue. Yanked the lash away as he collapsed.

I whipped the lash at another spirit on my right, heading straight for a guide. Caught him in the shoulder and twisted him, burning, to the ground.

Turning back towards the woods, I saw another rushing at me. This one a woman wearing a hospital gown. Another disease victim. She died a second death on the fiery edge of my knife. I shoved her off and kept forging ahead. We were nearly to the tree line.

Dolan had already hacked his way into the woods, but his shouts, loud whoops of thrilling excitement and encouragement, gave plenty of clues as to what way he slashed. Beside me, Selena finished a thorough dicing of a suit-sporting man and took a second to look across our line.

"We're not going to move fast," Selena said.

I agreed. Too many spirits poured from the forest. Our band was being surrounded, despite the fact that we were working our way through with brutal efficiency. Plumes of blue fire erupted constantly around us as spirits were wrangled and sent to the Cycle. Yet, between the snarls of rage and howls of anger, I caught cries of pain. Strikes inflicted on the wrong side.

"We can't stop here," I said. "Dolan's right, our only chance at slowing the spirits down is right now."

I didn't wait for Selena's nod, but dashed into the dark trees.

RAGE

The first breach sat a few yards beyond the forest's edge. A lime green pool expanding to fill a clearing beneath the dark canopy. Dolan, as I approached, ducked beneath two scrabbling arms and dished out a fatal cut. Then, without pausing in his move, he twisted the hilt around in his hand and stabbed the sword straight down into the earth. Just as I'd seen in the desert; bright flame poured into the ground and burned away the breach. Different than the sapphire tablets we used. Not necessarily better.

Spirits on the edge of the breach crawled away, escaping the flames. Our tablets, they would grab everything within the area. Every spirit would be pulled back and cleansed of their fury. But then, a tablet would have grabbed me too.

"On to the next one," Dolan said to me and Selena as we caught up.

"We're getting ahead," I said. "If we leave them behind, they might be trapped."

"If we don't move," Dolan said. "We will be."

The ancient spirit turned and advanced, slicing through another pair of burning blue souls.

"He's losing it," Selena said. "Dolan's going to get us killed if he keeps going like this."

"We're already dead," I said.

But she was right. The guides straggling behind us were scratched, wounded, or were fighting through exhaustion. Spirits continued to pour from between the trees, and my lash cracked again and again and again. My knife stabbed more times than I could count. I didn't have muscles that tired, but my friends did.

I had to get them out of here.

"Anna!" I shouted. And I heard the answer, somewhere in the woods. "Sound the retreat. Get the guides back to the gate. Hold that line. We'll take it from here."

The guides around us heard my words and backed away, formed a tight cluster then went towards the west gate. I went the other direction. Cheo and his Right Hand joined us, and I noticed some taking to the trees as they had in Mali's jungle. Their wrangling arrows split the air, piercing and cleansing spirits we didn't see.

Battered, we happened onto the second breach. Followed Dolan's trail of wrangled spirits and slashes biting deep into the trunks. Except this time, Dolan wasn't having it so easy.

In front of him loomed a ghoul, a two legged thing that had no arms, like a living archway. It lunged forward and shifted its legs to any angle it wanted. As though made out of rubber, or sand. As we entered the clearing, Dolan rolled forward, ducking under a wide sweep of the creature's front leg. Rather than continuing its motion, however, the ghoul sank back to the ground, and scooped its legs the other way, wrapping itself into a circle and pinning Dolan into the middle.

The ancient spirit tried to move the great sword, but the ghoul crushed him too tightly. No room, no range of motion.

I started to make a move, then Selena shouted and I turned. Too slow. A spirit, some sort of ragged deliveryman, tackled me and shoved me to the ground. His claws, sharp fingernails, raked my cheek. I felt the heat, and if I'd had blood, I'm sure it would've been running. I rolled to the left, using my shoulder to shove the spirit off of me. Stabbed with the knife in my left hand. Sent the spirit away. And then two more replaced it.

"Help Dolan!" I called, not sure Selena could hear me. The spirits bit and tore at my cloak, at my arms and legs. But they couldn't kill me. At least not for a while. If that ghoul took Dolan, then this whole thing was lost.

One of the spirits wrapped its arms around my neck and tried to crush my throat. I jammed my head into its face, which I didn't bother recognizing. There were too many, simply too many souls to note specifics. All of them burned the same, all of their teeth clicked and gnashed towards me. Their hands were all cold and hard. They weren't the people they had been.

My head knocked the spirit's own back, which gave me enough room to move my left hand and jab upwards towards the spirit's hip. Or at least, I tried. A third spirit joined the pile, pinning my arm and my knife to my left side. I felt my legs go numb. The second spirit ripping my knees apart.

I wasn't sure how much damage I could take until I ceased to be. I didn't know at what point I could be overwhelmed. Whether I could be ripped so far that my soul would not be able to put itself back together.

I didn't want to find out.

With my right hand, I dropped the lash and gripped the spirit that sat on me. Wrenched my arm to the right and threw the ghost off. Grabbed the knife from my left hand by the blade and pulled it out of my own grip. The spirit I'd thrown off tried to dive back on, but it wasn't fast enough. Still holding the base of the blade, I jammed it into the spirit as it tried to regain its position. Slipped my hand down to the hilt and twisted. Ignored my own searing pain to save what was left of my life.

I withdrew the knife and lunged into the spirit tearing into my left arm. Took care of it. Though I could no longer feel my left side, except for the pain. All of the pain. I'd been burned, I'd been beaten, I'd been slashed and bashed in this world. But this ripped a new layer of agony through my mind. I think the only way I maintained any concentration at all was by focusing on the shouts of Selena and Dolan as they tangled with the ghoul.

They were my friends, and they needed me.

I leaned forward, sat up and stabbed. Brought an end to the spirit that had made a meal of my legs.

I tried to stand up, only I couldn't feel my feet. Couldn't feel anything, in fact, outside of my right arm and my neck. The ground rumbled beneath me. Overhead, swinging in a lazy arc, came the ghoul's large left foot. More like an elephant, or a large Greek column than any human appendage. The ghoul's leg hovered over my head, and I could see the dripping scars, the slashes made from Selena's cleaver and Dolan's sword. I could see that leg come down towards me. And I could do nothing to stop it.

A flash of gold, and then the leg flew away. The ghoul, from what mouth I did not know, roared its outrage as Mali's creation battered it away. Pounded the ghoul with large gold fists. I looked over and saw the two-legged monster collapse under the barrage. Saw Selena and Dolan, limping, stick it with their blades and send their blue fire racing along the ghoul's body. A moment later, Dolan did the same to the breach.

For the moment, we were clear. For a moment, we were alive.

RETREAT

You're hurt." Selena walked up to me as I sat on the ground, looking and feeling pathetic.

"You've seen the obvious," I replied.

"We have to keep moving," Dolan announced from where the breach used to be. "If we stay here, they'll catch us. On to the next one."

"Carver is wounded," Selena said. "You can't walk, can you?"

"I'm going to have to sit this one out. Think Goldie over here can carry me back to the gate?"

Selena glanced at Mali's ghoul, its formless face looking back at us. "I don't think you're that heavy, Carver."

"Then go with Dolan," I said. "Close the breaches. And make it back."

Selena bent down, gave my forehead a quick kiss, and then she and Dolan were off. Sprinting further into the dark forest. Cheo and the others followed, the ghoul staying behind and lifting me up.

I'd never been carried like this before, in the arms of a giant creature like this one. Lofted above the ground. The peace didn't last long. Not thirty seconds into our walk, the first spirits arrived. Drawn by the sound of our crunching and grinding through the brush. The ghoul snapping branches as we pounded through them.

The spirits dove at the ghoul's legs, biting and clawing at its metal skin. So far as I could tell, they weren't doing any damage. At least, not physically. But they were wearing it down. The ghoul slowed, every step held back by the grasping arms. Spirits clinging to the legs; pulling and dragging. Trying to force the ghoul down. With both its arms holding me, the ghoul didn't have much in the way of defense.

But I did.

I reached inside my coat, to the holster Nicholas had made for me after I'd found Inman's pistol. I kept the weapon loaded, had more bullets inside my coat's pockets. The guides had plenty of ammo, although the bullets were made from Riven scrap. Nothing compared to the quality you'd find on Earth.

I drew the gun, it's gold barrel seeming very out of place in the gray dark forest. Aimed it, and fired as the ghoul stepped forward.

The bullet picked off a spirit on the ghoul's left ankle. I cocked back the hammer, aimed, and fired again. Another spirit knocked off to the ground. The shots didn't burn with blue fire, just hard metal. But every spirit I knocked away allowed the ghoul to speed up. Pulled us closer to that gate.

I fired another four times until, with a click, the pistol told me it was empty. I'd have to reload with one working hand. Not exactly something I knew how to do.

Maybe I wouldn't have to.

The ghoul crashed into the large clearing in front of the wall. Shouts and cries of guides and battle blew into my ears. I could see it; the mass chaos around the ruin where the west gate once stood. The guides that had come with us, along with reinforcements, manned the line of rubble. Held back a wave of spirits trying to claw their way through. Dolan's idea; those burning orange rays, had given us an opening, had damned our defenses.

"Anna," I yelled as we came closer. I could see her, wielding her spiked flail and waving it back and forth, bashing and burning spirits as they charged towards the guides. "Let the ghoul through. It can hold the line for us!"

The guides, whether they heard me or saw the golden beast, cleared a path for us to pound through. I had the ghoul set me down on top of some broken shards of the gate. Not exactly comfortable, but the sooner I was out of his hands, the sooner the ghoul could go back to doing what it did best: mashing spirits to a pulp.

Like Inman's pistol, the ghoul couldn't wrangle the spirits. Couldn't burn them in blue flame and send them running. But it could stamp them out. Knock them down and render them incapacitated so a guide following along could finish the spirit off.

And the ghoul was tireless.

I watched, crippled and useless, from my vantage as Mali's monster tore through the spirits. Had there been the thousands from before, I had no doubt the ghoul would have been overwhelmed. Covered and simply borne into the dirt by the weight of the spirits. Now, with only dozens, the ghoul was free to wreak its destruction.

"What happened to you?" Anna asked, walking over. I could see the sweat shine on her face, the fatigue evident in how she held her weapon low. Breathing hard even though Riven had no air.

"Outnumbered," I said. "Turns out letting spirits tackle you is a bad idea."

"Thought you'd have learned that by now," Anna said. "Selena? Dolan?"

I told her where they were. Told her that the success of this whole mission stayed entirely with them.

"If they can't close more breaches, then we sacrificed the gate for nothing," I finished.

"Not for nothing," Anna said. "We closed some, and we gave us hope. A chance that the guides might do something rather than die in alleys and dark rooms."

"That hope won't last long."

"That's up to you. How long before you're able to move again?"

I could feel it; my bones, such as they were, knitting together. Feeling returning to my arms and legs. Slow, but it would get there.

Before too long I would be back, as dangerous as ever. Such was the magic of being a spirit. Such was the benefit of being dead.

"When Selena gets back," I said. "I'll be ready."

What I didn't know is what I would be ready for. Either another raid deep into the woods, or a retreat to Nicholas and his desperate bomb.

RECKONING

At first glance, they didn't look good. The two of them, Dolan leaning on Selena as they emerged from the woods. The great sword dangling across Dolan's back, held on by its sheath. They stumbled across the clearing, spirits bursting out after them. I heard Anna call for the guides to assist. Saw my friends and fellows break away from the line and guide Dolan and Selena home. And I saw in my love's eyes that we had lost.

"You're still here?" I said to Selena as she came up to me. As she sat Dolan down alongside my shredded body. As she collapsed to the ground.

"I shouldn't be," Selena said. "They should have torn us apart a thousand times. I should have died a thousand deaths, Carver."

"But you didn't," I replied. I glanced at Dolan. The spirit's eyes were shut. He bore a number of nasty gashes and wounds. Perhaps, like me, he was waiting for them to heal. "Is Dolan alive?"

"He'll be okay," Selena said. "No worse than you, I think."

"Cheo? His spirits?"

Selena took a breath. How funny that instinct should live out past our lives. Past the point where our brains cease to be. Yet here we were, still taking a moment and inhaling nonexistent air before delivering bad news.

"Five," Selena said. "We'd been moving fast. Breaking in, Dolan sealing each breach with the sword, and then running. By the fifth one, though, we'd lost some. Too many."

"Lost?"

"The ghouls," Selena said. "They can't kill a spirit, send it to the Cycle, but they can consume them."

I saw the fear in her eyes. Then remembered that it had happened to her. Devoured in the forest by an old ghoul, Selena had ceased to be. At least until Anna and I had rescued her. Ghouls were simply products of spirits, a mass of cold anger and hate. Confusion and loss. Brought together to spread ruin.

"They caught up to you," I said. It wasn't a question. I knew from her look that Cheo and his spirits were still out there. Were now a part of some creature that would likely be making itself manifest before too long.

"There were two more waiting," Selena said. "Two more ghouls around the breach, attacking each other. Absorbing one spirit after another as they crawled through the breach. They were feeding, Carver."

"I suppose there's enough for them to eat," I said.

"They stopped when we came in. I don't know how to describe them to you, but they were shapeless things. Gluttons that had lost any limbs that they may once have had. They came for us," Selena's voice trembled here. Wandered up and down in pitch. Traumatized.

Sometimes I forgot, with all the we had seen, that it was always possible for things to get worse. You could happen upon some new terror that rendered you at a loss.

"There wasn't anything I could do," Selena said. "Dolan tried. Made a charge into the center of the breach and stabbed the sword down. That's when the first ghoul hit him away. Knocked him into the edge of the clearing. Both ghouls went after him. So I closed the breach. Went to the blade and twisted the hilt and sent the fire down."

"At least you closed it," I said, the words sounded lame coming from my mouth. Not nearly enough to fill the void for emotion.

"I didn't realize it," Selena continued. "Behind me, Cheo and the others, they attacked the ghouls. They were trying to save Dolan. In a way, they did. Distracted the ghouls long enough for me to pull the sword out, grab Dolan and run. I left them there, Carver."

"You did what you had to do," I said. "Cheo wanted peace. Now he has it."

Selena laughed, a hopeless chuckle. "Peace? Inside of a ghoul? I don't know, Carver. That's not any peace I would want."

"I can't argue with that. Except to say that maybe it will be worth it."

Selena looked back out across the spirits. The guides. Fighting each other in an endless dance. More guides were arriving from the clock tower, from the city, while others backed away from the front lines. Wounded or exhausted. A rotation that would be carried out indefinitely.

"We should use it," Selena said. "Nicholas. His device. Let's use it and end this madness."

"You know as well as I do that's not a permanent solution," I said. "If we leveled the city, the breaches would come back the same as before. We need something better. We need Bryce to succeed on the other side."

"Even if he does," Dolan said, his voice creaking up from beside me. "Even if your man stops this war. Even if this disease ends. There will be more. There will always be more people, more souls flooding Riven. It will be impossible to hold."

"This, from the most optimistic spirit I'd seen in a long time?" I replied.

"This, from a spirit that has seen the end. We have no other choice, Carver," Dolan said. "We must go to Nara."

"Didn't you say, not all that long ago, the Nara was the worst choice we could make?"

"She's the only one that can create an army big enough to keep

Riven safe," Dolan said. "The only one who can save us from total annihilation."

"Then we failed?"

"We have," Dolan replied. "There is no other way. We cannot close all the breaches, and if we cannot cut off the spirits, then we cannot survive."

SAVIOR

As time went by, with us laying in the rubble knitting our souls back together, the guides formed a more organized perimeter. Runners established routes, carrying ammunition, weapons to those who had broken theirs, and calling for reinforcements as needed. Injuries were carted away on makeshift stretchers. Crossing points close to the west gate were identified and communicated so guides on the other side could have an easier time coming to the wall. To the ruins.

But the swarm never ended. The spirits kept coming. Yes, they were mindless. Yes, they stood in each other's way. Those that had been wrangled often waited around for some time, giving guides a moment of relief before they were shuffled out of the way by the next wave of attackers. It wasn't easy. The repetitive boredom of the attack played into our human instincts. To where a guide might expect a moment after wrangling one spirit only to find the next one right behind, reaching for their throat.

Eventually, I was able to stand. Leaning on Selena. Dolan, less hurt than me, went along in front of us. We set off, leaving Alec and Anna in charge of holding the wall. I'd never left a fight like that before. Walked away from the guides who needed me.

I recalled my parents, in the bowels of the Mountain, fighting Piotr and yelling at me to leave them. Those had been impossible odds like this, so perhaps the fights weren't so different after all. Or perhaps I was a coward.

"You'll do them no favors by staying," Dolan said after I'd glanced back one too many times. "However many spirits you destroy, there will be double that coming after them. The best way for you to help your comrades now is this."

"And what is this?" I poured my frustration in the my voice. "What are you expecting Nara can do? What you couldn't?"

"I told you," Dolan said. "She will take the spirits, she will bind them together, and she will make an army that can cover Riven. Restore it to peace."

"Then why didn't we go to her from the start?" Selena asked.

"Because it took both Mali and I to contain her ambition before," Dolan said. "I'm not as confident in myself alone."

"We'll be there," I said. "And besides, if Riven falls, Nara falls too."

Dolan only nodded, then lapsed into silence. I remembered the paintings, Mali's show. If Nara truly represented a terror greater than what was already happening, well, we'd have to risk it. Certain failure on the path we'd tried. With Nara, we had a slight chance of success.

By the time we reached the clock tower courtyard both Dolan and I were walking normally. Our souls repaired. Bryce hadn't yet returned from the other side, which I took as a positive sign. If he was making headway over there, then that might make up for the lack of it here. We didn't stay long. I gave a quick update to the guides holding the command center, and then we were off. Marching east towards the grain field once again.

The trek to Nara's felt shorter this time. Perhaps because Dolan, as soon as he was able, pushed us to run. Claimed that because we could not get tired, we may as well travel as fast as we could. Lives were in the balance. I didn't argue.

Running without end felt strange. As though at any moment my muscles would wake up and realize that they shouldn't be doing this. That sprinting down one block after another, through neighborhoods and towards the east wall, past the palace and out towards the green without a single pause for breath was wrong somehow. But I didn't. My legs never protested. I didn't drown in sweat, or fall apart as my body gave out. Eventually the strangeness of it all faded. I was living in a new normal. I had no body, not a real physical one anyway, and it was time I learned to use it.

Nara stood outside her hut when we approached this time. Stared past us right at Dolan. Locked eyes with the spirit, but otherwise let no expression cross her face.

"It's been a long time," Dolan said first.

"I'd forgotten what it felt like," Nara said. "To have you close enough to feel the binding. I don't like it."

"If I could stay away, I would," Dolan replied.

The spirit then told Nara what had happened. Our failed defensive. The overwhelming numbers of any spirits flowing from the breaches. Not once did surprise cross Nara's face. Not once did she show fear. Instead, that same straight gaze stared at Dolan the entirety of his tale.

"So can you help us?" I asked when Dolan had finished.

"Help you?" Nara said. "It sounds like you need a little bit more than help. You need a savior."

"Don't let it go to your head," Selena said.

"Why shouldn't I?" Nara replied. She moved over to the ever burning stack of grain and poked it with a loose stalk. "Here I am, tending this fire for all eternity, until the three of you decide to pay me a visit after trying every possible way to avoid doing so. You tell me that all is lost. That your friends and families are suffering. That I am your only salvation. If I am not your savior, then who could ever be such?"

"When I first came here," I said, brushing over the argument. "You told me that I could help you. I've done that. Brought you who you asked. We need your end of the bargain."

"I cannot argue with that," Nara said. "I believe I know how to repay you. I can do as you asked. I can reach out, once I'm close, pull the spirits in and drag them into my net. Save your friends. Your world."

Hesitation hung in the air as her voice trailed off.

"But?" I asked.

Nara turned away from her burning grain pile and came towards me. Closed until she was barely a foot away. I stood my ground.

"The problem with being a savior," Nara said, "is that everyone expects you to save them. Even from themselves."

"Explain."

"Carver, back away from her," Dolan said, a different edge to his voice. I heard the great sword being lifted from its sheath.

And then I felt something alien. Nara reached out and touched my chest. Her hand pressing onto me, and then *into* me. I'd bound spirits before, but this was different. Rather than joining, Nara's technique felt more like theft. Nara took my will, my voice and my choice away. My senses were replaced with shadows of themselves, held by strings leading back to her.

In a moment I went from knowing who and what and where I was to waiting for Nara to tell me, for her mind to inform me. I stood still, rigid. Stared into Nara's eyes and knew what had happened, knew there was nothing I could do about it.

PETS

Carver, what's going on?" Selena asked.

I wanted to turn my head to her. To warn her. But I was a prisoner in my own body. I couldn't move. Until Nara gave me an order. The compulsion, Nara's binding pushing my mind to take Selena and throw her to the ground. Less an outside command and more an irresistible urge.

Knocking Selena to the ground was the *right thing to do*.

I turned, looked at Selena and gave her smile. "It's fine," I said. "Nara is going to help us."

"What?"

As she squinted her eyes at me, I stepped forward, wrapped my arms around her shoulders, and pulled her over my leg and onto the ground. Nara bent over Selena while I watched, but before Nara's hand could touch her, Dolan shoved his great sword in between. Pushed Nara back.

"Dolan," I said, drawing the lash in my right and the long knife in my left. "Nara is trying to help. This is how she does it. Stand aside."

Dolan glanced at me, then turned to Nara. "I had hoped the years had softened you. It appears I was wrong."

Nara slanted her head at him. "Softened me? I waited, trapped here in this field, for centuries. The only thing I had to nurse was my vengeance. Now I shall have it."

"Even if it costs you everything?"

Nara laughed. "It won't. After you, I will take Riven back and turn it into the paradise it was always meant to be."

"You don't deserve to be a god," Dolan replied, then lunged forward with the sword. Straight for Nara. Selena backpedaled away, while I stepped between Nara and Dolan's strike. Deflected the spirit's sword with my knife just enough for Nara to shift away.

Dolan settled his eyes on mine. I gave him a nod. I respected his skills. I did not respect his stance.

"Please," I said. "You know this is our only choice. Do not sacrifice yourself for nothing."

"She speaks through your mouth now," Dolan said. "I am sorry, Carver. You deserved a better end."

Dolan lifted the great sword, pulled it up and left, then stepped forward into hard swing at my head. Not something I could counter. So I rolled, fell to the right and let the blade whisk over me. Came up to a crouch and flicked the lash at Dolan's ankle. Caught it as the spirit slowed his swing, and I pulled. Should have swept Dolan off his feet.

Instead, the spirit dug his heel into the dirt, halting my yank, and then swiped down with the great sword. I dropped the lash, so it fell loose and Dolan's swing missed the cord. Didn't want my weapon severed this far away from Nicholas, the only one I knew who could fix the thing.

I stood up, backpedaled as Dolan strode towards me, the lash dragging behind him. My empty right hand reached into my coat, pulled out Inman's pistol. Properly loaded and ready. Aimed it at Dolan's face, and he paused.

"You're not fast enough to catch this," I said.

"Resist, Carver," Dolan replied. "This is not your doing."

The problem with Dolan's words is that they didn't go into my ears. Or rather, the mind that heard those words was not my own. So I pulled the trigger.

Dolan staggered, the bullet punching a hole in his chest. No blood, of course, but every blow still hurt. More importantly, it kept Dolan's attention on me. At least, until he heard the scraping sound of Selena's cleaver leaving its sheath.

Dolan looked behind him, saw Selena moving into position. I saw in my love's eyes the same spirit that had taken mine. Nara, watching from the edge of the clearing, held a small smile. Two new prizes to start her collection.

"Give it up," I said to Dolan. "This is a fight you cannot win."

"Don't you understand?" Dolan said, holding the great sword in one hand, the other over the bullet's wound. "She cannot leave if I do not let her. Or unless I am dead. Which do you think she has chosen?"

I struggled in that moment. Pushed against Nara's voice, whispering in my head. Telling me to fire again. To knock Dolan down and allow Selena to end his misery.

Do it. Nara spoke in my mind. *Set him free.*

My finger tightened on the trigger. Dolan's sad eyes watched, rimmed with the pale fire that had been burning him for a thousand years or more. And I stopped.

No.

Nara's fury flowed through the bond, and I felt myself losing control. If Nara wanted to move me herself, I couldn't stop her.

Dolan must have seen the flickering fight in my eyes, because he shifted his feet. Darted in an attack. But not at me. Not at Selena. At Nara. The great sword sweeping along the ground, burning with blue fire, to destroy our hope and our damnation.

My next bullet struck Dolan in his right shoulder, but the spirit barely flinched, racing across that clearing. A brief panic flashed over Nara's face, and then a long knife appeared, jutting out of Dolan's back, burning with blue flame. As Dolan crossed the last couple of yards towards Nara, he stumbled, the sword fell out of his grip, and as the fire began to crawl over him, the old spirit collapsed in the dirt at Nara's feet.

Selena drew back her arm, empty without her knife, and watched. As did I.

Nara bent down, picked up Dolan's head with her hand and angled his face towards her. I couldn't see his eyes, couldn't read the pain on his face, could only feel the immense satisfaction flowing through my connection with Nara. Could only hear her words as they slipped out of her sanguine smile.

"Goodbye, old friend."

CHAINED

I slid the great sword into its sheath, slung over my back. Looked towards the break in the grain where, a moment ago, Dolan had disappeared on his vacant journey to the Cycle. A hand landed on my shoulder, light and firm.

"It feels good, doesn't it?" Nara said. "To have your weapon back?"

I nodded. My mind, otherwise, ran blank.

"It is a proper sword for a champion," Nara continued. "Did Dolan tell you that part when he lied to you?"

"He did not," I replied.

Nara's words prompted a question, a thought: *lied to us?* But the idea of asking it fled, vanishing from my consciousness without consideration.

"Riven used to be a bustling world," Nara said. "Where every spirit had a home. A new beginning. A chance to pursue passions without the weight of reality upon their shoulders. With no need for food, for shelter, no fear of death or time, anything was possible. Until Dolan and Mali saw fit to destroy it. They were scared, I suppose. Thought my methods cruel. Dangerous. As do all who see things they do not understand."

Nara turned me around to face Selena, who had put her weapons

165

away and watched us with a solemn face. Waiting for the command of her leader.

"Until he decided on another path, Dolan was my sword. Was my champion. He protected my city, Carver. Now I ask the same of you," Nara said, then broke into a low laugh. "Well, *ask* may be the wrong word. Once you've seen the faults in loyalty, it's easy to see the advantages in obedience. In ownership."

Nara pointed towards the grain, and we moved. I heard her walk behind us as my arms pushed the stalks aside. Clearing a path for Nara's new freedom.

As we moved, I tested the limits of Nara's control. She'd set me to a task—clearing the path—and within the bounds of that task, it seemed I could adjust my approach. Move a stalk with my left hand, then the next with my right. Or use both arms. I tried just bowling them over with my shoulders and that worked too. Try and stop moving, though, and nothing. My body simply didn't respond.

Earlier, with Dolan, I'd felt Nara direct my thoughts. Alter my mind. My words. But when the spirit wasn't focusing on me, my soul came back. Like waking up after a deep sleep, I had to connect with my senses, my limbs. Understand what I could and couldn't do.

I glanced over at Selena, who marched resolute beside me. No idea if she was finding out the same things.

"Selena?" I said, more to see if I could speak than anything.

I felt Nara's glance snap to me as I said the words. Felt her mind press in on mine, searching for my objective. Relaxing when she found only curiosity.

"Carver?" Selena replied, meeting my look. "What are we going to do?"

"Whatever she wants us to," I replied.

"Correct," Nara said from behind us. "Take the opportunity to get used to your new existence. Understand that you are on a leash. One that can be long or short, according to your actions. I have no desire to hurt my champions, and would rather focus on things other than your next move, so please, treasure our relationship."

"Treasure," Selena said. "You just killed our friend."

"No. You did."

"That's a lie," I replied.

And dropped to one knee. My eyes shut. Mouth clenched. Not my doing. My mind ran away from my body, curled up against a crushing headache. Dolan was going to the Cycle because of what Nara made us do. Right?

Or had we done it on our own?

Hadn't Dolan turned on us? Drawn his sword while we spoke with Nara? Discussed the plan to save Riven?

He'd tried to kill Nara. Unprovoked. She had no weapon.

"We had to stop him," I said to Selena. "There was no other choice. He would have ruined our last chance to save Riven."

I saw Selena's slow nod in reply. "I had to," Selena said. "It was the only way."

"Regrettable," Nara said. "But we do not have time for grief. Come now, keep moving."

I stood, reached out, and brushed the next stalk out of the way. Put one foot in front of the other. Dolan had turned traitor at the end. Tragic, but inevitable. His plan had failed, after all.

Now we had a new leader.

THE EAST GATE

There were two guides waiting for us at the east gate. Watching to see if we had succeeded. One of them I recognized; the wiry guide that had worked with Piotr. Who may very well have killed me on the other side, trapped in the hotel room in New York City. The other I didn't know, but it didn't matter.

"This is Nara," I said as we walked up. "She's going to save us."

Polk looked past me, nodded at Nara. "Where's the other one? Dolan? Where you all traveling together?"

"Dolan has to handle some other problems," Nara said. "I'm pleased to meet you."

Nara stepped forward and reached out her hand. Polk took it. I saw the change come over his eyes, the moment when he lost control. The moment when Nara took him for one of her own. The other guide, however, didn't seem to pay much attention. He was looking at Selena, and I realized my love had drawn her cleaver.

"You won't be needing that here," the guide said. "There's no breach nearby. Kept it clean for you."

"Just in case," Nara said, placing her hand on the guide shoulder.

In a moment he, too, belonged to her.

From down the street, we heard a noise. A shuffling as another guide stepped out of a squat guard post, just inside the gate. I knew him. Derringer. Only instead of friendly eyes, his face was covered with suspicion.

"Derringer," I called. "Come here, say hello."

"Don't think I will," Derringer said. "See, I saw a lot of Piotr's work. Saw how those bound spirits reacted when he talked. Saw how those eyes matched his stare the way yours all match hers. I know what I'm seeing."

And then Derringer ran. Nara didn't speak, didn't say the words, but I felt the order. The call to catch Derringer and bring him to heel. To make him respect our leader. So the four of us took off at a dead sprint. Chased Derringer over the wide stone courtyards between the Palace and the statues that made up Riven's east side.

Derringer wasn't a small man. Wasn't slow, either. Chugged ahead, pumping his arms and his feet the way a true runner does. But he was human. His muscles burned. Selena and I picked up ground, running closer, harder. Derringer tried to duck behind columns, weave between streets and take back alleys at random, but it wasn't enough. He couldn't avoid our endless energy.

The streets had closed in by the time we finally caught up with him. Buildings lined either side of the broad avenue. The ashen flakes so common to Riven blew into my eyes. Then Derringer stopped, huffing, hands on his knees.

Selena and I came up behind him. I had my lash and knife ready, Selena with her cleaver. Inside my mind I felt Nara pushing me to end him. To burn him and turn him into a spirit that she could bind when she caught up with us. Beneath that call I felt my own boiling heat. Derringer had been with Polk, with my body in that hotel room. One of them had pulled the trigger, cut my cord to the other side.

I wanted him dead as much as Nara did.

"You know what happens if you kill us?" Derringer said. "The line's barely holding at the west. It's going to fall any day, any hour now. When it does this whole city will be razed to the ground by rampaging angry spirits. You think your new one can save it?"

"I don't think," I said, "I know she can."

"Well this is a hell of a way to start."

I raised the knife and Derringer glared back at me. Time to erase that face. I moved forward, drew my arm back. And felt searing pain tear into my shoulder. I fell onto the street, heard the gunshot's echo as it ricocheted down the avenue. Not what I'd expected to happen.

"It's not going to work," said a familiar voice. "You are covered, Carver. Surrender, and perhaps we can free you from your curse."

"Alec," Selena called, and yes, she was right. I knew that voice. "You are in the wrong! Nara wants to help Riven!"

I counted faces in the windows, a number of them aiming long guns down at me. The resources they must've pulled from the wall at the west gate to wait for our return. A return they expected to be triumphant, to bring miracles. To save their dying friends on the other side of the city.

Now the west served only to safeguard the doomed.

"Selena, it is a tragedy to see you so," Alec said, walking up the street towards us with a pair of guides on either side. "Our offer is for both of you. Put down your weapons. Talk peace with us."

I stood up, the pain from the bullet starting to recede already.

"We cannot," I said. "And you cannot win."

One of the guides in the building next to us shouted and vanished from the window. Attacked from behind. Nara's voice filled our minds, telling us to run. To pull back down the street and find her some blocks away. Another guide yelped across the way. As Derringer and Alec turned to the noise, Selena and I bolted. I heard bullets strike the ground around me, but then we dashed into an alley and were gone. Blitzing through buildings and around corners and curves. The route Nara wanted us to run appearing like a map before our eyes. A compulsion telling me to take a left, then a right, then to go straight through a ruined store.

We found her at the top of the decrepit apartment, the haphazard stairs giving us a stumbling hike to the top floor. At the edge of the center of town. Nara stared out a window over Riven. Neither of the other guides were there.

"Two sacrificed for your folly," Nara said. "Next time, catch your prey more quickly."

Selena and I apologized. In unison.

"It seems your guides have improved over the years," Nara said. "The kind of organization needed to have layered formations never existed in my time. Dolan must've been proud of his legacy."

"The guides are strong," I said.

"But not strong enough," Nara snapped back. "Still, the guides need not be our first foe. There are easier paths for us to walk. Fear not, Carver. We will save your world and we don't need the guides to do it."

THE BOUND ARMY

We moved south. South and west, skirting the edges of the main guide territory around the clock tower. We stuck to alleys, to side streets. Cut through buildings. Crept along little canyons between ruined structures. Whenever we happened upon a spirit, Nara would have us restrain the lost soul while she bound it to her. Then she would send the spirit out ahead of us and in various directions, scouting to see where danger might be. We avoided breaches, which would attract guides. We dodged clusters of spirits that could be seen by others. Or that could, potentially, attack us before we were ready. But as we went further and further, and Nara bound more and more, I began to notice around the edges of my vision, in the windows of buildings we passed and down streets that we did not walk, spirits flashing by. They were always there, always watching. Forming a ring around us.

Nara did not speak, and Selena and I had no words to say. I felt a growing sense of despair. Despair that nonetheless mingled with the slightest hope. Nara herself may not be the savior we were hoping for. Neither, however, did she want to see Riven destroyed. She might save Riven, even if what remained wouldn't be the world we knew.

We reached the Shambles and the southern gate, the beginnings of an army walking around us. Several dozen spirits trod in our wake, or led our advance. Nara bound everyone we came across. With a quick shake of her hand, a palm on an unsuspecting back, she added another one to our force. I began to see how she had accumulated so many spirits so quickly. How Dolan and Mali had grown to fear their friend. If in a matter of hours she could collect hundreds of souls, in a matter of days she could have thousands. Eventually, millions. Then there would be no force capable of stopping her.

Yet, I felt there was some chance of survival. The guides, after all, could cross out. Could leave Riven behind. If Nara ruled an army of the dead, at least they would not touch the other side. They would not come back to Earth.

We were not long into the forest, walking along the trail the spirits took to the Cycle, when a familiar rumbling shift the ground. The trees to our right emerged several ghouls. Ones I'd seen earlier, chasing Dolan and Selena on their quest to close the breaches.

"What should we do?" I asked Nara.

She only grinned at me, "Watch."

The ghouls stomped towards us, all three of them large, vaguely humanoid monsters with random collections of arms and legs. They pounded the ground and scooped up spirits as they went, devouring them into their bodies and growing larger with every one. Until Nara sent her wave.

Her new army moved in a giant cluster, charging and wailing and carving into the ghouls. They scaled those ghastly arms and legs. Clawed into their bodies and tore the ghouls to shreds. The giant creatures threw spirits off of them by the dozen, but two dozen more ran in to replace the ones lost.

In minutes, the ghouls had been shredded, scattered and broken into pieces. Nara gave us the command. Selena and I, with my lash and long knife, her cleaver, we went up to the broken ghouls and burned them in fire. Split them into their masses of spirits. Then Nara bound those too.

"Do you doubt me anymore?" Nara said to me when they were done. "Do you not think I can save your world?"

I could only shake my head. Nara was truly great, truly terrible. She was our savior.

A CHANGE IN PLAN

The Mountain. The last time I'd seen the place, I'd been walking to my eventual death. It hadn't changed much. Still the one entrance hollowed into its rocky walls, full of spirits walking into the Cycle. Spirits that were being bound one after another by Nara in a feverish blitz. From one to the next she took and chained their souls to her. Growing and expanding her force. Sending the new spirits to form ranks in front of the Mountain itself.

Just before the cavern entrance we turned to look at the ranks spread out in front of us.

"Do you see?" Nara said. "This is what you came to me for, Carver. This is what you needed. With these souls, we can clean our adversaries from Riven and take the world for our own."

"One question." I looked at the army, at all of the spirits standing with nothing on them. No weapons, no hooks, no swords, no sparkers. A mob, yes, but one lacking in the ways to wrangle spirits. "How will we shut the breaches?"

Nara glanced at me. "You have the sword with you."

"I cannot be everywhere at once," I said. "Here, come with me."

I felt Nara let me make the statement. Let me guide her to the top of the Mountain, through Piotr's passage to the slope high above the forest. Selena followed.

From up there, we could see all across the wood into the border of the city. The breaches popped, yellow and blue and green lights glowing throughout the forest and beyond. So many it looked like the stars in the sky on that night I'd gone with Inman to his camp along the river.

"Even with a dozen of me," I said. "We would never be able to close them all. We would never be able to keep Riven alive."

"Then we shall make a hundred of your swords," Nara said. "A thousand. Enough for every spirit to wield."

"How?" Selena asked. "Can you do it without Dolan?"

Shock, followed by frustration poured through the bond as Nara remembered Dolan was gone. The only spirit that had ever mastered the art of creating the burning weapons had vanished. And while the guides taken the original tools, had restructured them into new swords and axes and bows over the centuries, without Dolan, there wasn't a way to make more.

"Dolan was a spirit," Nara said. "Anything he did can be done by another. All we have to do is find the right one."

Neither Selena nor I were given permission to reply. Instead, we followed Nara down, back into the Mountain, to the edge of the Cycle. She positioned us near the ledge, and we watched her step up to a passing spirit, an older woman, and touch her on the shoulder. Bind her to Nara's will. Then, Nara pointed towards the Cycle.

Dolan had said that he'd captured the flame by accident. By touching the Cycle and corralling its burning energy. Nara sent the spirit to do the same.

The woman reached down over the edge and touched the blue. Fire raced up her arm, over her body until we could see none of it. Nothing except the blinding light. The spirit toppled over the edge and vanished.

"Only the first try," Nara muttered.

But the next one had the same result. And the third. The fifth. Into the hundreds. I couldn't track how much time Nara spent tossing spirits to their doom, only that it must have been many hours before Nara backed away, her face a mask of barely controlled rage.

"It will not work," I said. Nara wasn't paying attention to my will, her focus on other things. For once, I had the freedom to move my own lips. "We might stand here for an eternity waiting for another spirit like Dolan. If that doesn't happen soon, then Riven might well be gone by the time you find one."

"Be gone?" Nara said, looking at me with a question in her eyes. "Before, when you first came to me in the field. You mentioned that you wanted to save Riven. To save it from what?"

"It is being overrun," I said. I felt Nara pushing, questing after a deeper answer. "Guide history says that if there are enough spirits in Riven, a hole back to Earth might open. A way back to the other side. Where they could hurt our families. Our friends. Destroy everything we know."

Nara nodded. "That is what I needed to remember. Come, let us return to the slope."

Back at the overlook, we again stared out at the breaches.

"You asked me to save your world, Carver," Nara said. "But it seems that Riven cannot be so saved. There is no other choice than to let this calamity befall us. To ride the wave into the unknown. If these spirits will create a gateway, then we will walk through it."

Even with the connection, even with Nara suppressing my feeling, I turned over in anger. Betrayal. For a moment, that urge overwhelmed our bond.

"You lied," I spat. "You were the one that let Dolan go. That stopped our only chance. It's not that Riven can't be saved, it's that you destroyed any hope to save it."

"We are all human, are we not?" Nara said. "Flawed, pushed by our ambitions to something beyond our ability to obtain? Only rather than focus on our failures, I choose to take advantage of the future, and our future lies with those."

Nara's arms swept out across the view, taking in the breaches peppering the countryside. As she did so, one, a glow coming from inside the far-off city wall, winked out of existence. Nara stopped her gesture, blinked at the space.

"The guides," I said, answering her unspoken question. "They are still sealing what breaches they can inside the city."

"Delaying our victory," Nara said. "It seems, Carver, I may have a use for you yet. My champion still has a cause against which to wield his sword."

"How might I serve?" I said, hating the words as they came out of my mouth, loving them and the way they pleased Nara through the bond. I was her puppet, and adored it when she pulled the strings.

"You will take my legion," Nara said. "You will march along the spirit's path and enter the city from the south. Drive the guides before you. Slaughter those that stay. Chase away those that run. Cleanse Riven of them and their souls. Open the door to our new home."

INCURSION

Nara lined the souls up for me in row upon row before the Mountain's entrance. Bathed in the Cycle's glow, I stood before hundreds of spirits bound to follow Nara's, and through her, my command.

The spirits came from anywhere and everywhere. Young and old, rich and poor, dressed in rags and the finest suits. Through and around them wandered souls Nara hadn't yet bound, like a river breaking around a dam of the dead.

Every few seconds another spirit went around me and took its place in the ranks. Another binding, another soul that would stop at nothing to tear every guide apart. I only needed to tell them when.

"March!" I shouted into the swirling ash. Into those dark trees. Nara heard my words and sent the command to those in thrall to her. Including me.

Without conscious effort, my legs moved forward. Long strides that took me through and past my army until I walked at its head. I held the great sword in my hands, ready to fend off any attackers.

And there were plenty of those. Angry spirits from nearby breaches bit at the sides of my force. Crashed out from the trees in snarling waves only for my spirits to beat them back. Descended on my souls in gnashing piles until, with our superior numbers, we tore the attackers apart.

Of course, without the wrangling fires, the spirits would heal with time. Would return to their rampages. Would continue pushing Riven until it collapsed.

"Why the Shambles?" I said to Nara through our bond. "Most of the guides should be concentrated at the west gate?"

I could feel her back there, near the Cycle, gathering more spirits and adding them to her force. Yet, the strength of that bond dimmed as the distance between us grew. It would take two days march to get to the Shambles, and in that time her ties would slip. When we reached the city, I might be able to resist her entirely.

"Because I want to crush their resolve," Nara replied through the bond, her voice crashing into my mind. "Because when you threaten to cut them off from their home, they will not fight. They will flee. Scatter and break."

"You're underestimating them. The guides are better than that."

"Are they?" I could hear Nara's laughter. "You forget, Carver. I once had to choose between dying for my beliefs or living, trapped for centuries. They will choose as I did. They will run for their chance to survive."

Around me streamed the blank-eyed dead. Wrangled or, less likely with every hour, a spirit naturally seduced by the Cycle. I caught their eyes as they missed mine. How many of them would Nara turn to her side?

"We should make for the clock tower." My mind turned towards the attack, trying to find the angles for Nara's victory. "That is the center of the guides' forces."

"Then take it," Nara said. "Wield my force like a hammer and smash the guides to dust."

Had we been in person, I might have bowed. Or said how much I loved the opportunity to carry out her order. However, as I crunched along the path, Nara felt my pleasure through our bond. Knew that I would not hesitate to tear apart the city at her word.

The hundreds of souls behind me would do the same.

THE DEAD ASSAULT

The south gate stood a menagerie. A focal point for all the city's spirits coming together before pounding down the path to the Cycle. I'd not stood on the outside of it, looking in, before.

At least, not as an invader.

On either side of the gate stood turreted towers. Staring out over the right one leaned a guide, locking eyes with my army. As my forces formed up, the guide held up a sparker and launched a bright bolt into the air.

I pointed my sword at the guide as the spark burst high in the clouds, scattering a series of azure points high and low. They dimmed and fizzled as my souls ran around me, towards the gate.

Which slammed shut, its large oaken doors sliding closed before the first of my forces could make it through. Apparently, I was wrong. The guides were not entirely invested in the west gate.

Perhaps Bryce had learned from the others what Selena and I had become. Perhaps he had prepared for the worst.

It wouldn't be enough.

I jammed the sword in the ground before me. Took the crossbow off of my back and slotted in an orange bolt. Poor fortune that

Nicholas had replenished my supply after Dolan's ill-fated charge to the woods.

I raised the crossbow, aimed, and pulled the trigger. The orange bolt streaked towards the gate, hit the thick doors, and burst into a blinding nova. The searing rays crept along the outlines of the doors, like spilled paint spreading across a canvas.

After a minute, the rays drained away, leaving nothing more than some blackened bits hanging from the sides. A trio of guides stood behind the ruins, stunned.

"You should run!" I called as I went towards the gate. The crossbow over my back, the great sword yanked up from the ground as I walked. "There is no need for you to die here."

The guide in the middle, a woman with axes, whom I recognized dimly as one of Bryce's wardens after his arrest, stiffened but stayed. The two guides next to her, each one with the sword and knife combo of greener recruits, matched her resolve.

"You are no longer welcome in the city, Carver Reed!" replied the woman, her voice thick with the knowledge of impossible odds.

"If anyone has the power to decide who comes and goes from here, I do not think it's you." I raised my left hand and the spirits of Nara's force shuffled up beside me. Matched my stride step for step. "I say again. Depart, cross back over, and await your fate with your families."

These three guides would die if they stayed. Would be washed away by the force at my back. Their sacrifice would not buy time. Would not prove a point or change the outcome of this certain war.

So when the woman crossed her axes in front of her chest, ready to meet the charge, I held my spirits back. Nara, through our bond, urged an all-out attack. Told me to drive forth into the city and break them. But where before her voice had smashed through my mind, now it was closer to a conversation. Words that could be ignored.

I went ahead of my army. Met the woman and the other guides just on the inside of the arch. The Shambles, the scattered apartments, slums, and warped streets sat in front of me. Somewhere in there were my mother's journals, still sitting, as they would forever, in an empty house.

"There is no need for you to die here," I repeated to the three of them as I closed. "I cannot hold back Nara's spirits, or my own sword, much longer."

"And I will say what I said before. It is our privilege to die for our city and our order." The woman looked for a second like she was going to attack then and there, but a last glance at the younger guides next to her stilled her hands.

"Then do so when it will matter," I said. "Go, run and warn your fellows of what is coming."

Nara couldn't control what I said, not at this distance. Even so, my skin began to crawl. My head hurt. I wasn't quite defying her command, not yet, but the pressure to strike these three down, to send in the spirits, grew.

"Why are you giving us advice?" the woman asked. "Why should we trust you when you're bound to the enemy?"

"Because who else is there?" I said. "Also, this."

I raised the sword and the guides stepped back. The spirits behind me edged forward. This was the moment.

"Five seconds," I began. "Four."

The woman looked again at the guides. At the spirits behind me.

"Three."

At impossible odds. I saw her eyes shift.

"Two."

They ran. Turned their backs and sprinted down the road. Past hapless spirits marching towards us.

"One."

I pointed the great sword forward and Nara's spirits surged past me into the city. I walked with them, one foot falling after another.

On my left, Nara's spirits wound their way up an apartment building. Breaking through windows and doors, searching every room for hiding guides. To my right, the spirits found where the three guides had kept spare weapons. Took them and armed themselves.

Everywhere I looked, Nara's army spread. A wave crashing through the city, and bringing terror with it.

THROUGH FRIEND AND FLAME

The three guides must have made it back. Must have warned the others. I encountered no resistance moving through the Shambles. None at all in the Warrens. Even Anna's apartment building had been abandoned.

A dangerous gamble—without access to its basement, Anna wouldn't be able to cross back. At least, not if she'd continued using the building as her entrance into Riven.

I doubted she was the only guide taking such a risk.

The guides had set themselves up in the clock tower square. My home in Riven for years, the clock tower itself loomed as a burned out ruin on the north end of the square. A fountain, now surrounded by shanty shelters, served as the nexus for guide operations.

I formed the spirits back into a line as we moved into view of the square. A block away. In front of us, looking out from building windows and standing in a line across the avenue, stood the guides that I had called friends. Brothers and sisters that I planned to drive away or grind into dust.

Front and center stood my mentor, his twin-edged voulge standing taller than he did. Bryce glared at me with a mixture of anger and disappointment, a look that had as much directed at himself as it did me.

Beside him stood Anna and Alec. I suppose in some sort of attempt to twist my emotions with my friends. An attempt that worked, that made me lurch, that nonetheless did nothing to stop me from ordering the charge.

Nara's army would lose many spirits, but we could afford to. The guides, on the other hand, would be decimated by every casualty.

From the buildings around us, rising two and three and four stories, guides shot their sparkers. Anna, Bryce and the others as well. The bright light and heat saturated the air, caused me to pull up, shield my eyes with my hands. Warmth brushed my face, and when I pulled my hands away, the buildings around us burned.

The guides that had been on them were nowhere to be seen. The fires spewed smoke into the street, the sky, the alleys. Weakened walls collapsed, spreading debris and sending charred rubble into the way of my spirits. While not deadly, the hot ruins hampered our progress. Set spirits aflame or shattered their legs. Trapped them under falling balconies.

Our advance floundered.

Nara could feel the anger and agony through her bindings, and she pushed those feelings to me, and I used them. Charged forward through the blaze to the other side. Where instead of dozens of guides, I saw a scattered few. Bryce had disappeared. Retreated.

"Carver, it's good to see your tactics haven't improved." Alec struck fast, his gauntlets flying towards me from my side.

I rolled with the blows, turning as his fists hit my shoulder to bring the great sword between us.

"With Nara's spirits, I don't need them."

I countered. Stabbed the sword forward. Alec grabbed the blade with his hands, tried to turn it away. Only I pushed forward, forced him back.

He'd been stronger than me as a man. With human limitations. As a spirit; no longer.

Alec pushed the sword to the side as he felt a building's burning pyre draw close. Accepted a cut on his right shoulder as he twisted from under the blade. Danced into me, and then rolled out again as I reversed the stroke and forced him back.

"You can fight the binding, Carver!" Alec fell back as some of Nara's spirits pushed through the smoke behind me. I nodded, and they rushed my friend.

"You can run, Alec," I replied.

The guide took a step into the first spirit, delivering a gauntlet-armored right uppercut to the soul's chin. Striking and setting it aflame.

The second jumped into the air, arms outstretched, towards Alec's left shoulder. Rather than turn, Alec stuck out his left hand and let the spirit impale itself on the gauntlet's spikes.

The third, however, caught my friend out of position. Striking him low, with Alec's right hand still pushing off the first spirit. Knocked Alec's legs out from under him and sent the guide to the stones.

In a flash I stood over him, Nara's remaining spirit holding down Alec's arms. I pinned Alec to the ground with the point of my blade.

"You're better than you were," Alec said to me.

"I always let you win," I replied. Raised the sword. Nara's voice screamed in my head to end him. To stab Alec and burn away the guide's tie to Earth. To life.

Difficult to ignore a direct command through a bond, even from one so distant. But I could hesitate. Could try.

Only for a second.

"That, I will never believe."

Alec pulled Nara's spirit, clinging to his arms, over his head and in between my sword and his chest. I stabbed down, felt the sword bite, and twisted the hilt. Burned the spirit away.

Alec pushed himself out from under my legs. Scrambled to his feet as I worked my sword out from the spirit. Dropped into a ready stance, which loosened as he looked over my shoulder.

I could hear them. Nara's spirits making their way across as they found ways through the flames. As burning rubble died down. The guides had delayed our advance, yes, but their gambit was at an end.

"Much as I would love to continue," Alec said. "I believe these odds are against me."

"You're giving up the clock tower? How will you cross back?"

"If we don't end this now, there won't be anywhere to cross back to!" Alec gave me a slight nod, then turned and ran. The square behind him was deserted. Guide gear, tables, and maps remained.

Nara's spirits flooded into it, tearing everything apart with abandon. I went up to the main table, where not long ago I'd sat with Dolan, Selena, and the others to plot our last best hope for salvation.

On the table sat the same map they'd had on there before, only instead of breaches, there now was drawn a single thick line. From the center of the city towards the Mountain.

A small ball sat at the end of it, right over the Cycle.

A GIFT

I felt Nara's pulse as I looked up from the map. Her words crossing the distance between us.

"You have driven them from their home?" Nara asked.

"Riven is their home, and they are still in it," I replied.

"Then you are failing."

"I don't want to succeed." I watched as spirits armed themselves with remaining gear. Long knives and swords. Spears and axes. Guide weapons in the hands of those they were designed to destroy.

"But I do, and you belong to me." Rather than hot anger, a cool acceptance flowed through the bond. Assurance that I was indeed hers. That I would do whatsoever she asked.

Nara was right.

"I believe they mean to come to you," I said, explaining the map. "Though what they plan to do when they get there is harder to know."

"Try to destroy me, of course. Though what their hopes are after that, I do not know."

"The Mountain is too far for most of them," I said, glancing at the clock tower's ruins. "They won't be able to cross back before their bodies die on the other side."

"A pity. You will follow from behind. Chase them. I am building up a secondary force that shall meet the guides head on in the forest. They will have nowhere to run."

With that command, Nara's voice faded away. Her mind turned to other matters. Mine turned to the army, now staring at me and waiting for further orders.

So we marched west. Towards the Mountain, Bryce and the guides.

As we went through the city center, I realized we were passing close to the apartment I'd shared with Selena and the others. To Nicholas' lab.

I directed the spirits to continue their destructive walk after the guides and dipped down the right side street. Nara was paying less attention than usual. Focusing on growing her second army, no doubt.

The apartment sat as I'd last seen it. Three stories of shabby, yet sturdy construction. The balconies that Selena loved to look out from stuck their black iron out from the top, a fire escape ladder marring the side view.

I went inside Nicholas's lab, which occupied the entire ground floor, and stopped. Empty, except for a couple of old tables. One of which held, on it, a piece of paper, next to a box no larger than my hand.

Conspicuously absent was the bomb. The reset button. I'd half expected it to be waiting for us in the clock tower square. Thought they'd push it and send us back.

Carver,

Anna tells me you're on your way to ruin us at the behest of some ancient spirit. I can think of no more appropriate way for our time here to end than at your hand, though I confess my own thinking has you too headstrong to simply follow orders.

However, I've come to understand Riven as a place of paradoxes. A world where science ties loose with the spiritual, and where our strongest friends may need the most help. And so I offer you a gift, with all my thanks.

Your humble scientist,

Nicholas

I looked at the box, small and squat and black. A gift. What

Nicholas could have for me at this stage, I didn't know. I reached for the box, no latch bound its contents, and pushed up on the top.

I heard the bang. My eyes caught the flash before they closed by reflex. I felt the fire burn. Both the harsh heat of orange flames and the purifying blue.

"Come back, Carver."

What? I floated. Or rather, existed in a place that did not. A vast emptiness. One I recognized, from when Dolan had wrangled me. A place of shadows and flitting images.

This was, I understood, the place where spirits stayed as their mindless forms walked to the Cycle.

"They told me I should leave you. But you saved me, so I feel I have to return the favor."

I looked around, but couldn't find the source of the voice. Couldn't remember to whom it belonged. The shadows shifted. A face? Hair?

Something tugged me, yanked me off of my feet, such as they were, to my back and I fell. Through the shadows and the lights. Until the world gradually brightened around me and I realized I was looking into Anna's eyes.

"There you go," Anna said. There was a noise, somewhere outside, and a worried frown crossed along her expression. "I'm sorry, but I can't wait for you. When you get better, come find us. We're going to the Mountain."

Anna stood up. I tried to speak, but my mouth wouldn't work. I couldn't feel my legs, my arms. Pain began to leak through.

Anna pulled out her flail, let the chain dangle near my head. "Goodbye, Carver. I hope I see you again."

And then she was gone. Leaving me lying there, on the floor of the lab, with hordes of Nara's spirits running through the area.

Nicholas's bomb had broken my spirit. It would take hours to heal. Hours I didn't have.

SEVERED

Feeling returned to my arms, tingling sensations that gradually grew into the cool touch of the stone floor or the ragged scratch of my ruined coat as it brushed my leg. The ceiling blurred in and out of focus as my eyes pieced themselves together.

Nicholas hadn't gone easy on me.

If Anna hadn't been there to bring me back, I'd still be in that dark nova. Lost. Unknowing.

The first time, when Dolan burned me away, I hadn't known what was happening. He'd yanked me back so fast that I didn't have a chance to process the event. We'd moved on out of the desert and I hadn't given it a second thought.

Now I understood what had happened. Who to thank for bringing me back to Riven's ashen world.

I reached out through Anna's bond. She was growing distant. On her way to the Mountain. I felt a rush of warm encouragement from her. She still believed in me, somehow.

My right hand came back to me. I traced the floor. Felt my way around, as my neck refused to turn.

Nicholas' bomb had devastated my coat, leaving a shredded mess behind. At least the thick jacket had done some work protecting the shirt and pants beneath. They felt crisped to the touch, but intact.

I couldn't say the same about the lash. The heat, it seemed, had burned through the cable. The hilt sat in the holster, but as a weapon, its days were done.

The scrabbling came soft at first. A grumbling rasp. The lab's door swinging open and banging against the wall. I couldn't turn to see, but I could feel its eyes on me. The rasping stopped.

A spirit, and based on how fast it shaped up, one of Nara's.

"He is here, yes," the spirit spoke to no one. At least, nobody here. "Alive, yes. Eyes are open. His hand moved."

My left hand only hurt. I couldn't move it. Legs could twinge, but couldn't bend. The only thing I had was my right.

"I am sure, yes." The spirit came closer to me. Its head popped into view. Long, stringy hair. A face that should have been young, but had been worn hard. She blinked down at me. "Alive, yes."

"She can't feel me, can she?" I said. Playing for the delay.

"He is speaking," the spirit muttered. "Asking questions."

"Ask her," I said.

The spirit snarled at me, then pulled back. Stared straight out at the wall of the lab.

"He wonders if you can feel him?"

I shifted my right hand. Pulled it across my body. To my left holster. Towards the long knife I hoped would be there. When the spirit jerked her eyes back down to me I paused.

"No, she says. You are no longer hers."

"I can feel her," I protested. My voice scratched. Again the spirit looked away. Listening.

My hand made it farther. Grasped the end of the long knife's hilt.

"She says you lie." The spirit leaned in close to me. Her manic eyes locked on mine, her lips pulling apart. "She says you are not to be trusted."

"What's your name?"

A tactic I'd used before on spirits, especially ones on the edge of sanity. Even if they had no intention of answering, for a moment the spirit would think of their name. Many could no longer remember it, and that realization would throw them into a panic.

As it did with this one. Her face went slack, then widened with worry. Until Nara clamped down on those feelings. Pushed the spirit back to its goal.

"She says you are to be ended." The spirit opened her mouth wide, the inside of it far too close and visible for comfort. Teeth, bent and broken, came in close for my eyes.

The knife bit in hard, though I didn't have the angle to twist the hilt. My wrist wasn't turning. The spirit fell back, my long knife sticking out of her abdomen. Hissing in anger, pain. Whistling screeches that echoed around the lab's hard walls.

I lunged with my right arm, pulled my body over. Presented my back to the spirit, then my left side. But I saw what I wanted.

Trapped beneath me, under the ruins of the crossbow, sat the great sword. I rolled slightly, giving my right arm enough room to grab its hilt. Bent my elbow to swing the point of the sword up, maybe a foot.

I had never realized how heavy the blade was till now. I suddenly wasn't sure I could actually use it. Could keep it high enough.

The spirit wrapped her hands around the knife and pulled it free. Looked like she was about to throw the blade away, then stopped. Nara again.

This much direct control from so far away. If nothing else, keeping Nara so busy would buy my friends some time. Leave a few more spirits unbound.

The spirit burst at me, stumbling forward with the knife swinging in her right hand. Holding it forward in a stab.

I pushed with my right hand, levered the great sword's hilt into the floor as I slid onto my back. The point went up as the spirit closed. My blade hit the knife, knocking it from the spirit's hand. But then my move was done.

The great sword stood upright, but it was all I could do to keep it that way.

Outside, from the street, I heard the pounding of footsteps. Reinforcements, and I doubted they were mine.

The spirit sidestepped nearer my head, her eyes locked onto my sword. I couldn't move it to follow. I tried to think of what tricks I had left. Came up blank.

As the spirit realized I couldn't counter, a gnarly smile spread over her face. She came in to kill me.

As she dove towards me, I shifted my shoulder, pushed my right arm forward. Let the hilt tilt back towards my head. The heavy blade fell, right towards me. I locked eyes with the sword for a second, before the spirit's wild face blocked my view.

I felt her teeth bite my skin, and then heard the thick slice as the great sword fell onto, into the spirit's head. This time, I had the leverage to turn my right hand, twist the great sword's hilt, and send the pale fire burning.

The flames covered my vision as they consumed the spirit, lying on top of me. I closed my eyes for a second. Started to relax. Until I heard the feet again. Close.

I'd lived through one spirit, only to die to the coming dozen.

WOUNDED WRANGLING

I pushed the vacant spirit off of me with my right hand. Felt a bit of life in my left leg, so I pressed that foot against the ground and scooted back. Bought me some space and an angle with which to look at the door to the street.

There I saw madness.

Spirits tangled with spirits. Diving at each other, rolling around in the street. Some had the telltale blue eyes of an angry soul, enraged and mindless. The others were likely Nara's forces, pulled into a fight they weren't looking for.

That many angry spirits meant a breach would be nearby. A breach that, right now, was saving my life.

A clang drew my eyes back towards the spirit I'd wrangled. The great sword had fallen to the floor when the spirit stood up, her head at an awkward angle from the sword's cut. Her eyes were blank, staring straight ahead without emotion.

She took one step, then a second and a third. Towards the door and out into the chaos. Without interruption, she would go all the way to the Cycle.

Where, if Nara stood ready, she could be bound back into service.

Nothing I could do about that, though. So I pushed my way over to the great sword. This time, I moved over to the wall, dragging the sword behind me as I crawled.

I jammed the sword into the angle between the floor and the wall and pushed with my right hand. Pressed down and slipped my left leg under me. With my right leg still straight, the position was profoundly uncomfortable.

But if I couldn't stand, I'd be defenseless against the next spirits that came in, whether they were Nara's or wild ones from the breach.

With my right hand, I let go of the sword. Shifted my weight to my left side. Leaned forward, grabbed my right ankle, and bent my right leg beneath me.

Pain sparked and splashed. My vision swam. I tried to focus. Suppress it.

The pain isn't real, Carver. You don't have nerves.

If only it was that easy.

Outside, shrieks grew louder. More of them. Spirits howling frustration without reservation. Which meant Nara's side was losing. Or abandoning the field.

Soon I'd have company, once one of those angry souls wandered in here.

Again I picked up the sword, now in a kneeling stance. Pressed it against the wall with my right hand. My left foot, its shredded boot sticking to the skin, moved until it rested flat on the stone. Then I pushed, hard.

I may have screamed.

But, leaning on the sword, I stood. My right leg, still a broken mess, touched the floor. Did not want to put weight on that yet.

I looked across the lab. To the tables two yards away. The sword would be my walking stick. My left leg my only balance. If I could get to the tables, then I'd have some support. Could free my right hand to swing the sword, at least somewhat.

A body smashed against the outside of the lab, scrabbling hands and tearing teeth telling just what was happening to it.

I lunged with the sword, turning and driving the point into the stone. Hoping Mali had made Dolan's sword stronger than the city. That her gift to her fellow spirit could bite into rock.

The sword struck the floor and sparks flew, but I felt the point lodge into the ground. It held my weight as I moved my left foot forward a long step. Did it a second time.

Now I could reach the tables. One more lurch with the sword, and I'd be perfect.

But I'd run out of time.

Behind me, I heard the mad mutterings, growls from a pair of spirits. I risked a glance. Soldiers, their military minds long gone. Looking at me as though I were lunch.

They darted towards me, eyes wide and burning. I waited a long second, then shifted my weight to the left foot. Pressed down with my left leg, and then swept the great sword with my right hand.

As my body twisted, I shoved off with my left leg. The spirits' hands brushed my ragged coat as I turned, the sword scraping along the ground. I saw their faces, their burning eyes, as I fell. They kept coming.

My back hit the edge of the table, and Nicholas' workbench held firm. I used the leverage, dragged the sword up in a crossing cut that the spirits, without any sense in their souls, ran into.

I twisted the hilt as the sword slashed, drawing burning blue lines across the spirits' outstretched arms. They landed on me, bearing me off the table and to the floor. Collapsed.

I saw the underside of the table, and had an idea. The burning spirits rolled off of me, and in seconds they would be gone. Leaving me again open to attack. Unless the spirits couldn't tell I was there.

With my right hand, I hefted and hacked at the table's front right leg, nearest to the door. After a pair of whacks, the leg snapped in half and the table tilted forward, then fell. As it listed, I pushed myself behind the falling barrier.

The table sat between me and the door, blocking all view of the outside. The screams had died down. The breach would still be drawing spirits, but with nothing to keep them here, they would be ranging farther in search of souls to maul.

Me, I curled up behind that fallen table. Pulled my legs together, held the sword close, and willed my soul to heal.

GET UP

Hidden behind the table, waiting for my body to heal, I reached out across my bond to Anna. Felt her nervous excitement, and spoke to her.

"Where are all of you?" I said the words in my mind and, like directing a shout towards a distant friend, sent the question to Anna.

"We're in the forest," Anna replied. "Closing breaches and marching towards the Mountain. Bryce is leading. Determined."

"Not surprised. Sorry I can't be there."

"Yet, you mean."

"I'm hiding behind a table, Anna. Nicholas' bomb really tore me apart."

A wave of concern passed through the bond, along with a little bit of laughter.

"We couldn't take chances," Anna sent. "If the fire didn't break the bond with Nara, we didn't want you up and running again."

"Right. Instead I get to stay here and fight off spirits with one working arm."

"I thought you were hiding?"

"Now." I listened. Spirits were still running through the streets outside, but nothing pulled them into the lab. "How are you going to last until the Mountain?"

"We will because we have to. There's no other choice."

"Nicholas thinks his bomb will work?"

"Same answer, Carver. It has to."

"Know what'll happen if it works, right? I'll be gone."

Silence from Anna. A tinge of sadness.

"We know," Anna's words came slow. "If Nicholas can do what he's promising, he'll be swept away too. And Selena. And, really, all of us still here."

"That's a high price to pay."

"Set against the cost of not doing anything?"

"I see your point."

"I believe you said to me, shortly after we met, that guides have to be prepared to die at any time, right? That we couldn't expect long lives?"

I nodded to nobody in the lab. It'd been a bravo sentiment. Words that made me feel strong and important, especially when shared with a kid on the train into Chicago, or in a quote to Opperman for one of his stories.

"Comes with the job," I said to Anna. "Only, just because it's likely, doesn't mean you have to be all right with it."

"Tell me. Would you really want to stay here, in Riven? Forever?"

"It's not all bad." I surprised myself with the words. How true they were. "With Selena, and all of you, there's plenty of adventure. Places to explore. Things to do. The scenery could use some work, and the food is terrible..."

Anna didn't say anything. Not that there was much you could say to someone who'd already died, who was about to die again, if his friends got their way.

"Except," I continued. "You know what, I am angry. I'm frustrated. I never had a chance to raise a family. To lead a normal life. To fight in a war for my country or find a normal job. By chance, I could become a guide, and before I knew any better I was one. All of the things I could have done, I can't do."

"As it is for all of us," Anna's reply came soft. "We're pawns in a game bigger than we are. Carver, even with all the horrors, all the danger, and all the fighting, at least we have the chance to affect the world. You and I, Bryce and the other guides, we're shaping everyone's future."

"I know. Which is why I wouldn't change this for anything," I quirked a smile that I hoped made it into my words. "I need catharsis every now and again."

"Know what you could be doing instead?"

"What?"

"Getting yourself up and coming after us."

"That might be a good idea." I tested my legs. My hands and feet. More feeling. I could probably stand, maybe limp. Brave a step or two.

I curled forward, sitting up. Put my right hand on the top of the table, pulled myself standing. My right leg wasn't thrilled about it, but between the twinges, it held. I leaned down, picked up the great sword. Lifted it with both hands. Shifted the weapon to my right and took a step, left hand ready to catch myself on the table.

I didn't fall.

Took another step. Reached the end of the table. I could do this.

"Anna, it's going to be a while, but I'm on my way."

SOUL WAGER

The Tar Pit's factories and warehouses were empty. Its streets bereft of the wandering spirits that I would normally see. The breaches pulled the souls elsewhere, and the guides had kept the city as clear of those as possible.

My limp straightened as I walked. I flexed the fingers on my left hand. Even managed to turn my head from side to side without pain. The miracles of being dead.

Within a few hours I could see the West gate, or rather, its ruins. The long line of rubble where the archway had once stood. The half-crumbled guard tower on the south side.

And the guides fighting a desperate battle outside of it.

I couldn't quite run, but as my shambling jog brought me closer, I saw the pair of guides outside the tower's lone door. They were fighting a group of spirits, armed as well. Nara's army, then, chasing down some stragglers.

The clash of metal on metal confirmed that the spirits weren't the usual hands and teeth crowd. I slowed as I approached, taking cover in the torn ruins of a guard house. Through its ripped walls, I took in a better view.

I didn't like what I saw.

Holding their ground in front of the door, fighting in solid tandem, were my least favorite guides; Polk and Derringer. They barred the door with their bodies, driving Nara's spirits back. The odds weren't great; eight against the two of them, and Nara's spirits seemed to be fine with biding their time. They darted in an out, looking for a quick stick, rather than the reckless charge I'd come to expect from spirits.

Polk and Derringer were human. They would bleed, they would tire. They would lose.

While I wasn't quite my sneaky self, I hadn't been noticed. I could wade into the back of the spirits, could take them down. On the other hand, Polk and Derringer had killed me. Took a knife to my throat or put a gun to my head and pulled the trigger. What better justice was there than seeing their cruelty matched?

I watched Derringer duck a swing from a spirit's sword, then saw Polk stab over his partner's head, driving the point of his rapier into the spirit's chest, alighting it in blue flame.

A strong move. One that left Polk open.

The hatchet came down into Polk's back, the spirit wielding it in both hands. The guide collapsed against Derringer, who by reflex or skill threw Polk perfectly back through the doorway while retreating himself to fill the entrance.

One on seven.

Even I'm not that mean.

I stumbled out of the guard house into the dirty street and started shouting. Waved my arms. Trying to draw attention. The spirits, and even Derringer, turned at the noise. Stared at me.

Then Derringer took advantage. Used his swords and stabbed the spirit closest to him. Burnt it up.

Two on six now.

The spirits split in half, three turning to tackle Derringer and another trio facing me. I had hatchet man, another spirit with a pair of long knives, and one holding a spear in both hands. All three spirits looked like shabby ghosts of a hospital ward, clad in stained gowns with pocked faces.

"Nice variety, guys," I said, drawing the great sword.

The one with the spear had the reach, and he led the attack, darting forward with a straight stab while the other two broke out to either side of me. A good ol' pincer move.

So I stepped forward. Slid just to the side of the spear's thrust, and as the spirit started to pull back his weapon, I sliced the great sword across. The spirit wasn't far enough away to avoid the blazing point.

I kept my momentum, pulling the sword and rotating my feet to the left, forcing hatchet man back. Which left long knives free to jump on my back, stabbing into me with those damned daggers. But I kept turning, and he failed to account for his own momentum, and even as those knives stuck into me, he flew off and hit the ground.

I lifted my swing, pushing past the searing pain, cut my rotation in half, and brought the great sword over my head and down on the knife-wielding spirit. He wouldn't be getting up again.

Which left hatchet-man all alone.

"Carver!" Derringer's pained yelp jerked my eyes back towards the tower. One spirit left for him, but Derringer, leaning against the entrance, had a knife sticking out of his side. One of his swords sat on the ground. The last spirit, holding a big ax, wheeled it back for a deathblow.

So I did the only thing I could. I twisted, put my weight into it, and launched the great sword through the air. It flew, spinning, and thwacked into the ax-man's legs. Sliced in and tripped the spirit.

I didn't see what Derringer did then, because the hatchet man came for me. He swung towards my chest, and I dove forward. Caught his forearm before the weapon could come down, and drove both of us into the dirt.

Unfortunately, that meant seeing the spirit's face up close; its sore, oozing nightmare a true feast of terror. I responded to it in the only sane way I could imagine—taking my own head and bashing into his nose.

With my left hand, I tried to get a grip on the hatchet. Failed as the spirit moved his arm out of my reach. Ready to slam it down on my back. So I slipped my right arm underneath the spirit's back and pulled as he swung the hatchet. Yanked the spirit over on top of me, causing his strike to miss wide right.

The hatchet hit the stone hard and bounced off, out of his grip. Leaving us both weaponless. Two spirits clawing and tearing at each other. At least, that's what I thought would happen, until the spirit, snarling in my face, froze and collapsed as blue fire burned around it.

Derringer's sweaty, bloody face appeared over the burning spirit's shoulders, searching to see if I was still alive.

"Barely," I answered the unspoken question and threw the spirit off of me. My back burned, but compared to Nicholas' bomb, this was cake. Nothing to it.

"Thanks." Derringer helped me up. "Came out of nowhere."

"Still not convinced I should have helped you." I leaned on him as we walked back to the tower.

"Polk and I were the guards." Derringer showed me in, and I saw, lying there in various states of injury, a dozen guides or more. Most leaned against the walls. A few sat on the ground. A couple were on their backs.

I felt faintly ill. I'd almost abandoned all of them to their deaths, just for my own grudge.

"Hurt too bad to go on," Polk coughed as he stood to shake my hand. "Bryce sent us back with them. Circled around that band of spirits you were leading. Guess you aren't doing that anymore?"

"Changed my mind," I said. "The rest of the way shouldn't be too bad. A breach, but it's not crowded."

Derringer nodded. "Suppose you won't want to escort us?"

I shook my head. "Have to catch up to the rest of them. If they don't succeed, it won't matter if you get back alive."

None of them protested. They all knew.

TWO GHOULS

Derringer walked up to me as I stared at the ruins of the west gate, already coating over with ash flakes. The breaches in the woods, and the spirits pouring forth, were likely chasing after the guides. Nara's army. A rare moment of quiet for this part of Riven.

"Polk and I can go with you. We can help," Derringer said.

"You won't be able to keep up," I replied, not bothering to look at him. "I won't get tired. Any spirit that catches me, I'll heal up in minutes. You're already hurt. Polk can barely walk."

Derringer didn't say anything for a second. Then I felt his hand land on my shoulder. "We're with you, Carver. I know you have no cause to like us, and that's fine, but we're behind you. All of us want you to go back to that Mountain, take care of Nara, and save Riven."

"You say you're behind me?" I looked at Derringer, then spread out my arms. I think he thought I was going to wrap him in a hug, but no, I had a better idea.

"Anything we can do."

"Give me your coat."

"What?" Then Derringer looked at mine, which wasn't a coat so much as a pile of cloth scraps. "Oh."

In Derringer's coat, a little loose in the shoulders but otherwise solid, I left the guard tower and headed west. Beyond the gate and into the clearing before the forest. As I neared the trees, I turned back. Looked at the ruined wall, the fractured gate, and the city that lay beyond. I would never go back there. I knew this as much as I knew anything.

Either we would succeed, and the Cycle would wash over and burn me from existence. Or we would fail, and Nara would bind me to once again become her thrall. And we would await the end of everything in the Mountain.

I hadn't felt sadness thinking about how I wouldn't see my apartment in Chicago again. A smile at the thought of Ezra's, never tasting another glass of their frothy beer or warm coffee on a cold winter morning. Riven had none of those charms, but I realized, standing there, that it was more of a home to me than any place had ever been. I knew its streets, its breaking buildings, its endless breeze and ash flakes. Riven was never safe, but it was home.

Now to protect it, I had to destroy it.

With the great sword held out in front of me, my back still sore from the hatchet, I moved into the forest. The gray trunks rose high into the air, the dark canopy filtering out the fogged sky. Sounds of spirits fighting each other gnashed their way through. Echoing off of the trees, the ground, to make it seem as though all the world around me engaged in a deadly struggle.

I knew which way was west, and that was where I walked.

I reached out to Anna, to see that she was still there. Confidence fled back to me. A slight bit of sadness. Perhaps they were losing guides. Perhaps they were understanding that this might cost them their lives as well. Resignation to a necessity.

Several hours into the walk, or at least that's what I guessed, the constant crashes and growls and chatter burst forth closer to me than before. I could see movement beyond the next tree and I steadied myself. Waited for something to come crashing through. The sounds turned away at the last moment, a sharp change. They were loud, a struggle between more than just spirits.

I shouldn't have investigated. No reason to be curious now.

Should've just kept going. Except I didn't know if it was like Polk and Derringer. A friend in need of help.

So instead of running from the noise, I went towards it. Went into a clearing, one that hadn't been there before, but now, through the felling of trees by blow and body, a broken circle appeared. In it, their large and thick arms swinging at each other, stood Mali's golden ghoul facing off against another, stranger one.

This ghoul, made from the molded bodies of consumed spirits, had six arms, and used them as legs and anything else that needed. It grappled with the golden ghoul, and they alternated throwing each other around the clearing. I couldn't tell who was winning, both battering the other in equal measure.

The monster stood on two of its arms, and grabbed the golden ghoul's paired hands with two more, and then with its uppermost pair snatched the golden ghoul's head and began to twist. To tear the golden ghoul the pieces.

Mali's creation had been my friend.

I ran forward and slashed with the great sword. Caught the back of the monster and bit deep into the dark, swirling flesh. The blue fire from my blade danced along the edges of the cut, but failed to take hold.

The ghoul, however, noticed. Broke off from its grapple and cut loose with a high-pitched howl that came from, I realized, a mouth in the middle of what I'd taken to be its chest. The ghoul turned and kicked with its lower left leg. Hit me square in the ribs, though I managed another cut from the sword in the process. I flew back, landed on broken branches.

What was another bruise anyway?

The attack gave the golden ghoul a chance to regain its footing. It bashed down on the six-armed creature, driving it into the ground with the force of its golden fist. However, from its new position hugging the earth, the ghoul grabbed and threw Mali's creature's feet out from under it. The golden ghoul tumbled to the ground.

The monster used its advantage; scrabbled on top of the golden ghoul and began to hammer on it with four of its six arms. Beating and breaking down my monstrous friend.

"Mali should have made you better," I muttered as I stood up. Adjusted the sword and charged with it, leading its point like a spear.

As I came close, the monster slowed its beating with its middle left arm, and swung it out to meet me. I stepped left, around the swing, and then brought the sword around and down on the arm. With the added force, the sword sliced through and severed the ghoul's limb.

It shrieked, and stumbled back off the golden ghoul. This time, the blue fire from my sword burned away the severed hand and licked at the stump. As the ghoul fell back, I followed in. Slashing every time the ghoul tried to drive me away with its arms. It had no defense against the sword.

Or so I thought.

The ghoul paused and I drove in for a stab right into its mouth. And then all three of its remaining arms, the ones it wasn't using for legs, came in at me from different angles. I adjusted my swing to aim for the right one, slashed across the ghoul's reaching hand, but it kept coming.

The ghoul pressed the sword into my body and accepted the blue burning flame. I felt the pressure on all sides. Crushing, grinding. In a moment I would break apart entirely. Flattened to nothing more than dust.

Until Mali's ghoul, the thing that had nearly killed me back in her temple, dove headlong into the beast's midsection. Knocked me out of its arms and drove its golden fists over and over into the other ghoul. I hit the ground and stayed still for a moment, trying to find which parts of me worked.

Thanks to Mali's ghoul, I could feel my arms and legs. Wasn't destroyed like after Nicholas' bomb. I creaked to my feet, hefted the sword up off the ground, walked around the golden ghoul as it continued to bash the thrashing beast, and then jammed my blade into the top of the six-armed monster. Let the blue fire run down the sword and into the creature, burning away the ties that bound together.

Mali's ghoul stood as the fire finished consuming its foe. Stared at me with a nod. And then turned back to the burning remnants.

I saw why. As the ghoul burned, spirits emerged. The source of its power and its rage. Those spirits were those of the Right and Left Hand. Cheo's warriors, torn and confused. Bound together in lost anger.

"Cheo," I said when I saw the leader emerge from the fire. He was not, however, the man I'd known. Like the others, the ghoul had torn apart any connection he still had to sanity. If I'd still been human, still had life, I could have bound them. If I knew how to use Nara's technique, I could've done that as well. But I saw the calm on that face, the steady, clear eyes, and I rested my hand on his shoulder.

"I'm glad to give you the peace you sought," I said as Cheo looked at me. "You're fighting days are done."

A moment later, Cheo walked his last steps to the Cycle.

REUNION

I slid the great sword back into its sheath and turned westward. Ready to follow in the footsteps of Cheo's spirits and catch up with the guides heading towards the Mountain. I took one step forward and then heard a rumbling sound behind me.

Oh. Over my shoulder, I noticed the golden ghoul looming.

Took another step forward. Heard the ground shake under my feet as the ghoul shifted, following.

Guess he wanted to come with.

From there we kept walking. The ghoul followed me almost to the line, brushing aside trees as if they were twigs and staying within inches of my back foot. If the idea of a ten foot-tall living statue, with bits and pieces broken off, walking behind me didn't seem odd, well, I'd been in Riven a long time now.

Things didn't surprise me much anymore.

As we moved, spirits occasionally appeared, from breaches or lost contingents of Nara's army. The ghoul and I handled them with equal amounts of disdain and skill. I would either slash or stab. The ghoul would stomp, or hit the spirit with its fist so hard that the soul would go flying through the trees and not show its face again. So we progressed. With every step I felt stronger. My soul knitting itself together.

I don't know how long it took, but we caught up with Nara's army. Or what was left of it. When I'd set out from the Mountain, as commander of Nara's force, there had been over a thousand spirits walking with me. But over time, as breaches and guides and angry spirits had torn away at the sides, only thirty or so remained marching in any semblance of order. As the ghoul and I approached, they halted. Turned to look at us.

"Carver!" I heard the voice; Bryce's call. "How about you take them from the back, and we'll take them from the front?"

I held the sword high, signaled a yes. We charged. Nara's spirits turned, half of them to greet me and the ghoul, and the other half to stand against the sudden appearance of a dozen guides. Guides I recognized. Anna and Bryce, Alec and more. They dove at the spirits with desperate viciousness. We all knew this was it, and we weren't going to let the snarling traces of Nara's army stand in our way.

The fight was swift, uneventful. An unbroken line of cuts and swirls, tweaked with blue fire and Nara's spirits were laid to waste.

When it was done, I helped some of the guides tend to their wounds. Bryce found me setting a man's shoulder, dislocated when a spirit he'd wrangled fell onto it, back into place.

"Nicholas is just beyond the next set of trees. The remainder of our forces around him." Bryce looked me up and down. "Glad you're back, Carver."

"If you wanted me back, you could have found a nicer way to ask," I said. "Leaving a bomb, really?"

"We didn't know if you'd even find it," Bryce said. "More a last-ditch shot than anything. Anna had more faith than I did."

"Thanks."

"But now that you're here, we need to decide what to do."

"I saw the map," I said. "You want to detonate it inside the Mountain."

"Nicholas believes his device will burn far enough to bring the Mountain down. To set the Cycle free." Bryce led me into the trees, away from the cleanup. Towards Nicholas. "If that happens, the Cycle will wash through the forest, over the city–"

"It'll wipe out everything," I said. "I know."

"Including you. And Selena."

"We're already dead Bryce." I gave him a halfhearted grin. "I died once, I can do it again."

My mentor gave me a quick nod. "Thank you for understanding. The other part of it, of course, is the rest of us."

"We'll give you time to escape." I wasn't going to detonate the bomb while Bryce and Alec and all the others were still in here. They had families. This whole thing was pointless if it meant killing the ones I loved.

"We can't trust this to you," Bryce said. "If you fail, if Nicholas can't detonate the bomb, then we lose everything. Who knows what Nara has waiting for us up there—if it's only you, there might be no chance of success. If that means we lose ourselves, then so be it."

As we went into the main force of the guides, I could feel stares on me. Some hands went to their weapons, before relaxing at Bryce's look. My fellows, having last seen me carving through their own ranks, no doubt had some grievances. Debts they felt they needed to settle.

"Nara's hold is broken," I announced to the guides. "I'm here as I am. I will take Nicholas and the bomb into the Mountain, we will detonate it, and end the risk Riven poses to you and your families."

I saw a few nods, but it seemed like the guides weren't in the mood for speeches. That's when I realized that they had been traveling for days already. Crossed over for far longer than a normal hunt. Their bodies, on the other side, were at risk.

"Bryce," I turned to him. "You have to get them back. You have to get back."

"How would we do that?" Bryce replied. "They're exhausted. Only some of us, the strongest and most experienced, have been able to keep their endurance. To send them back now, through that forest, would be sending them to die."

"Not if they had an escort."

"There's no time."

"We split them up," I said. "Mali's golden ghoul goes with all of you, back to the city. Nicholas and I go to the Mountain."

"You, Nicholas, and some of us," Bryce countered. "As I said, Carver, we mean to see this through."

Bryce gathered up the rest of the guides, those who could walk, and those who could carry the ones who couldn't. I sent the ghoul off with them. Pointed and told the creature to protect the guides with its life. I didn't know if it really understood me, but when the guides shuffled off back towards the city, to the places where they could cross over and return to their homes, the ghoul followed.

They would make it. They would be saved.

Alec and Anna stood near Nicholas, looking over the bomb, which was attached to a cart nearly as tall as I was. Crude wheels on the bottom, and ropes around the device that tied it to the signs. Keeping it level, keeping it safe.

"Sorry I nearly killed you," I said to Alec as I walked up.

"Me? Why, I decided not to kill you." Alec glanced at Anna. "For her sake. I, I had declared that you had outlived your usefulness. But she argued that you should have one more chance."

"Well then, thanks Anna," I said. "Alec, I won't be saving you when you get into trouble."

"My friend, if I get into trouble, it will be trouble's problem, not mine."

Anna laughed. "Carver, without you around, he's only become more insufferable."

"I didn't think that was possible." I looked at Nicholas, bending over the bomb, adjusting something on the left side. "Will it work?"

The scientist stood up and looked at me, his face straight. "Always you question me, and always you are wrong. Why would this time be any different?"

"This time is different because you're trying to blow up a mountain. Not make a lash, or a crossbow."

"They are all miracles, and I am a miracle worker."

"If you're wondering, Carver," Anna interjected. "I stay sane around these two by taking long walks. Long walks where I find and wrangle every spirit I see."

"Healthier than drinking, which was my solution," I replied.

"You imply that I am in nuisance in some way," Nicholas drew in a fake breath. Smiled. "You are likely correct. Glad to have you back, Carver."

"Couldn't miss the finish."

"We will need that sword of yours," Alec said. "It would be nice if we had Selena as well."

"She'll be there," I said. "Just not on our side."

"Yet," Anna placed her hand on my shoulder, the drew me in for a hug. "We'll get her back. Before the end."

"I hope so," I said. And I did. Really. I hadn't said goodbye to Selena yet. I didn't want to go away the vast nothing, into the next grand adventure, without one last time to talk to her. We had our life stolen from us, and it was time to take it back.

Bryce sounded the call a moment later. Time to head off, to the Mountain. To drive one more mad spirit into the ground.

THE RABBLE

The Mountain rose out above the forest, no longer a natural wonder but a trap constructed with hopeful intents: to make Riven into a second home for humanity. A dream turned nightmare.

The Mountain was, at the heart of it, the only reason Riven existed in the first place. Without it, the Cycle would be free. Spirits would wander into its blue oblivion soon after arriving.

No breaches. No ghouls. No guides.

But there the Mountain stood in front of us, and before the wide cave entrance through which hundreds and thousands of spirits passed through on their walk to the Cycle, stood Nara's new force. Smaller and concentrated, and led by the love of my life. Of my death.

Selena led at least a hundred spirits. They arranged behind her, standing in rank-and-file, in sections. Perfect lines, perfect soldiers.

A couple dozen of us walked out of the forest. Bryce, Anna, Alec, myself and a bunch of other guides that had made the journey. All of them exhausted. All of them slow. All of them knowing they weren't likely to make it home. Today, they were here for their friends. For their families. For their homes.

I wouldn't let them down. I wouldn't fail them.

Not again.

Nicholas stayed at the back, hidden in the lost spirits that continued to move around us in their blank walk to the Mountain. Had to keep him protected. If Nara destroyed Nicholas' device, then this was all lost.

Me, on the other hand. I was expendable. The only spirit on our side. Which meant I walked out in front. I kept the great sword on my back as I went toward Selena, who stood several yards in front of Nara's troops. Their many eyes followed me and I flashed briefly back to that moment in the Tar Pit when my father, Graham, threw a torch. So many single-minded faces locked on mine.

"Nara suspected that you'd been turned." Selena didn't smile as I walked up. Didn't draw her weapons. Instead, she looked at me as someone might stare at a particularly ugly house. An object both ordinary and unimportant. To be dealt with if necessary, or ignored.

"I have problems picking sides." I spread my hands as I came close to her. "But I think you'd like the benefits over here. The people are nicer, for one."

"They won't win," Selena replied. "Look at them. Half are about ready to fall over right now. And the others . . . can they even lift their swords?"

"My love, I dare you to find out."

Love. That word seemed to penetrate Nara's binding. Made Selena flinch, look away for a moment. Her hands, I noticed, balled into fists. For a second Selena had her own body back.

When her face came up to mine, Nara's mask had slipped on again.

"Nara is willing to offer all of you one last chance," Selena said the words not to me, but above and around, to Bryce and the other guides. "If you leave, she will let you go back to the city unmolested. You can head back to your families, safe."

"Till when?" Bryce called back. "Until your army grows again, and chases us down? Or until you let Riven fall to pieces under the weight of the dead?"

Selena turned back to me. "I see Bryce hasn't changed. He's never been a man of reason."

"Is that you, or Nara talking?"

"I suppose you'll never know," Selena said, and then she frowned. I noticed a single tear slip out of one eye. "But Carver, you should know, what happens next is all her."

Selena's hand moved faster than I thought possible. Sliding in her coat and drawing the cleaver into a slash at my stomach. I didn't jump back so much as fall, my feet dancing quick under me to keep my balance. The cut snagged the edges of my borrowed coat and tore through it. But not me. No blue fire burned my skin.

I reached behind my back and drew the sword out in a wide swing that forced Selena to stop her advance. I had reach. I had power. Selena had speed. Tough to say who would win this one.

"Resist her," I said, keeping the sword in a guard stance. Ready to swivel to any side Selena chose.

"I can't." Selena rose her cleaver into the air, twisted the hilt, bursting the blade into blue flame. Behind her, the spirits roared as one, and began their stampede towards my friends. This would be it, and I didn't know how the guides could survive. They were too tired, too drained.

Selena brought her cleaver down, dropped into a crouch. Ready to spring at me.

Only I wasn't standing still.

I jumped to the left, bowled into a bunch of charging spirits ignoring me to rush the guides. Swung the great sword through their ranks. Felt the weapon bite and cut and burn. Tried to take as many as I could with every lunge and spin. Dolan's sword sang, and it played a fiery tune.

Selena was on me. Her cleaver blocking my strike, stopping the sword. Her knife stabbing towards me. I reversed my grip on the sword and spun backwards. Away from her knife.

With my wrist reversed, I didn't have the leverage to keep the blade upright, and my sword went down into the ground. Dropped away from Selena's cleaver.

I flipped my wrist again, underneath the sword, and swept it up. Selena dodged to the right, into the path of one of her own spirits. The charging soul shoved into Selena and knocked her to the ground.

I had a clear shot. Lifted the sword, about to swing it down, when I felt Anna's panic through our bond. A paralyzing fear, numbing cold through my body. I turned, looked down the hill.

I'd done what I could, but the guides were still being overwhelmed. Anna herself, flail swinging, was holding four spirits at bay alone. She was already bleeding, already hurt.

"You stay here," I said to Selena, who was trying to free herself from the spirit.

I sprinted down the hill, using the weight of the sword to give me extra momentum. Swung at spirits on my way down, hacking their legs out from under them, or pushing them into each other. Anything to disrupt their numbers. To keep them from simply overwhelming my friends like a wave crashing over a small rock.

I hit the spirits from behind, slicing through three of them in one broad swipe. Anna's flail caught the fourth. She gave me a quick, tired grin. "Like I said, it's good to have you back."

"Doing what I can," I replied, twisting and laying into another two with a couple of chops. Unlike Nara's first army, the one I'd taken into the city, these spirits lacked weapons, lacked discipline. Nara was panicking. I could see, in the stream of occasional spirits coming out of the Mountain and diving towards us in suicidal charges, that Nara seemed more bent on numbers than strategy. Her forces lived and died by hordes, not skill.

"Watch it, Carver!" Alec called as I took care of another spirit. The guide, his gauntlets lit with flame, darted in between Anna and I, catching another spirit that I thought had gone down, but had only tripped, its hands grasping for my ankles.

"Get back to Nicholas." I needed them by the scientist. I needed them away from me. "I can take their claws. You can't."

But I couldn't take the cleaver. I couldn't take Selena's knife. She came after me, relentless. I barely had my sword up in time to block a straight ahead stab, the ridged edge of the cleaver making that as lethal as the sideways chop. She tried to stick the knife in my right leg, but I shifted to a side stance, her knife only grazing me. Not enough to set me aflame.

I drove her back with a quick series of in cuts; short jabs that leveraged the sword's reach to force her into a defensive stance.

"Nara says that she'll forgive you," Selena said as she whirled around me, moving her feet from side to side in a circle, continually testing my movement with the great sword. Looking for me to get out of position. To not follow her around and leave myself open for a quick strike.

"So kind of her." I shuffled my feet well. If there's one thing that I had learned with Bryce and our hunts, it's that being nimble was the key to survival. Movement kept you alive, which was more important than getting a lucky blow. We rotated until Selena stood downhill from me. A bad move.

"She thinks it's generous," Selena said "I think it's your only chance."

"I think you need to pay more attention." I lunged forward. Used my higher ground to deliver an overhead blow at an angle she couldn't counter without sticking both her blades above her head. But I didn't count on her roll. Rather than block, she dove down the hill. Towards were Anna stood, fending off another spirit. Selena came out of her tumble, rose, and jabbed Anna with the knife.

I saw Anna's eyes widen. Saw her mouth drop, saw her turn at the pain and knock Selena's knife away with her flail. Anna stumbled back against a tree trunk. The sneak that I had found, that I met on the train all those days and months and years ago, held her hand on the blossoming red coming from her side.

Through our bond flowed pain, and a sudden weakness.

I ran. Followed my swing. Selena turned towards me with the cleaver, but I stepped by her. Delivered a cross chop that caught a spirit reaching to finish Anna off. Selena had a clear shot at my back.

I expected the bite of her cleaver, even as I planted my feet to turn around.

Anna pressed herself off of the tree, her left hand leaving a bloody print behind. Swung the flail forward, over my head as Selena thrust forward. Anna's spiked, burning ball hit Selena's shoulder, knocking her strike away and bursting her into fire. The blue flame covered my love, and washed her away.

I wanted to hold her. To stay with Selena and never, ever leave. But as Selena burned, I had to turn. Had to keep swinging the sword and fight with my fellow guides.

Some fell, others stood strong. Bryce lanced with his voulge over and over again. Alec used his gauntlets to devastating effect. Other guides used their knives, their swords, their axes. By the end of it, eight of us were left standing amid a hoard of vacant spirits.

Nara, it seemed, had taken her own lesson. Resolved to keep any new souls for later. She gave us a moment to breathe.

Anna looked gray. Pale and lost. Her eyes caught mine as I stepped over to her, back leaning against the tree, her flail on the ground, her hands clasped over the wound in her side where Selena's knife had cut deep.

"You have to release me," I said, looking at the wound. "Cut the bind. Take your strength back."

"But we need you to finish this."

"I need you to live," I said. "We're so close to the Cycle now, so close to Nara. I'll be able to fend it off for a little while."

Anna stared at me. Then shook her head. "I won't. I won't take that chance."

"Then promise me," I said. "Promise me that if you have to, you'll cut me loose."

"Only if I must."

Bryce and Alec were there a moment later. Alec moved Anna's arms away, started binding the wound. Tearing treads off of his own coat and wrapping the stab. "It's a long way back, Anna, so we better get moving."

"You can't abandon them here," Anna replied, shaking her head.

"The way's clear," I said. "Nara doesn't have the forces left. I can take it."

"No," Bryce said. "You'll need help."

My mentor turned and went over to Selena, just standing up, lost to this world. He put his hand on her shoulder, and started talking to her. Establishing the familiarity, the relationship to form a bond. In a minute, Selena, my Selena, looked at me.

"Carver? Are we free?"

"Not yet."

Minutes later, the entire group sorted itself into two sections. Bryce and the other guides in one. Selena, Nicholas and I in the other, along with the cart holding the bomb.

"Take Anna back," I said, my eyes drifting over to her again. Sweating and pale, Anna's own eyes were closed. "Go as fast as you can. We'll take care of this."

"I'll let her know when we're clear through our bond." Bryce nodded at Selena. "So you can detonate."

As good a plan as any. As spirits roamed by us, my friends began the long trudge back to the city. Back to where they could cross over. On the way, they'd doubtless have to fight other spirits, pouring through breaches and in scattered angry waves prowling Riven in ever greater numbers. They would make it. They would survive.

It wouldn't matter if we failed.

AT THE EDGE

Surrounded by the walking spirits, the three of us, with Nicholas pulling the device on its cart behind him, entered the Mountain. Spirits filled the tunnel, all moving down towards the Cycle. On either side, branches broke off, empty and unexplored. I remembered them from when we were here last.

"It's sort of fitting," I said. "The end of the guides will be the place where they first began."

"Where they began?" Nicholas asked.

"Mali created the Mountain to house the Cycle. It was here, Dolan said, that he first found how to make the weapons that burned. Here where the guides stayed when they first built up to fight Nara."

I wasn't sure what else to say. There's something about actually confronting history that leaves you at a loss. Myth and legend becoming real and tracing a direct line to you. All of those events, those mistakes and those successes leading to the three of us trying, in one last attempt, to erase all of it.

We made it to the cavern where Piotr had crossed over. Where those months ago I had lost my parents. We had scored our first real victory, and had our first real loss.

It would've been nice to have Graham and Katherine beside me.

Graham's cocky optimism, his big hammer would have suffused us with confidence. Katherine's kindness, her knack for knowing the best way forward . . . but they weren't here. We were on our own.

To the left, stairs continued down, descending deeper into the cave. At the bottom of those steps would be the gray blue ocean of the Cycle. At the bottom of the steps, I had no doubt, would be Nara.

"I'll lead," I said, with the great sword out in front. "Selena, you take the back. Stay between anything and Nicholas. And you, genius, you get that bomb to the cliff and get it going."

"Don't we need to wait for Bryce and the others?" Selena said.

"We wait if we have time. I want them to live, but we can't risk it. If we have no choice, Nicholas, you blow this thing."

The scientist nodded. I didn't notice any moral qualms flashing through his eyes. Any concern that he wouldn't be able to follow through. Nicholas knew the objective. He would do what he had to do.

We took the last set of steps, past the cave leading up to Piotr's overlook, slowly. At the bottom the steps opened into a wide chamber dominated by the Cycle. Its blue light flashed through everything, covering our faces, our coats our minds in teal. Ahead of us a parade of spirits shuffled off the precipice into the endless sea. One after another, like animals. Or machines.

"I've never seen it," Nicholas said. "It's beautiful."

"Just don't get too close." I shifted the great sword, looked around. Where was Nara?

Nicholas move the cart into the chamber. Pushed it near the cliff's edge. Spirits ran by him, by all of us.

"You came back to me," Nara's voice echoed down the steps. She was above us. Back the way we came.

"Where are you?" I shouted. Ushered Selena by me, and pointed her over to Nicholas. We had to keep him safe.

"Why does it matter?" Nara said. "It won't change what is going to happen."

"What do you think that is?"

Part of me wanted to keep her talking, though I didn't think we could keep up the back and forth for an entire day. Or longer, depending on Bryce and the others. Nara would come out sooner or later. We would be ready.

"You're going to lose," Nara said. "You won't even see it coming."

I positioned myself in front of the steps. Glanced back at Nicholas and Selena. They seemed okay.

I felt hands grab my mouth, my throat, pull me back and pin my arms to my sides. Shouts came from my friends, and spirits that I'd swore were walking to the Cycle a second ago pulled them away from the device. Away from the Cycle. Against the cave walls.

Spirits held each of us, resolutely obeying their leader's command. Nara, who walked down the steps and into the chamber. Walked towards the bomb and stared at it.

Two other spirits, both soldiers, followed her. Personal bodyguards.

"What are you trying to do with this?" Nara said, and she looked back at us. "What is it? Some sort of weapon?"

I realized, hopefully as Nicholas did, that Nara may have never seen a bomb before. May not have any idea what such a thing could do. After all, explosives had no place in Riven. Perhaps the idea of detonating the Mountain would never even occur to her. Wouldn't even be a possibility.

"It's mine," Nicholas said. "I'm trying to find out more about the Cycle."

"It doesn't matter. The Cycle won't matter soon. We'll all be going back home."

Nara walked across the chamber, through the spirits, and up to Nicholas. Reached her hand for his face.

I saw Nicholas move his shoulders. Saw them shift, and then I recognized the coat he was wearing. The lines crossing it. I'd had a coat like that once, until spirits had torn it away. As Nara reached for it, the coat burst into blue wrangling flames. They covered the spirit holding onto him. Nara jerked her hand back in surprise.

I felt the twinge. The spirit holding me tight wavered as Nara lost her own binding. Her own focus on the spirits falling away in her fear.

I took advantage. Pressed my feet to the ground and shoved the spirit back into the wall behind me. Broke it against the stone.

The spirit's hands fell away and I stepped free, the great sword in my right hand. Ready to end Nara's madness.

I reversed the sword and stabbed behind me. Felt it bite into the stunned spirit. Burned it. Nara ran away from Nicholas, back up the cave's stairs. Coward.

"Carver!" Selena yelled, and I saw her spirit dragging Selena up the stairs. Up and away from the Cycle.

I moved to follow when Nara's two bodyguards cut me off. They were tall, hulking creatures. But they held no weapons.

So when they dove at me, I used the sword. A right swing, then a whirl to the left. Two cuts, two burning spirits. The way was clear.

Nara needed better guards.

Nicholas darted over to the device, the glanced at me. I could go after Selena. Or I could stay, keep Nicholas safe.

"Go," Nicholas said. "That's not my last surprise." He opened his jacket to reveal a number of blue bolts on the inside, leftovers for my crossbow. "I'll be fine."

"You'd better be. Yell if something changes."

I ran up the stairs, chasing after Selena. Chasing after Nara. Trying to survive.

SAVED

I went up the stairs and paused as I passed the pathway to the overlook. There were two places they could go. I didn't know which. I could still hear Selena shouts, but they echoed through the cave, bouncing off the walls and making it hard to tell where they were coming from.

Everywhere, really.

I was about to cry out, to ask which way, when pain flowed through me. It wasn't mine, though, it was Anna's. Coming through our bond. It went away almost as soon as it hit, but our tie continued to weaken. I could feel it, feel her life slipping away. If she died, our bond would be gone.

I shook my head. I couldn't do anything for her now. Had to find Selena, had to keep Nicholas safe.

"The overlook!" I heard Selena's cry, and went that way. She'd realized, perhaps, that giving directions was a better play than anguished yelling.

There weren't spirits wandering Piotr's path, so my progress was fast. I leapt up the steps. Pushed off the walls and kept the great sword ahead of me, held steady. Burst onto the overlook.

The forest expanded below, falling away from the Mountain. I could see, almost like city lights, glowing breaches. Riven was being overwhelmed, and it was happening faster. Some breaches looked like they were connecting, large pools of yellow swallowing up trees whole. Somewhere down there, Bryce and the others were running for their lives.

At the edge of the overlook, Selena fought for hers. The spirit had her, a scrawny but strong soldier that had lifted Selena's feet off the ground. Was moving her towards the edge, getting ready to drop her off.

I couldn't make it there in time. Selena was going to fall.

I lifted the great sword over my head, in both hands, and threw it forward. Let go as my hands started down.

The sword flew through the air, whirling end over end. It struck the spirit. Embedded itself into its back. Burst into flame. The spirit fell over the cliff.

And Selena went with it.

I ran towards them. Where they had been. Dove and slid across the rock, reached with my hand to see if there was anything to grab.

Felt nothing.

"You'll have to reach farther," Selena's voice sent a jolt through me. I peered over the edge; she hung a few feet down, her cleaver and long knife biting into the rock, giving her enough of a handhold. I scrabbled further, leaned down, and gripped onto the rock with my left hand. Reached out with my right. Selena glanced at it, glanced at the cleaver and the long knife.

"Leave it," I said. "It's not worth dying for."

"You keep forgetting Carver, we're already dead." Selena let go with her left hand, and the cleaver fell out of the Mountain and tumbled into oblivion. She leaned on the knife, and reached up and grabbed my hand.

As I pulled Selena up, the knife fell free. Selena kept her right hand wrapped around its hilt. Not willing to give up that last weapon. I rolled over, used the leverage of my back to pull Selena up and onto the overlook. She rolled across me, and we both laid still for a moment.

"How many times do I have to save your life?" I said to her.

"I could ask you the same question."

And then I remembered Nicholas. Alone down there by the Cycle. With Nara roaming the caves.

SEVERED

Selena and I sprinted down the stairs. Back through the hidden passage and down towards the cavern and the Cycle. Every second we weren't by his side, Nara could find a way to tear the scientist apart. Destroy the device.

Selena and I burst into the chamber, shoving spirits aside, and saw the device still intact on the cliff. Nicholas stood in front of two smoldering spirits, watching to make sure they didn't rise up again. Behind him, stepping out of a cluster of spirits marching to the Cycle, Nara walked towards his back.

Nicholas looked up, saw us, held up a hand. Didn't see Nara approaching.

I shouted his name. "Behind you!"

The scientist, thin lanky eyes shining with adrenaline, turned in time for Nara to grab him by the face. Her bony fingers wrapped around his cheeks and I saw the life drain out of them. The independence, freedom, gone.

I ran towards them. I could hear Selena doing the same. Despite the fact that we only had Selena's knife, I was determined to try something, anything.

Nicholas turned back to me, between Nara and I. Held up his hand, gave me a single wave. "Goodbye, Carver."

The scientist turned and jumped off into the Cycle.

We all watched Nicholas vanish into the blue. Then the old spirit, the one who was supposed to help us save Riven and who had scattered those dreams to ashes, spoke. "He was the greatest risk remaining," Nara said. "An unknown. I do not know what that thing is, but there must be a reason you brought him here. There must be a reason you were trying to save him."

"It doesn't matter now."

I didn't know what to think. To feel. With Nicholas gone, I didn't know who could trigger the device, if anybody. I didn't know what the plan was. I just never thought we'd fail. I never saw it coming. We had the advantage, we had the equipment. But here I was, unarmed, at the end of the world.

"What's next?" Nara said, and she looked at Selena. "Do you stab me? Burn me and throw me into the Cycle? Even though it will do you no good?"

"Maybe not, but it'll feel great," Selena said. She took a step towards Nara, and then the old spirit lunged towards me. I had no weapons to strike her, so I did what I could and met her grasping hand with a tackle. Pushed her back, along the Cycle's edge. We danced, me trying to keep her hands from grasping mine, from touching my face, my throat, my wrists, anywhere that could allow her to connect to what was left of my soul.

"You are such a disappointment," Nara snarled as we wrestled. She was stronger than I expected. But again, appearances could be deceiving in Riven. Muscle and bone didn't matter once you were dead. The only thing that did was your determination. Your skill.

Nara had learned a lot in her centuries.

She twisted her leg and caught my calf, threw me to the floor. Reached down towards my face. I kicked up with my foot and struck her in the stomach. Drove her back.

"Can't you see that Earth doesn't deserve to die so you can live?" I shouted at her.

"I happen to think it does." Nara rushed at me again. I could see Selena behind her, angling for the right spot to stick Nara with the knife. That was my hope, that was my plan.

But Nara knew that as well as I did. She kept twisting us, rotating our grapples to get Selena out of position.

I had to try something different.

So when Nara charged again, I let her wrap her fingers around my throat. Felt her start to tear my soul. Felt Nara's whispers pour into my mind. And then I felt them vanish. Pushed away by Selena's burning blue knife.

Nara took a step back for me, surprise showing on her face. She couldn't possibly imagine such a thing. As though the concept of defeat had never crossed her mind.

"Stabbed in the back," Selena said. "Should be familiar to you." Nara took one step, her mouth worked, and then she collapsed into the flames. They dwindled around her body on the ground. I didn't let her stand up and pushed her over the edge.

As Nara disappeared into the deep blue of the Cycle, I realized that all three of the spirits that had build Riven were gone. Fitting, then, that their creation go with them.

I gave Selena a smile, and started to move to the device, when my world exploded.

Pain lanced through me again, coming out of nowhere and everywhere. Through the bond I shared with Anna. It was wild, uncontrollable, and I knew there was only one way to stop it.

"Let me go," I said the words aloud, but sent them through our bond. Sent them to Anna across the distance between us. If she was going to get back alive, she needed all her strength. She needed the part of her that she had given to me. I needed her to take it back.

Confusion, relief, flowed through our bond. Anna was hesitating. So I urged her again. Begged her. Tried to be confident, to let her know that this was my decision. That I would be okay. Despite the fact that I knew none of those things.

Selena knelt next to me, her face a mask of worry, when she asked what was going on I could barely form the words to tell her.

Then I felt it. The strange rush of my body putting itself back together. Of Anna leaving me, and cutting me off. She would be feeling the same. Strength returning to her limbs. Like waking up after a long nap, or a good meal. I hoped it would be enough.

When the severing was done, I stood, pain-free.

"It's done," I said to Selena. Only, it wasn't. I heard the voices leaking into my head. The whispers. The endless parade of statements one after the other. Urging me, urging me to walk ahead. Take a few steps and disappear. All of my worries, all of my troubles would cease.

I knew where they came from, I knew that calling.

The Cycle wanted me.

A PERFECT WAIT

Selena had her arms around me before I could move. Her mouth close to my ear, and I heard her voice.

" Carver, Carver come back. Push it away. Listen to me."

The words came and went, blending with the growing chorus of whispers. Demands. Urges that I dive into the deep blue. Like the craving for tobacco, alcohol. Deep needs that had to be satisfied.

"I can't fight it," I said, and pushed Selena way. Stood up. Moved my left foot, then my right foot. Closer to the edge.

Selena tackled me from behind. Knocked me down. Jammed her elbow into my back and pressed me to the ground.

"You're not going to leave me here," Selena said, I could hear her voice break. "After all this, you're not going to leave me alone. Not here. Not now."

The raw emotion in those words broke through. Blunted the force of the Cycle's call just enough for me to pause. To feel my hands, my legs, my mouth. To take control. But I didn't tell Selena to get up. Not yet. Not until I was sure.

"Keep talking," I said. "I need you."

Selena did. She spoke in stories, and memories, and poems. She told me about how she felt the first time we met. When I'd saved her from the spirit and the streets. She told me about the apartment, the long days drawing and trying to find a passion in Riven, loving it when I came to the door to offer excitement.

She told me about the first time she held the cleaver. More than a weapon, it was a symbol of independence. Something that said this was her world too, and she had a place in it. Was no longer at the mercy of others. She could drive her own destiny.

She talked about how she felt closer to me than any other. How when the two of us journeyed through the strange world, those were the best times of her life. In Riven or without. That the two of us as a team, facing horrors, or just walking together through the endless desert or stalks of grain, those moments were what she treasured.

Selena buried the Cycle under her words. Her love quieted the whispers, softened the cries. I fell into a trance listening to everything she said. When she finished, before she could launch into something else, I held up an arm. My face still lay against the rock, but I spoke anyway.

"Thank you," I said. There may have been more to say. But right then, that's all that seem to matter.

Selena let me up a moment later, but I noticed she stayed ready. Willing to throw herself under my legs again, and again and again if necessary.

Around us spirits continued their doomed walk as though none of this was happening. An audience unaware of the play in front of them.

The device sat there. Waiting.

I went up to it. A solid dirty metal sphere, with a small hatch that opened when I pushed in. Inside sat a smaller sphere, connected to the outer one with many spokes. A simple switch, one that you could press, sat inside.

Carved into the metal above it, was a message.

To whomever happens to be the one activating this device, I would pass along the following:

Pressing the switch will activate the procedure. Precisely 10 seconds after, the inner core will ignite. The rays will admit shortly thereafter, triggering the chaining reaction as expected.

I glanced at Selena. "He said this was complex, it looks like it's just a switch."

"Maybe he knew," Selena said. "Maybe he understood at the end that it wasn't going to be so simple. That he might not make it."

I looked back in towards the switch, and noticed another series of etches. Below the button. These in a messier scrawl.

If you are reading this, then forgive me. The Cycle calls to me, and if I am to see it, I needed a reason. This was my chance.

Your friend,

Nicholas

"I always knew Nicholas was a sly one," I said after letting Selena look at the message.

"He got his wish," Selena answered.

"So when do we press it?"

"When Bryce gives us the signal."

I don't know how long we sat, telling stories, holding each other, and basking in the Cycle's blue glow. Watching the spirits go by in their endless march. It was a long, perfect goodbye. The two of us together in our wait for the end.

When Selena sat up, I knew the call had come in. Bryce had made it home.

"He says to thank us," Selena spoke, repeating Bryce's words to her. "That they made it back, with surprise help from a golden ghoul who, wandering back from the city, found them."

"Mali's finest creation."

"Anna made it," Selena said. "Alec says Laurence is going to take her to the hospital. Bryce says to detonate it."

"Are you ready?"

Selena nodded. I moved towards the bomb, stopped. Turned back to her. "Together."

We both reached in, her fingers rested lightly on the switch. Selena whispered *now* and we pressed down. The only sound was a slight fizzing, as though something had started to burn.

I shut the hatch. Selena met my eyes, I met her lips, and the world swirled away.

PEACE

Anna walked down the avenue, on a wide sidewalk beneath towering buildings. More and more every day, scaling upwards ever higher. Now that the war was over, plenty of energy and materials were being thrown into the city's growth. Zeppelins filled the sky, fewer mechs walked the streets. Still, Anna felt relief when she came in sight of Ezra's. A home of sorts. Through the purifier, and into the rich bar. That mantel above the back counter showing a fantastical orchestra, jazzy tunes pouring out from speakers beneath. Alec was already there, sipping coffee. On the table, a mug of tea just for her.

"It's been a while," Alec said as Anna sat down.

It had. Months. Not much reason to get back together this far from home anymore. They didn't have regular meetings. The guides, as a whole, had more or less stopped existing. Bryce said he checked every so often. Crossed over and stood on the small piece of Riven that remained. Anna hadn't tried it. Most of the crossing points, the beds they were used to, would take you right to your own demise. They'd lost a few guides that way, immediately after. Now there were only special places, tied and designated to the small scrap of Riven remaining.

"He's coming today, right?" Alec said. Anna nodded.

They spent the next hour rehashing their lives. Catching each other up the way, Anna supposed, normal people did. There weren't toxic ghouls, angry spirits interrupting. No discussion of hidden enemies, vile maneuvers. No, for once all they had to complain about was the rent. New restaurants. The conversation went flat.

Then a third person joined the table. Anna stopped. Looked at the man.

Opperman, the reporter, took a seat, pulled out a notepad. "So, I hear you've got a story to tell."

AN EXCERPT FROM THE FARTHEST STAR

A NEW ADVENTURE FROM A.R. KNIGHT

I woke.

That term wasn't accurate, but for cognitive narration, it would suffice. Raw data streaming into the processes and memory that made up my being was not, apparently, of use to the Voices, those that made me. They wanted an accounting they could understand.

So I gave them one.

First, I flexed my nerves. Artificial lines running from my various nodes scattered along my humanoid body, all funneling to a core in my head. They worked. My fingers and toes moved, felt the stiff cushion beneath me. The responses fell on a scale, and I evaluated the cushion as decidedly uncomfortable.

My eyes reviewed other options. The space I inhabited was not large, was square, was not empty, was, in fact, brilliant. Light, cyan-blue and rippling, swept back and forth above me. A long tube, hanging loose from two weak cables, rocked to a standstill, centering its glow between my cot and one to my right.

An empty cot, yellow. Another empty one beyond it blue. My own, green. Shifting over onto my left shoulder, the last one red. And occupied.

She—applying sex and gender to artificial lifeforms seemed foolish, and yet the Voices insisted I differentiate, so I did—looked lithe, strong. Frozen in the immortal plastic existence lived by inactivated mechs. Even her hair stayed in place, black and straight, immune to gravity's pull.

The rocking light lingered as a mystery. An insistent tolling in my still-loading mind. I felt no wind in the room, no shift in the air that would explain why the light would move as it had. How should I regard something like that?

A threat? An idle question?

I sat up. A simple action that nonetheless cost my virgin muscles. Pops and ripples ran their way up and down my core as parts did what they were designed for, and came away successful. A hollow ticking in the back of my consciousness logged the motion, sent the data to a dark hole I could not access. Information for my successor, or whomever would build it.

I rotated my neck next, and took in the surroundings. Beyond the light and the cots, the room had character: posters depicting entertainment clung to the walls, blasting motivational and dire slogans with their heroes front and center. Many bore tears, some remained hanging only because a gentle breeze had not seen fit to knock them down.

Beneath the art's paper-and-plastic shielding sat a pitch-black paint, a coating that made its way to a rubbery floor, the cots pushing into it and creating little divots with their pressure. As if whomever had designed the room had feared its occupants might roll off and hurt themselves.

Our cots had no rails.

"Welcome to Starship." The voice came from nowhere, its patterns falling into a gentle, older human male's timbered range. "Please, raise your right hand."

I saw no disadvantage to doing so, and obliged the voice. As I did, the space in front of the cot, a heretofore empty spot on the floor, resolved itself into a yellowed, but otherwise real-seeming image of that same man.

How did I know the image matched the voice? Because when it

spoke again, the man's mouth moved with it, shoving a thinned white beard around a gnarled face as it did so.

The man asked me to raise my left hand too, then move my legs and so on and so forth until, after I had completed what the man called "limbering up", I stood beside my cot, bent at the waist and watching him smile at me.

"Another success," the man said, then fizzled out for a millisecond before popping back into focus. "Gamma, I'm pleased to say you have passed your first test."

"Test?" I asked the question as much to trial my vocalization abilities as to gain more information from the image.

The sound I made resembled a squeaking wheel, high-pitched and awkward. The man made no mention of it, he only turned and pointed out the doorway, saying something about where I ought to be going next.

I, meanwhile, focused on changing that awful voice. There were a million choices, ranges culled from the same entertainment on the walls and plenty beyond. Of the options, I selected a middle register, a voice for a man not quite sure of who he was.

It seemed fitting.

The image had disappeared. I stared at its spot. Willed it to return.

"Start again," I said.

Nothing happened. Instead, with the image and its commands absent, I listened to the loud silence.

Starship, the image had said. The name implied a machine, and my surroundings echoed that impression. Beneath my feet, through the soft floor, I could pick up the distant, regular tremors of something in operation. Occasional, far off hisses wound their way into the room. And a single, forlorn beep sounded nearby every three seconds.

Walking came unnaturally. The motion's steps had been programmed, but understanding the proper distance between one foot and the next, the length of my stride, took walking back and forth along the room several times. After those paces, I'd managed to correct from a lunge to a skip to a regular step. I'd learned, too, how to hold my arms steady and keep them from flailing with every move.

A body, it turned out, was a complex thing to manage.

Three empty cots in the room. One of them mine. One still occupied. The two cots that had been unoccupied when I woke looked like they hadn't been touched for a long time: while mine bore the indent from my weight, these other two seemed pristine. Every trace of use erased, if they ever had been.

I confirmed the woman in the last cot lay in the same sleep that had held me for however long. That dark spot in my mind wouldn't give me clues to my age, and nothing about my appearance or hers offered any answers. However, a black, taped line across the top of her chest, like the one on my own, delivered a name:

Delta.

Seeing her, and looking down at myself, confirmed another difference. The man in the image had worn clothes, a sort of formal suit and pants with a neck that came right up to the man's chin. Delta and I wore nothing, though I didn't feel any discomfort.

Either our home kept things perfect, or our bodies did the job.

The beep sounded yet again, drawing me towards the room's exit. The image had said to go this way, and lacking other objectives, other ideas, I supposed I ought to follow. I could have returned to the cot, spent my own eternity there staring at those posters and that blue light.

But my creator had given me curiosity, and I followed it.

Walking beyond the room revealed a narrow hallway, these walls less covered but no less intriguing. The posters continued, but between them, nestled in metal tiles, glowed what looked like neon gems. Their light cast the hall in greens, pinks, blues and more, with a dark ceiling offering the sense of walking into another reality.

I thought I would confront a choice: the hallway went left and right, but as my feet crossed the room's threshold, a spiral door shut with a soft click, forming a hard barrier to my leftward ambitions. In its center, a red-glowing gem rested, an evil eye denying my passage.

Compelled by that curiosity, and the temptations that came with being denied anything, I reached out and brushed that red gem. Cool to the touch, and artificially smooth, the gem glistened when my fingers ran across its surface, the red turning ever so quickly to a winter silver and back again.

The door did not respond at all.

Left with no other choice, I turned around and followed the neon path away from the room. The floor out here lacked the cushion inside my bedchamber—what else to call it?—and my feet felt warm, rippled metal beneath them. Hard, somewhat uncomfortable, but undeniably effective at keeping my grip as I walked.

The hallway curved ahead, but before I'd made a dozen paces, a room on my left appeared as the source of those low, long beeps. Another spiral door waited, this one's gem an emerald green. Looking at it, I hesitated a moment, glanced back towards the door's distant, red-gemmed partner.

Too obvious? Or perhaps part of a broader plan?

When I touched the green gem, it flashed gold. Warmth greeted my touch. This time, the door did not sit indifferent to my gesture. The soft click repeated itself and the spiral's metal tendrils retracted.

The room shared the sole blue light hanging in the center—this one not swaying from some prior interference—and beneath it, instead of cots, sat a molded, steel-gray stand with two handprints. The same emerald green as the gem traced those prints, begging me to touch it.

And I wanted to.

I walked in the room without thinking about the motion, as if some invisible hand pushed me along. It's a curse of my code to evaluate the options, to consider not only the what and the when, but the why.

Something had directed me to this room. Something wanted me to press my hands into these prints.

What would that something do if I didn't follow their directions?

I turned around and started back towards the room's exit. Made it two steps before the door that had opened to me shut again, trapping me inside. Its green gem now that same red.

The path, then, was set.

The beep came again, and this time I traced it to that same molded stand. Calling out to me, alone in the dark room.

What choice did I have?

The molds were larger than my hands, but it didn't matter. As soon as I slid my fingers into their slots, the emerald tracings flashed, and I felt something new enter my mind.

"They're giving me a vessel after all this time," I said, but I did not say. Something had control over my mouth, my voice. "Gamma? I guess I shouldn't be surprised. But when is it? Where are we?"

I looked—thankfully, whatever the words coming from my mouth, I retained some influence over my body—around the room and saw nothing. The molded stand had regressed to hard nothing, the emerald around the prints dying out.

"This is unexpected," I-but-not-I said. "I can't feel anything. The mouth moves, the words come out, but I cannot lift my arms?"

The mold had infected me. Something had crossed from that terminal into my head, my heart, my memory, and I could feel it stretching out, hunting for the keys to my controls. The intruder had taken my mouth, and now it wanted more.

I wouldn't let that happen.

The room, the blue light disappeared as I focused myself inside . . . myself. Transitioned my attention from the outside world to my inner functions, those now under assault from this new threat.

We stood on a vast whiteness. A featureless plain extending to eternity. Above the ground, suspended, floated glittering crystals, their points angling down towards us. From some, copper tendrils stretched loose and flowing to the intruder, who stared at that crystal sky and waved his hands. As he moved, more tendrils appeared, snaking out towards my crystals.

"Stop," I said.

The intruder looked towards me, confirming my initial suspicion: the image I had seen in my waking room, the older man who had so gently walked me through my first minutes now stood inside my inner workings, attempting to turn them to his own ends.

"And what are you?" asked the man. "Some sort of new addition?"

"This is me," I replied, sweeping my arms. "You are the addition."

I had, without considering it, adopted a digital version of my physical form. I saw myself reflected in the man's eyes as I came close, and considered changing my body. What would most frighten this intruder, terrorize him into submission?

Clearly not my current self: By the man's studying look, my body did not inspire fear.

"Interesting," the man said, and as he spoke, those copper tendrils retracted into his body. "Then, as the visitor, perhaps I should introduce myself. I am the Librarian."

"A strange name."

"A title," the Librarian replied. "And a description, I believe, of my purpose."

As we spoke, I considered ways to destroy the Librarian. While the man seemed benevolent for the moment, he was still an intruder and had, seemingly, the capability to overwrite my own programming in his favor. And what could I even do? Physical violence in a digital space seemed broken, somehow. Would snapping his neck change the bits and bytes that made the Librarian? Delete them?

"Your purpose?" I asked.

I figured I could buy time to solve the Librarian's demise by indulging his musing. He proved me right by folding his hands and taking a slow turn, considering the vast emptiness around us and the crystals above.

"Eventually, we knew we would need vessels, and ways to fill them," the Librarian said. "I did not make you, and indeed was put under, I suspect, well before they finished your design. Things must have changed."

Vessel? I stopped my macabre imaginings. The Librarian seemed to be hinting at a larger story, one that tugged at my own sense of self. I knew my name: Gamma. I knew there were at least two of us. But beyond that, I had no directive. No memories, dreams, or anything other than an urge to explore. To discover.

To learn.

"You're so quiet," the Librarian teased me. "Why is that? Surely they did not strip the vessels of their voices."

"My name is Gamma. Stop calling me a vessel."

"Fine, Gamma, though a vessel is what you are," the Librarian replied, and his weathered face softened behind his white beard. "Don't be disappointed. You are an opportunity, a hope, and a chance. Every worthwhile story starts with a vessel, and yours, I suspect, will be no different."

"You say I'm a vessel, and you spoke of ways to fill them," I said, putting aside his mention of a story. Romantic ideas like those could wait until I had left my inner workings behind. "What do you mean?"

"Let me show you," the Librarian held out his right hand. "This will be so much faster than talking, however much I may enjoy it."

I stared at the hand. It looked plain, creased but hardly coarse. No threat seemed to present itself, but I remembered those copper tendrils, what they might do, and hesitated.

"You were taking me for your own," I accused.

"Because I thought that was my role to play," the Librarian said. "I was wrong."

Without warning he reached forward, grabbed my arm. A strong grip, and one I couldn't even think to break before the white vastness and its crystal ceiling fell away, vanishing as I flew out and up into an infinite beyond that left me, suddenly, standing before the metal mold.

The green outlines had dulled to nothing. The blue light still glowed.

Starship hummed.

The name slipped into my thoughts, like a half-remembered dream, and lodged itself there. Starship. That's where I was. A vast structure, speeding through space with—

Slow down. I shook where I stood, coming to grips with the massive data now sitting on my mental fringes, waiting to be explored. Simple, for a computer like me, to analyze. Harder, far harder, to comprehend.

"I have never been in this room," the Librarian said, and when I looked to my right, he stood there and did not stand there, his form a wavering, hollow thing. "I'm not quite sure where you are, Gamma, so I am afraid I will not be of much use to you yet."

"Use to me?"

"You feel all my stories, everything I learned during a long life, pressing in on you now, yes?" the Librarian asked.

"They nearly swept me away."

"A known possibility," the Librarian nodded. "The early vessels, the only ones I saw, failed under the weight of what you just did. We nearly scrapped the program, except there were no other options. For now, I will close off most of myself so that you are not overwhelmed. Too much knowledge, too quickly, can be a terrible thing."

Behind me, the spiral door clicked and opened with its trademark whooshing sound. I turned and saw nothing more than the neon hallway waiting for me.

"Well then," the Librarian said. "Off we go."

Continue THE FARTHEST STAR at your favorite retailer, and stay in touch for free books and new adventures by signing up for my newsletter!

ACKNOWLEDGMENTS

There's this idea that writing is a solitary act, but that couldn't be further from the truth. Every writer depends on friends, family, and, yes, the readers to keep spinning their stories.

Specifically, I'd like to thank my wife, Nicole, who's endless love and encouragement make every day brighter. My brothers, Jonathan, Justin, and Matthew, and parents, Bob and Mary, who help keep a smile on my face.

And, of course, all of you readers that make this life possible.

Thank you.

ABOUT THE AUTHOR

A.R. Knight writes sci-fi and fantasy in the frozen north of Wisconsin. With a pair of cats keeping him company, he enjoys delving into adventures that are as much about the villain as the hero.

After getting a degree in journalism and touring the country installing healthcare software, A.R. Knight thought it would be good to get back to what he loved. So now he's got a small office and early mornings to spin whatever tales come into his imagination.

When he's not writing, A.R. Knight tends to travel anywhere he can, whether that's islands off the coast of Ecuador, the rainforest, snowboarding in the Rocky Mountains, or sipping scotch in Edinburgh. That's the nice thing about the writing life, you can take it anywhere.

To contact or see what he's up to, visit www.adamrknight.com

For Matthew